T0016253

PRAISE FOR DEMON

'A taut and gripping tale that deftly skewers the perfect balance of crime, thriller and horror. Intriguing, disturbing and impeccably crafted – I was riveted from the first page' Lucie McKnight Hardy

'*Demon* scared the bejesus out of me, beating even *Hydra* on the fright factor. Matt Wesolowski is the master of horror, of mixing folklore with urban myth and real life. Terrifyingly good' Louise Beech

'Matt's real skill is in finding a deeply human story and twisting it with the paranormal, touching the reader and scaring the wits out of them at the same time. In my mind, he's one of the best storytellers of our time' Chris MacDonald

'Another masterclass in writing by Mr Wesolowski ... Like binge-watching your favourite TV show – twists, turns, creepy, emotional, sad, scary. Ticks all the boxes for fans of horror and crime thrillers ... The story Matt weaves is addictive and is cleverly pulled together by the end of the book. His skill at doing this is phenomenal ... These books are brilliant' Dale Robertson

'Matt Wesolowski manages to give all the different episodes their own unique voice and shows a genuine skill in storytelling ... A brilliant author and a series of books that are quite simply PERFECT' Kendall Reviews

'Ussalthwaite – on the face of it a beautiful, rural village – has its own very unusual, dark and cursed history, and the author is gifted at conjuring up a chilling backdrop for this excellent series' Trip Fiction

'The most chilling episode yet I think. It had all the horror elements and more ... The setting is one of the most graphic and unsettling I have read about in a long while. I might never look at a stone in the same way again. Nor will I ever enter a cave in Yorkshire' The Book Trail

'I'll be rereading these books forever, and if there were 150 more of them I'd happily spend a year reading nothing else' Sublime Horror

'This series goes from strength to strength thanks to the author's exceptionally descriptive writing and his vivid imagination. His plots are original, terrifying, disturbing and deliciously dark ... I absolutely loved every page of this compelling read' The Book Review Café

'Another excellent entry in such a strong series' Bride of the Book God

'Creepy, chilling and unnerving storytelling at its finest … completely unpredictable and absolutely fabulous' Little Miss Booklover

'This author deftly weaves a crime story, creepy paranormal elements, and current social themes into every one of his books ... Completely unexpected and so satisfying' Goodreads reviewer

'An unusual and clever plot, and as to be expected, CREEPY. Harrowing at times and absolutely brilliant. However, I read it too quickly and I am already dying for another instalment in the Six Stories series' Goodreads reviewer

PRAISE FOR THE SIX STORIES SERIES

'First-class plotting' *S Magazine*

'Bold, clever and genuinely chilling with a terrific twist that provides an explosive final punch' Deidre O'Brien, *Sunday Mirror*

'A genuinely genre-bending debut' Carla McKay, *Daily Mail*

'Impeccably crafted and gripping from start to finish' Doug Johnstone, *The Big Issue*

'The very epitome of a must-read' *Heat*

'Haunting, horrifying, and heartrending. Fans of Arthur Machen, whose unsettling tale *The White People* provides an epigraph, will want to check this one out' *Publishers Weekly*

'Matt Wesolowski has just the formula to meet your self-scaring needs' *Strong Words Magazine*

A masterly piece of storytelling, very sinister, deliciously entertaining' *New Books Magazine*

'A dazzling fictional mystery' *Foreword Reviews*

'Readers of Kathleen Barber's *Are You Sleeping* and fans of Ruth Ware will enjoy this slim but compelling novel' *Booklist*

'Matt's books are fantastic' Ian Rankin

'Matt Wesolowski brilliantly depicts a desperate and disturbed corner of north-east England in which paranoia reigns and goodness is thwarted … an exceptional storyteller' Andrew Michael Hurley

'Beautifully written, smart, compassionate – and scary as hell. Matt Wesolowski is one of the most exciting and original voices in crime fiction' Alex North

'Endlessly inventive and with literary thrills aplenty, Matt Wesolowski is boldly carving his own uniquely dark niche in fiction' Benjamin Myers

'Frighteningly wonderful … one of the best books I've read in years' Khurrum Rahman

'Disturbing, compelling and atmospheric, it will terrify and enthral you in equal measure' M W Craven

'Wonderfully horrifying … the suspense crackles' James Oswald

'Original, inventive and dazzlingly clever' Fiona Cummins

'A complex and subtle mystery, unfolding like dark origami to reveal the black heart inside' Michael Marshall Smith

'A captivating, genre-defying book with hypnotic storytelling' Rosamund Lupton

'A chilling, wholly original and quite brilliant story, *Deity* is utterly compelling, and Matt Wesolowski is a wonderful writer' Chris Whitaker

'A gripping exposure of the underbelly of celebrity and obsessive fandom with lashings of supernatural horror – *Daisy Jones and the Six* gone to the dark side. I couldn't put it down' Harriet Tyce

'Insidiously terrifying' C.J. Tudor

'Dark, twisty and incredibly clever. Matt Wesolowski is an author to watch!' C.L. Taylor

'A dark, twisting rabbit hole of a novel. You won't be able to put it down' Francine Toon

'Matt Wesolowski is taking the crime novel to places it's never been before. Filled with dread, in the best possible way' Joseph Knox

'Matt is one of the powerhouse authors at Orenda who continues to deliver a new style of telling a story that can't be copied … and if it was we would immediately know it was Matt who has inspired the work' Claire Sheldon

Demon

ABOUT THE AUTHOR

Matt Wesolowski is an author from Newcastle-Upon-Tyne in the UK. He is a former English tutor for young people in the PRU and care systems.

Matt was a winner of the Pitch Perfect competition at the Bloody Scotland Crime Writing Festival in 2015. His debut thriller, *Six Stories*, was an Amazon bestseller in the USA, Canada, the UK and Australia, and a WHSmith Fresh Talent pick. *Hydra* was published in 2018 and became an international bestseller. *Changeling*, the third book in the series, was published in 2019 and was longlisted for the Theakston's Old Peculier Crime Novel of the Year. His fourth book, *Beast*, won the Amazon Publishing Readers' Independent Voice Book of the Year award in 2020 and was followed by *Deity*.

Matt lives in Newcastle with his partner, young son, several tanks of rescued goldfish, a snake and a cat. Find him on Twitter @ConcreteKraken and Instagram: MattJWesolowski.

The Six Stories Series

Six Stories

Hydra

Changeling

Beast

Deity

Demon

Demon

MATT WESOLOWSKI

ORENDA
BOOKS

Orenda Books
16 Carson Road
West Dulwich
London SE21 8HU
www.orendabooks.co.uk

First published in the United Kingdom by Orenda Books, 2022

A catalogue record for this book is available from the British Library.

ISBN 978-1-913193-98-0
eISBN 978-1-913193-99-7

Typeset in Garamond by www.typesetter.org.uk

Printed and bound by CPI Group (UK) Ltd, Croydon CR0 4YY

For sales and distribution, please contact info@orendabooks.co.uk

'This glen was in very ill repute, and was never traversed, even at noonday, without apprehension. Its wild and savage aspect, its horrent precipices, its shaggy woods, its strangely-shaped rocks and tenebrous depths, where every imperfectly-seen object appeared doubly frightful – all combined to invest it with mystery and terror.

No one willingly lingered here, but hurried on, afraid of the sound of his own footsteps. No one dared to gaze at the rocks, lest he should see some hideous hobgoblin peering out of their fissures.'

—William Harrison Ainsworth
The Lancashire Witches

'They had engaged in mortal combat with one another, they had cooked strange ingredients over a smoking and reluctant flame with a fine disregard of culinary conventions, they had tracked each other over the countryside with gait and complexions intended to represent those of the aborigines of South America, they had even turned their attention to kidnapping (without any striking success), and these occupations had palled.'

—Richmal Crompton, *Just William*

Please be aware before you proceed that this book contains fictional violence against children and animals that may cause some readers distress or upset.

—Matt Wesolowski

Dear Mum,

You would have hated it today. You would have bent down and whispered in my ear, 'Look at the fucking state of that.' I loved it when you used swear words, Mum. You only ever whispered them. Sometimes I whisper them too. I do it in bed, when Dad's clattering round downstairs or outside having a smoke.

I whisper them and sometimes I cry. But not that much and definitely not when Dad's there.

It was the village fete today, and it looked properly empty without your stall there. There was all this bunting everywhere with Union Jacks on it. That was new.

It looked shit, Mum, haha!

Everyone stared at me when I walked in, like I had two heads or something. I thought, *Look at the fucking state of that,* in your voice, and I swear I felt your hand on my shoulder, I smelled your hair, felt it tickle. Heard all the beads in it jangle.

I could almost smell the incense that you used to light and put on your stall. Loads of people bought it as well, Mum, I remember that. I saw one of those little brass Buddhas you used to sell on Nelly Thrunton's windowsill the other day, so there. To be honest it was really weird – the first fete without you. They had one of those pig roast things where your stall used to be; a whole pig on a spit over this grill thing, and you could see its face and everything. You would have been properly annoyed. I held my breath when I walked past it, just like you would have done.

There wasn't any of those goldfish in bags as prizes on the whack-the-witch stall, you'll be pleased to know. I was worried that they'd bring that back, but they must have listened to you for once. There was loads of little kids lined up to have a go. I don't know why they all go so mad for it – it's proper lame: the stick is foam, the witch isn't even scary and if you miss her, Mr Diamond gives you a bag of sweets anyway. What's the point?

Mrs Bellingham had her jam stall, and all the old biddies were fussing on about it. She had this mad new flavour – gooseberry and lychee, or something, and all these little samples on bits of toast, like in the supermarket. But I didn't have one.

I've still never heard anyone my age say 'old biddy' either, Mum; that was totally one of your old-person things. When I walked past, they all turned to look at me with their sad eyes, like sheep. None of them said anything though, none of them asked if I was OK or was I having a good day or anything like that either. I heard them all whisper as well – *pss-pss* behind my back.

I remember when you got mad once and said that it was full of snakes round here. Now I think I get what you meant. But I think they're more like sheep: old and white and fluffy and boring. Don't tell Dad I said that.

Mr and Mrs Hartley were wandering round like they were the bosses of the fete, as usual, and everyone was shaking their hands and saying how lovely it was, and I wanted to say it was *fucking shit*. Imagine, Mum, if I'd gone up to them and said that. There was nothing to do, really, just boring stalls and food. I wanted to buy a cake, and I joined the queue, but then everyone said I should go to the front and it was proper embarrassing, so I just left because I couldn't be bothered with them all looking at me and saying they were sorry and all of that. I did go to the book stall, because Mr Womble (remember how you used to call him that?) was the only one who didn't look at me with stupid sheep eyes. He was too busy with his pipe, and his face was all red, and he was wearing this massive jumper, and he smelled of burned paper. His hair still grows out of his ears and nose too, in those great big clumps. I bought a new *Just William*, which he said I could have for 5p because the cover was all hanging off. It was *William the Fourth*, which I've not got yet.

I just went home after that.

Dad sent me out after tea to 'play with my mates' because

he had stuff to do, but he didn't know I had *William the Fourth* in my back pocket, so I went to the secret place to read it. I saw the new lad on the way. He was walking over from Stothard's rec, where they all play football. I bet he's just like all the rest of them round here, a right wazzock.

No one saw where I went. I was smart: went one way then doubled back on myself up through the dip in the top field and along the ditch. No one was there, they were all playing football. It was peaceful. It's always peaceful there, Mum, and I sat in the shade and read *Just William*, and I cried a bit, Mum, but only a little bit, and only because I remembered when you used to read *Just William* to me. When I read it, I heard it in your voice.

I'm going to start taking a cushion with me, but what if someone stops me and says, *What are you doing?* I'll say, *I'm taking my cushion for a walk, thank you very much!* That's the sort of thing you would say, and you would laugh and you would have said, *That showed the old fuddy-duddies.*

Remember when you told me Richmal Crompton was actually a woman, and I didn't believe you? I didn't think a lady could write stories like *Just William*, and you said no one else did either, and no one would have read it back then if she hadn't changed her name to sound like a man. You told me I need to always look out for that sort of unfairness in the world, because it's still here, you said, it's still everywhere.

I waited until I had stopped crying before I went home, but it was dark by then and I was worried that Dad would go mad, but he was snoring on the sofa when I got in, so I read just one more *William* story, and I remembered that time we made liquorish water and I pretended to like it, and Dad said, 'What's this pond water doing in the fridge?', and we couldn't stop laughing.

I thought I'd write this just before I go to sleep. School tomorrow, worse luck.

Goodnight, Mum. Xx

http://www.missingpersonsteam.uk

Ussalthwaite

England

North Yorks. Police

[View sensitive images]

Gender: Male

Age Range: 30-50

Ethnicity: White European

Height: 175cm (5 ft 8 ins)

Build: Medium

Body or remains: Body

Circumstances: Deceased male found within cave area of Ussal Bank Kilns, Ussalthwaite

Hair: Brown

Facial hair: Beard

Distinguishing features:

Tattoo – unspecified – left arm – image: 'Celtic cross'

Tattoo – unspecified – left forearm – image – 'unspecified tribal design'

Possessions: None.

The Demonic Duo Have Served Their Time in Hell

Leonora Nelson

The men who were once children have served their time. Now has the idea of revenge replaced a need for justice?

A caveat before I even start, before I'm accused of being a hand-wringing Marxist or some kind of war-crime sympathiser: the crime perpetrated by two twelve-year-old boys in Usalthwaite, North Yorkshire in 1995 was abominable. Some might say unforgivable.

The idea that one or both of the 'demonic duo', now men in their thirties, will be named leaves a nasty taste. If doing so is not a dog-whistle to provoke some kind of vigilante justice, then what is it? What is the purpose of exposing people who have served their allotted time and have been judged to be successfully rehabilitated into society?

The 'demonic duo' have rightly paid for what they did; they are figuratively and literally not the people they used to be, but that may never be enough.

The word flittering though social media is that a member of the public has discovered the identity of one, if not both killers, and is prepared to reveal them for the highest price.

Whoever's going to do this needs to take a long, hard look at themselves and decide who the demon really is.

Episode 1: The Bad Place

—There was only one remotely bad part of Ussalthwaite, and it wasn't exactly bad. It's like anything really, there's a rotten apple in every batch. .

It's just outside the village. You have to go over Ussal Top, a big steep hill covered in heather, to find it. Not really Ussalthwaite village I suppose. Well, that's where they found him the other week, that man.

Have they found out who he is yet?

Dear me, his poor family.

When I was a girl, most of us were happy just messing about on the hill or wandering down to Barrett's Pond. It's lovely down that way; there's a meadow and bluebells on the banks in spring. That's where we went when there were too many older ones on Ussal Top. There were reeds and you could find frogs or catch sticklebacks in jam jars. We'd take sandwiches and scones that our mams had made. It seems mad now, doesn't it? Can you imagine parents letting their little ones wander round a pond trying to catch fish with jam jars these days? It would never happen.

Nowadays, they're just sat inside on their phones, aren't they?

Back then though, our mams and dads told us to get out the house and be back when it got dark. It was that safe around here. We had all we needed, the sun and the fields and each other. Paradise on earth. That's Ussalthwaite alright. That's the real Ussalthwaite.

We weren't daft, neither was our parents. If I wasn't home at or before 5.30pm on a Saturday or if they even thought I'd been to the kilns, I was grounded for a month and probably got a whack on the arse with a slipper too. Of course, everyone always went and played at the kilns on Ussal Top. The one place you weren't allowed to go. The bad place.

That's kids for you. That's about as naughty as it got in Ussalthwaite when I was a girl.

Things are very different now.

Welcome to Six Stories.

I'm Scott King.

The voice you've just heard is that of long-term resident of the North Yorkshire village of Ussalthwaite, Penny Myers. Penny says she has not and will never live anywhere else.

Ussalthwaite is the epitome of 'God's own country', although, considering what happened there in the seventies and again in 1995, the terms seems ironic.

Now it has seen a suicide. A man, still unidentified. This series, however, is not about him. Not yet. But it was the discovery of his body that brought me here, to this small, picturesque village nestled in the stunning Yorkshire countryside. But this suicide is sadly not the first time tragedy has struck here.

Before we travel to this beautiful village in the middle of nowhere, let me say a few words about what we do here at Six Stories.

We look back at a crime.

We rake over old graves.

I'd just like you all to know that I'm no expert, I have no degrees or PhDs in criminology or psychology. I'm not trying to change laws or challenge beliefs. This podcast is like a discussion group at an old crime scene.

Six perspectives on a crime; one event through six pairs of eyes.

In this series, we're going to talk to six people who were there at the time of a terrible tragedy; a tragedy that, despite the weight of what occurred, was very swiftly forgotten. It's inexplicably difficult, even today to find much on the subject of the strange events of more than twenty years ago that sent shock waves through this peaceful, rural Yorkshire community.

Sometimes, looking at the past can have consequences for the present. Sometimes our raking disturbs a plot and sometimes people don't like old graves disturbed. I can understand that. Some graves should be left well alone. Sometimes we don't need to pull to pieces things that are better left to rest.

Like, perhaps, this one.

It was here in Ussalthwaite, on a bright morning in September, 1995, halfway along a secluded bridleway, under the shade of some trees, that a local man walking his dog saw what he thought was rubbish bags that had been tossed into a small stream. It took a few moments for the man to realise exactly what he was looking at.

Twelve-year-old Sidney Parsons had endured a severe beating; he suffered broken ribs, cuts and internal bleeding, and his small body had been laid, face down, in running water. A rock was embedded in the back of his skull, it had been thrown with so much force.

I don't derive any pleasure from giving such gruesome details about the fate of Sidney Parsons, but I think it's necessary that you know how violent the attack was on a boy who'd simply been sent to the shop by his mother and never returned.

—It's never been the same round here since then. I would have said that Ussalthwaite was the perfect village. I really would. Then this happened, and no one'll ever forget it. Not as long as they live.

Ussalthwaite, nestled in the heart of the North Yorkshire Moors National Park, is stunning. It's a bit of a time warp – cottages nestled along cobbled streets. Walking around, you can almost hear the strains of Dvořák's Symphony No. 9 on the coal-smoke tinted breeze. Flowers tumble from every window box and spoiled cats loll on windowsills.

The moors themselves were formed in the Ice Age; uplands, lowlands, moors, coasts and cliffs.

Bronze Age and Roman remains have been found across the wider area of the National Park. There are decommissioned nuclear fallout shelters from the cold war era, too. Nature swallows the past swiftly here.

A few remote sheep farms dot these wild uplands, and rivers gurgle through patches of woodland. Time passes here with the flowering of the heather – the cry of the curlew and the golden plover marking the slow turn of the seasons.

But not 150 years ago, this vast landscape of hills and heather hummed with industry. The steam of rail-building met the black smog of the mines; furnaces roared and steam power shunted ore and coal further north and to the coast.

The village of Ussalthwaite itself had a brief flirtation with ironstone mining in the mid-1800s, before the rock went dry. The industry finally left in the 1920s. Just a spatter of the mining cottages remain.

There are remnants scattered in and around Ussalthwaite from its industrial past; the shadows of trams and railways wind past ruined chimneys and monolithic slag piles. Hay meadows now encroach on the remains of pump houses, and the metal grates that seal the ancient pits are grown over.

This land is good at forgetting.

Its people? They wish they were.

—I'm good at this whole Zoom chat rigmarole, you know. You have to be, don't you? We're not immune to Covid, even all the way out here. I set up the Ussalthwaite WI Zoom meetings to keep our spirits up. There's a few of the older ones who are house-bound or frail, and it's a lifeline for them. It brought light here during that dark. If we hadn't embraced technology, it would have been the end for a lot of us. Mind over matter, isn't it? We might be falling apart out here, but our brains are tough as old boots.

I talk to Penny Myers via Zoom. She sits in a comfortable-looking armchair. Like most of Ussalthwaite's residents, Penny is well off, and her home is neat, polished and cosy. She's less and less able to move about much these days, but she can still run online bingo like a pro.

Her carer wanders past in the background occasionally. He's keeping an ear out to hear what I'm asking; he's making sure Penny doesn't upset herself.

I somehow doubt that's going to happen, but it's early days.

—I sometimes wonder: if our parents hadn't been so adamant about us not going up to the kilns, then maybe we would never have passed that down to our kids, and none of it would have happened? I dunno. You can't stop badness; you can't stop the devil being the devil, can you?

There are many different stories surrounding Ussalthwaite and what happened there in 1995. I guess I'm here to pick out which one, from six, is true. So where do we begin? Let me tell you a little about the kilns. In fact, no, I want to give Penny that honour. She lived through the horror.

—Well, you can see 'em online, of course. The kilns on Ussal Bank.

People usually catch them proper nice, with the sun shining on them or else the sky all purple behind them, but when you're up close, they're not all that picturesque, I'm telling you now.

There's a stretch of cliffs about a mile as the crow flies from Ussalthwaite village, over the hill and onto Ussal Bank. This was the main site of the mine, back when the ironstone stood out from the cliff face itself. The kilns are less like an oven, more like a sort of viaduct shape – a line of great stone arches built into the side of the cliffs. They're ominous; a row of ten black tunnels, about twelve feet high, earth and slag tumbling from their entrances. Frozen in time. Crumbling, grey brick.

—Me granddad worked in the kilns: he used to burn the ore in the furnaces, to get it ready to be sent up to Durham to be smelted. Some nights, when there was a storm, he used to take me dad and his brothers up onto the moor to watch the lightning hit the cliffside. He used to tell them it was as black as the gates of hell in there. He said he was lucky he never had to go into the mine itself. He said a devil lived down there, under the hills. There were a load more people in the village when me granddad was a lad; more houses as well. Most of them, he said, worked in the mines. They had some funny old stories, I can tell you that for nowt.

—*What kind of stories?*

—I think he was just trying to scare us kids, you know? Part of a grandparent's job isn't it, to tell tall tales? One story he always used to tell was about poor old Pat Wood, who lived down Pitt Cottages. Poor fella. Blind as a bat from the mine. Probably had early dementia as well, God rest his soul. Me granddad used to say that there was a story in the pubs that Pat Wood was one of them what saw something in the mine. You see, by the 1920s, it was getting harder and harder to get hold of that ironstone, and they had to dig further and further into the hill. The companies were laying off more and more lads, because there was no more work as all of it was gone. Pat Wood, me granddad said, was on the final shift down there when there was an incident.

—*What sort of incident?*

—Stink damp. It's gas what can build up inside mines. Toxic it is, even a little bit of it. They dunno how long it was poisoning them down there, in the deepest part of the mine, but they told their gaffers there was a smell. Rotten eggs. Hydrogen sulphide. They should have got them out of there right away. They should have known, but no one listened. No one believed them, thought someone was playing practical jokes. Pat Wood was the only one what lived. The rest of the poor buggers died within a few weeks; bronchitis. It was a tragedy. After that there was a strike. The company went bust and they filled in the mine. Good riddance.

—*You said that Mr Wood saw something.*

—That's what me granddad used to say. That was the tale they passed round in the pub. I daresay it was a story soaked in too much ale and not enough work, but it used to scare me as a kid. And me dad used to tell me he saw Pat Wood out and about, every so often, when he was little. Used to scare him something rotten, staggering around and shouting about summat from a long time ago buried down there. Pat said he seen a terrible, long shadow when there were no men to cast one, heard summat laughing under all that rock. Poor bugger.

—*It sounds like a combination of dementia and the long-term effects of the gas, perhaps?*

—Aye, it does, doesn't it? Me granddad used to tell us the old tale to keep us in check. He said that those miners had been poking their noses in places they shouldn't have been down there in the dark. He said if we did the same we'd end up like them. He said there's things down there that no kiddie should be asking about, and that's as far as he would go.

—*What do you think now?*

—It's not a very nice story, is it? I guess that's why we were told to stay away from the kilns and all. I think there was a bad feeling about the whole place. It's what happens when there's tragedy, isn't it? Stories begin, rumours start, shadows get longer.

The shadows of Ussalthwaite and the kilns are especially long. The next tragedy surrounding the place is just as speculative as that of Pat Wood.

—There was some young girl who came here on her holidays back in the seventies. What was her name – Julie? Something like that. Well, she ended up in one of those … what do you call them these days? Not an asylum, but you know what I mean, don't you? They reckon she'd been poking around in them kilns when she was here, messing with things better left alone.

It's a story I've heard, but one we need to leave aside for now.

As early as the late 1980s, Ussalthwaite became a sought-after place: the affluent bought holiday cottages and second homes here. Refurbishments began on many of the old mining houses and barns. Wood-fired hot tubs and decking began to replace allotments and blackberry bushes. Then a wave of new families moved into the village, bringing with them prosperity. The old farmland was bought up and developed, barns were converted and new ones sprung up across the barren moorland.

—You can build what you like here, paint it all over, but I'm telling you now, them kilns are a bad place. That's where they waited for him, those two. They waited for young Sidney Parsons up at them kilns, and that's where they battered him; then they dumped his poor little body in the stream to die, like he was nowt more than rubbish.

The kilns are still there today, crumbling and silent. There's no heritage trail or public information boards; no neat fences politely holding back the public, like at similar, more tourist-friendly sites, such as Rosedale.

The beauty of the area can swiftly turn ominous – with a rainstorm or fog. And at night, when the wind howls across the barren hills of heather, the stories of a devil living beneath Ussal Bank suddenly don't seem so farfetched. As we'll come to discover in this series, there are many more stories about the kilns, stories hidden in the shadows of their vast silence. Stories older and deeper than the deadly stink damp lurking beneath the hills.

—So you see, we've had horrors stories, here in Ussalthwaite. But in ninety-five we got a new one. Those two boys and what they done to Sidney Parsons. And I think it's scarier than any of those old stories my grandad told us.

We take some time to have a tea break. Penny's carer pops up in front of the camera and tells me he's going to turn off her video and audio for a few minutes; give her some time to refresh herself. That's understandable; we've painted a picture of a place and now we need to delve down into it.

The event that made the name Ussalthwaite infamous occurred in September 1995. The savage murder of a young boy. By two children.

A horror. There's no other word for it. Horror upon horror. But we need to find a place to start, which is why I want to begin with Penny.

—I think it'll be good to just get it over with.

—*OK, thank you, Penny. Now, when did it all start, for you?*

—It all started at the kilns. They're spooky; even on a sunny day, those kilns were dark and damp. But they weren't deep; just ten feet or so into the hill. We dared each other to go right to the back, where it got darkest and you could feel all that ancient rock pressing you in. It was dangerous; and it's only by the grace of God that no one got hurt worse than a black eye or a scraped knee.

There was loads of stuff from the kilns – bits of smelt and iron ore all over the place that we picked up. You had to hide it from your mam and dad, mind, cos that would be evidence you'd been up there. There was other stuff too, all the waste – rock and crystal from deep underground. People found even older stuff too – arrowheads and that from the Bronze Age.

Slag heaps from the iron mines in the area render all sorts of treasure at sites like these. It isn't unusual to find Roman and Bronze Age artefacts; bits of pottery and weapons, blackened by age, dug up from the mine and discarded in vast heaps of earth.

—We all wanted them for show-and-tell at school; or we played with them.

—*Are there many of you left – the families from back then?*

—Not many from when I was a girl, no. Most people upped and left after what happened here in ninety-five. All these along my street are holiday houses these days. There's one or two of the old 'uns like me what are still here.

—*I've been past and seen the Hartley house. No one's bought that one, have they?*

—No one ever will either. It needs knocking down, demolishing;

its bricks ground and scattered on the moor. Folk still avoid walking past there. Even today. I still feel sorry for them two. Ken and Jennifer. All they ever did was good, and look what happened to them.

Penny's correct; people do avoid the Hartley house. I sat in my car yesterday, parked up on the tiny, single-lane road that winds through Ussalthwaite. Pretty little terraced cottages sit on banks on one side; a stone bridge leads over the green rush of the River Fent to a wooden-walled community centre with green, anti-climb fences around the edge of a 4G football pitch. A crumbling church with restored stained-glass windows sits atop a squat hill surrounded by ancient tombstones wreathed in ivy. I saw no cars drive past, and the passers-by made a point of crossing the road when they came to that particular house, the former home of Ken and Jennifer Hartley. It's at the very end of the row, and sits in the shadow of a sprawling plum tree in its front garden; the branches look like dense, black fists covered in knobbly wooden claws. The windows of the house are boarded up, and there's a metal grate on the front door. The front garden is a mass of rotted fruit and dead leaves. It's a huge contrast to the affluence of the rest of the village.

—I'd say the Hartleys were the first well-off folk what moved here. They were professionals, both of them, educated. Lovely couple. They gave Ussalthwaite its heart back, them two. Always planting flowers and litter-picking – getting the local kids involved, too.

—*How many children did the Hartleys have?*

—None of their own. I think there was a problem there, but you don't ask, do you? It's not good manners.

At least before the event of 1995, what's been reported about Ken and Jennifer Hartley is nothing but complimentary. By all accounts, the pair were good-hearted pillars of the community. It was the Hartleys who started up a Neighbourhood Watch scheme and encouraged other residents to report crime. They lobbied for funding for local transport and a new community hub. Penny tells me that Ken and Jennifer Hartley brought a genuine sense of pride back to Ussalthwaite.

—They brought back some of the old ways, them two. That's why folk took to 'em so easy, see? We started up the harvest festival again, and I tell you what, that was lovely.

—I have listeners from overseas who might not know what a harvest festival is. Can you paint a picture of what it was like?

—Oh it's a very English thing, isn't it? When the heather across the moor turned purple you knew it was nearly harvest time. When I was a girl it was a big event, the harvest festival; all us kids dressed up as pumpkins and onions. Folk showed off their cabbages and parsnips and whatnot that they grew on their allotments. They used to have animals on show as well; the sheep and the cows and that. Cider and a band. Country dancing. When I was a girl, we had Morris men swinging their hankies and jangling their bells. It was lovely. But times move on, don't they? No one had nowt to show, and the harvest festival just faded away. When Ken and Jennifer brought it back, it were new. More charity-based, with everyone bringing tins of food for the old folks and the infirm. We've been collecting for the food banks these last few years.

—It sounds like the festival brought everyone together back in the nineties.

—It really did. We were a community again. They started it off, the Hartleys. Good people.

We're going to stay in the nineties. By the time the Hartleys had brought the harvest festival back and were renovating their house, Penny was in her forties, with her own children. Her husband played in the Ussalthwaite brass band, something else that had been set up by, you guessed it, Ken Hartley.

—Can we talk about the…

—Those boys? Aye. I know. I've been dancing, haven't I?

—Actually, no. You've painted a solid picture of Ussalthwaite back in 1995. It's what we need – some context.

—The thing is, this story is just horrible, it's sad; you know those crime stories where there's a detective with a drink problem and it all gets tied up at the end? Well that's not this story, it's not what happened here in ninety-five. So I'm sorry if I go on a bit, because it were terrible, and I'm going to tell it like it is. Like it was, I suppose.

But it's not going to have a nice bow on it at the end, I hope you know that?

—I know.

There's a long pause before Penny goes on. Her fingers grip the arm rests of her chair, her eyes gazing past the camera of her laptop, through her front window, I presume, over the empty street and into the horizon where spring sunlight dapples a Yorkshire sky. I wonder what memories are coming back, what this digging will unearth. I feel like those miners going deeper and deeper for the iron ore. How deep is too deep? I wonder. What good is there in opening this old wound? Taking an old woman back to a place of trauma?

—It all began with that one what came to live with the Hartleys. Robbie, he was called. Robbie Hooper. No one knows what he's called now, do they? The other one, Danny, he was from here. An Ussalthwaite lad, born and bred. He lived up top – over the bridge. His dad were a farmer. Sheep. He was from one of the old Ussalthwaite families. Richard Greenwell. Quiet man. Spoke only when he needed to. They had a dog, Jip – lovely old thing with odd eyes. Danny went to school with our Elsie – that's my daughter. As far as I know he were nowt to talk about really. Just a quiet farm lad. Didn't really have much to do with no one else. Got the bus with all the other kids up to the school. But then his poor mother died, God rest her soul. I don't think he ever got over that.

The death of Saffron Greenwell, Danny's mother, and particularly the way she died, rocked the close-knit village.

—I'm not one to speak ill of the dead, but she was a funny one, Saffron Greenwell; one of them sixties flower children, she was. She did massage and that, yoga and – what was it? – some kind of healing, I daresay. Whatever that is. Summat to do with your auras and whatever. She made a living from it. Right popular with tourists. She travelled all over to see her clients, you know. She was back and forth, all the way to Harrogate sometimes.

Saffron Greenwell was a self-employed yoga teacher and therapist; she also practised reiki and crystal healing. Her list of clients in the North Yorkshire area was extensive, and she was considered, in alternative-therapy circles, to be one of the best.

—Well I'm not one to say what she was doing but Sally Bentley, who lives on Bramwell Court, says she was up on the top floor one night, rocking her Anthony to sleep, and she looked out the window and saw Saffron Greenwell and someone else, she couldn't make out who it was, walking down from Ussal Top. Saffron, she says, was naked as the day she was born! One o'clock in the morning and all.

I never knew how she and Richard got together. Chalk and cheese they were. And after that, I don't know why he even kept her. Maybe it was for the boy? Who can say? She wasn't exactly a good example for him. Lighting fires all over the land, telling folk she had a right to do what she liked. No wonder their Danny turned out the way he did. No wonder he done what he did.

It was in December 1994, the day after Boxing Day, that Danny Greenwell, then ten years old, found his mother hanging from an electrical cord in one of the barns. As far as I'm aware there was no note. Her death was ruled as suicide. There were no suspicious circumstances.

—She were the one who kept everything going on the farm. Danny's dad, Richard, was a sheep man, like his dad and his dad's dad. All he knew was the fields and the flock, so when she died, he suddenly had a young lad to care for too. Poor thing. We tried to help, all of us, made him food and that, but they didn't want to know. Kept themselves to themselves. Threw it all back in our faces.

But what happened with Sidney was nowt to do with what happened to Danny's poor mother. He only turned when that Robbie arrived. It was Robbie what changed him, I swear on me old mother's grave.

Robbie Hooper arrived in Ussalthwaite in February 1995. He was the same age as Danny Greenwell and Sidney Parsons: twelve.

—There was summat different about the lad. Ken and Jennifer

Hartley told anyone what would listen that Robbie was coming to live in Ussalthwaite for six months. They thought that being out here in the middle of nowhere, out in the sticks, in a small community, would be good for him. They never said that much about him before he arrived though. I think there was summat going on behind the scenes with him, you know?

From what I have managed to piece together, Robbie Hooper was the child of a family friend of the Hartleys. The Hoopers lived far away from Ussalthwaite, in Gloucester, and had suffered their own terrible tragedy. Robbie's parents Mildred and Sonny were involved in a car accident. Mildred sadly died, and Sonny lay in critical condition in hospital. Robbie, their only child, had nowhere to go, so through some kind of arrangement ended up staying with the Hartleys. I want to stay with Robbie's arrival in Ussalthwaite, two hundred miles north.

—Now don't get me wrong, that man and his wife, they were saints, taking in the boy like that. They had patient hearts, the pair of them. I remember Ken saying to us that children need patience and kindness in order to thrive. He told us that Robbie would need a little more from all of us, from the community – he needed kindness, understanding.

—*Were the people of Ussalthwaite obliging?*

—Oh yes, of course we were. Everyone respected the Hartleys. They were grateful to us. Not like Richard Greenwell, who shut the door in our faces when we tried to help.

Penny's not sure when exactly Robbie Hooper arrived but his presence came without fanfare. One day he was in Ussalthwaite.

—I remember our Elsie pointing at him from her bedroom window. Hers was up at the front, looked out over the street, and I was putting away clean washing when she says, 'There he is, Mam.'

I don't know what I was expecting, really. He was a bit funny-looking I suppose, all hunched and hulking with a big forehead. He was walking past our place wearing a rucksack and he must have sensed us watching, because he looked up at us and smiled.

I know what you're waiting for – there was something in them eyes;

that gaze chilled me right to my bones? Well there was none of that. He glanced up, saw me stood at the window with a load of washing, and all that was wrong with him was some gaps in his teeth. Then he just kept going, went about his business. I have to say, it was an anticlimax.

—*How do you mean?*

—Well, there was this great, big build up wasn't there? The Hartleys telling us all how we had to be kind and that; all this mystery about why he's even come here in the first place. I was a little disappointed if I'm honest. Not a lot goes on round here, you see, so young Robbie was the talk of the village. I asked a few other mams who had kids at St Catherine's what he'd been like in school, and they all said he was quiet, 'just keeps hisself to hisself'. I swear that's all I ever heard from anyone about this Robbie. I think no one really knew what to do. He wasn't one of our own – none of us really knew what we were supposed to do for the lad. We couldn't go round bringing soup and stuff, could we?

Penny says that no one really saw much of Robbie at first, save for when he walked to the bus stop or back up the road to the Hartleys' house at the end of the street.

—I feel like maybe we all could have been a bit kinder; gone out of our way to talk to him, made him feel welcome, you know? I think everyone was waiting for someone else to do it. It would have seemed odd though, wouldn't it? All these adults talking to a young lad like that.

—*What about the children in the village? Did they have anything to report about Robbie?*

—I asked our Elsie, and, well, she was at that age where she was getting awkward, self-conscious, all that, and she wasn't going to walk up to some strange new boy she didn't know and make friends, was she? Maybe when she was little, but not then. No, she didn't see much of him. Even on the bus and in school, he was quiet, she said.

The local secondary school, St Catherine's, is a thirty-minute ride on a school bus that picks up young people from the surrounding area. Penny tells me this bus ride is where many friendships are made.

—So when he starts at St Catherine's, Robbie starts getting the bus with the rest of them, including our Elsie. She's a bit older, year ten by then, and sits at the back with all her mates, listening to their Walkmans and that. She says no one picked on him, no one took much notice of him really. This little quiet boy. Then one day, when they go up the hill past the farm where Danny Greenwell lives, to pick him up, Danny sits next to Robbie. That was the start, as far as I know anyway.

Penny explains that she doesn't know a lot more about the relationship between Robbie and Danny. She saw them around together over the next few months, but paid them little mind.

—I used to see them round the village a lot more, especially on the weekends – wandering off to the pond or, as it turned out, up to the kilns. I never thought much of it, to be honest. I was glad the lad had made a friend. I was glad that the other one, Danny, had found someone too. I thought it was good for both of them.

Penny tells me that she wasn't aware of any interaction between Robbie and Danny and Sidney Parsons, their eventual victim.

—I honestly think if they'd been after Sidney from the start, we would have known about it. I would have heard something in the queue at the supermarket or after church. Folk looked after their own round here, especially a kid like Sidney Parsons.

From what has been made public about the case, Sidney Parsons was relatively popular around Ussalthwaite; certainly everyone knew who he was and looked out for him on account of his epilepsy and a learning disability.

—Back then we didn't know what to call it. I don't know the right words and I don't want to upset anybody. He was a bit … slow, you might say? A bit delayed? He was a smiling, happy sort of boy, would do anything for you if you asked him. You know the type? Lots of people made sure no one took advantage – cos they do, don't they? People take advantage of folk who are a bit … well … less fortunate. It wasn't like Sidney didn't have friends of his own though. He hung around with poor Terry Atkinson from Butterwell Court.

We'll come to what happened to Terry Atkinson in due course. For now I want to keep things in relative order. Robbie arrived in the village in February 1995 and soon made a connection with Danny Greenwell. A few months later, in the summer, some strange incidents took place in the village.

—Oh it was like a biblical plague, right here in the village. Horrible things. I've never seen anything like it.

Penny's talking about an infestation of flies that descended on Ussalthwaite overnight, sometime in June 1995.

—We couldn't sleep; they kept setting off the security light, there was that many of them. I've never seen anything like it in all my life – thousands of them all over everything. Those citronella candles you burn on holiday were changing hands for hundreds of pounds; the shops were all out of fly spray. We all had to stay in with the windows closed – they would get in your hair, your mouth if you dared go outside. Everyone was tense the whole time cos you always felt like there was one crawling on you. We looked out of the window and saw them swirling in the sky like a flock of birds. I get the shivers thinking about it now.

Our Elsie says there was a horrible day on the school bus. She said that there was a group of lads who sat at the back – older ones, and they were always shouting things at Robbie and Danny. She says that one of them, she can't remember who, turns round and tells them if they keep going, they'll be sorry.

—*Robbie or Danny said this?*

—Right. She says these lads all start laughing, and the rest of the bus was laughing too. But then suddenly it slows down, the engine stops and everything goes dark.

—*On the bus?*

—On the bus. It was them flies; the bus had driven into a big cloud of them, and they were all over the windows. She said it was like a moving fog, millions of little bodies slithering all over each other. She thought they must have got into the engine or something.

Then of course, poor Sidney Parsons starts fitting, doesn't he?

—*What kind of a fit?*

—He starts shaking, and the kids round him are screaming. He was lucky he had his mate with him, Terry Atkinson, who knew what to do – looked after him until the driver gets the engine going again. Elsie said he had the windscreen wipers going to shift them. They finally managed to get Sidney to the hospital and the kids to school.

Then, after a few days, they were gone, the flies. Folk were sweeping great big clods of them from their windowsills and off their ceilings for about a week afterwards.

It happened again. Just a few months back. Twenty-six years later. On the anniversary of that poor boy's death – another load of flies. Horrible. Just horrible. It goes to show that there's summat not right going on. The flies come back, and then that poor man. What's the common thing here? The kilns, that's what. That bad place.

It was reported at the time that, on the twenty-sixth anniversary of Sidney Parsons' murder, Ussalthwaite was once again engulfed by a plague of flies. The official explanation was the flooding of the River Fent, which flows through Ussalthwaite; the standing water left on the moors, and the lack of activity there and on the river during lockdown, allowed the concentration of a mating swarm of a non-biting midge known as the chironomid.

Let's go back to 1995.

—It wasn't long after that the disturbances began at the Hartley's place. Word gets around quick in the village, so soon everyone knew about them.

—*When did you first hear about what was happening there?*

—I knew the folk next door to the Hartleys. They were an older couple: Fiona Brown and her husband Henry. Henry, the poor soul was bed-bound; on his way out.

I remember chatting to Fiona after church one Sunday once the schools had gone back. She was pale, drawn, all of a flutter. Not had enough sleep, poor thing, and she said it was all cos of the racket.

—*From next door?*

—That's right. She said she'd been hearing all sorts, the most ungodly din. Great, big, clomping footsteps she says. But not on the floor. They was all over the walls, like someone's walking on them. It went on and on, all bloody night. She didn't sleep a wink.

—*Did the Browns complain?*

—I think, what with the boy coming and his situation, they didn't want to make a fuss, you know? Maybe it was him playing up, but with what had happened to his parents, and being in a strange place and all, that was understandable, wasn't it?

I told her to have a quiet word with Ken. I was sure he'd understand. But there was just something about the way she looked at me then, like she was scared. She said she didn't want to make a fuss. She just needed to tell someone on the quiet, just to let it out, she didn't want to be the one what kicked up a stink about this Robbie. She didn't want to be the one who looked like she wasn't accepting him, see?

I don't want us to get too far ahead of ourselves, but I do want to mention another strange thing that Penny remembers happening around this time.

—Our Elsie was walking back from the shop one night with a bag full of fish and chips for us, and she says when she passes the Hartleys' place, she saw a light on in an upstairs room, and there was a figure there, framed in the window, looking out. Nowt weird about that, is there? But just then the Hartleys' car pulls up in the drive, and Ken and Jennifer get out, with Robbie. They've just got home from somewhere. She says she looks back and the window in the house is dark again. Maybe it was just her imagination? It unsettled her though, I know that.

These events – the flies and the figure in the window – could have logical explanations. And neither of them have any direct connection with Robbie. However, things were about to get darker and more disturbing in the village.

—We started hearing things from folk in the village, just mutterings, you know.

—*What sorts of things?*

—About them two, about those boys: Robbie and Danny. Tom Diamond, who owns The Coach Inn, swore blind he saw two boys on the bridge over the Fent when he was closing up one night. It was late, nearly midnight – and this was a school night. He said he recognised Danny Greenwell, but the other one, presumably Robbie, was stood in the shadows. Danny was leaning over the edge, staring down into the water, he said. Tom was about to call out to them, ask them what they were doing there so late at night, but when he looked again they were gone.

And then there was Nancy Bellingham. She had some hens, you know, in her back yard. She made jams and cakes what she sold at markets and that. She had one of those little honesty boxes at the front of the drive where she put eggs, sometimes some chutneys. Folk could leave a donation and take what they wanted. It was for the tourists and the folk passing through. Well, she said, she'd put the eggs out one morning and a couple of kids on their way to school swiped them.

—*Did she see who it was?*

—She said it looked like that Danny Greenwell and his pal.

—*Robbie?*

—That's what she said. Thick as thieves them two – they swipe her eggs and go running off with their hoods up. She wouldn't have minded that much, boys will be boys and all, but it's what they did with them what made her so cross. Poor Mr Worrell from the bookshop – he was weeding in the graveyard at St Luke's, and the pair of them bombarded the poor man and ran off, laughing like drains, he said.

—*And this was definitely Danny and Robbie?*

—Well, Nancy's seen them from the back, and Mr Worrell, his head's in the clouds, but he said it was two boys their age. And then we found out that a few weeks before all that, the pair of them, Danny and Robbie, had got into big trouble with Ken Hartley.

—*What had they done this time?*

—He'd caught them bunking off school. They'd been up at the kilns, and Danny's father had caught them and brought Robbie over to Ken, who grounded him.

—How did you find out?

—Oh, it was talk of the village. People had seen them sneaking off from the bus stop and up over Ussal Top. Two figures, they said, creeping in the shadows, walking in the ditches under the trees, hiding behind the dry-stone walls. Everyone knew that kids weren't allowed to go up to the kilns, but those two, they acted like they didn't care, that the rules didn't apply to them. Our Elsie said they'd found something up there and were showing it off on the bus. Some artefacts. We all thought it was arrow heads, maybe some bits of Bronze Age pot or whatever. Whatever was going on, the pair were getting a reputation in the school as well as the village.

According to Penny, Elsie and a few other former pupils at St Catherine's, these two year-seven boys from Ussalthwaite had begun causing real problems for the teachers and other kids in the school.

—What exactly were they doing?

—Our Elsie said that pair were forever stood in the corridors outside classrooms or in detention. Everyone was surprised because when Robbie first came to the village, he was just this quiet thing with no mates, and Danny, he was just this loner that most people felt sorry for. But Elsie says it got worse and worse with them two. She was a few years above but kids talk, don't they? According to her, them two were always making noises when the teachers' backs were turned, then they started throwing things. Rubbers, pencils, rulers. She said you could always hear them arguing as well: 'It wasn't me, miss! I didn't do anything, sir!'

—Did Elsie ever see anything happen with her own eyes?

—Elsie told me that once she saw a whole stack of paper go flying across the art room when she went in to deliver a note to one of the teachers. She said Robbie and Danny were sat at the back, but they looked scared, she said – they looked as shocked as everyone else. But that pair not only had to stay in over lunch time to tidy it up, but they were put on after-school detention for arguing that it wasn't them. Now I'm not daft, there's always going to be lads playing up in school, but it was getting ridiculous. Then it got downright disgusting.

—*Disgusting?*

—Look, I know you're supposed to be kind, aren't you? You're supposed to show understanding to kids like Danny who'd lost his mother only the year before, and to Robbie – well, we all knew his situation. But apparently them two were doing all sorts of stuff on the field at break time – eating insects…

—*What, really?*

—Well, you don't know for sure with these things – you know what kids are like. But our Elsie said that Robbie was showing off, sticking spiders in his gob and chewing them up. She says she watched Danny Greenwell catch a Daddy Long Legs, pull off its wings and eat it in front of a load of kids. That wasn't long before we had that plague of flies you know. Everyone said those two would be having a feast.

—*Was anything done about this, at the school, I mean?*

—What were they to do? Back then, there wasn't the interventions and that you get now. They weren't being violent or anything like that, not straight away. They were just … odd. Ken Hartley and Richard Greenwell had to go for meetings at the school a couple of times, but I don't know what came of that.

Penny says that these stories spread like wildfire through Ussalthwaite and many people gave the two friends, Robbie and Danny, a wide berth. Some shopkeepers wouldn't allow the pair inside and if they wanted something, they had to send someone else in with their money to buy it for them. The children of the village, however, had a rather different view.

—Oh you know what little boys are like: frogs and snails and puppy dog's tails. They all thought that Robbie and Danny were great. Of course they did. Their mams thought very different though and made sure they stayed away. Left them two to make trouble by themselves.

—*To be honest, as unpleasant as it sounds, Robbie and Danny's behaviour sounds like pretty standard twelve-year-old lads trying to cause trouble, wouldn't you say? It seems like quite a jump to what came next.*

—Well I'm not the one to ask, because I don't know what happened exactly. But he left. Never came back.

—*Left? Who do you mean?*

—One of the teachers up at the school; a trainee, I believe. Mr … what was it now? Mr Graham, that was his name.

I've tried to find Laurence Graham but to no avail. From what I've been able to piece together, he was a trainee teacher at St Catherine's High School on his second placement of his training year. Mr Graham was in charge of a number of classes from various year groups, including one that contained Robbie and Danny. No one at St. Catherine's was prepared to answer much else about Mr Graham, so we'll have to go with what Penny Myers heard.

—He was young – quite popular with the kids as far as I know. Elsie had a few friends who he taught in her year.

—*You say he left.*

—That's right; one day he was there and the next, gone. Refused to return, apparently. All because of them two: Robbie and Danny.

—*I guess it must have been the level of disruption…*

—Oh it wasn't that; it was much, much worse. And it wasn't his classes that they made a misery. The poor lad had just bought a house in Ussalthwaite, him and his girlfriend. Those two little terrors made their lives a misery – knocking on their doors and windows all hours of the night, and following them home. They had a little one as well, a newborn, as if their lives weren't tough enough.

There was a few incidents, apparently, when she would be walking the pram late at night – you know how it is, trying to get a newborn to sleep – and those two, Robbie and Danny, would be following her, hidden in the shadows, behind walls. Leaping out at her. They just kept going, every night, every weekend. Mr Graham, he started joining her, for protection, like, but that didn't stop them. If anything it made it worse. Those two would appear at the end of the street, hoods up, or they'd follow behind them whispering horrible things, insults at them.

The poor man was a wreck by the end, our Elsie says; walking round that school like a zombie, with those two laughing at him the whole time. They almost broke him.

—*Why though? Why target Mr Graham and his girlfriend? What exactly had they done?*

—That's what no one really knows. All that I've heard is that Mr Graham was trying to teach the class about the old witch burnings what went on in Yorkshire in the 1600s. Mother Shipton and all that. Robbie and Danny took exception to it for whatever reason, and that was it.

After that; after Mr Graham packed his bags and left the village. That's when folk round here began to realise there was summat not right with them two.

—But surely someone could have done something? These were two twelve-year olds.

—That was the thing. No evidence; we didn't have all that CCTV you get nowadays back then. No one ever seen them, save for Mr Graham and his missus, and of course the boys denied everything.

The plague of flies in Ussalthwaite occurred in late June 1995. By the time the summer holidays started in August, after what happened with Laurence Graham, Robbie and Danny's reputation in the village was in tatters. Ken and Jennifer Hartley tried grounding Robbie, telling him he and Danny were no longer allowed to associate with each other, but to no avail. The two always found a way to get together. If anything, Penny says, forbidding their friendship only seemed to make it stronger.

—Them two were always away up at the kilns. God only knows what they were doing up there, but at least it meant that they weren't causing bother in the village. We were all a bit worried, what with the summer holidays coming up, what would happen. If them two would start targeting someone else. We never thought it would get as bad as it did. Never in a million years. I wonder if there was more we could have done?

According to Penny, the summer holidays passed in relative calm. Rather than there being trouble to do with Robbie and Danny directly, there were a lot of rumours and strange stories bubbling under the surface in the village. A shadow had fallen.

—The Browns, who lived next door to the Hartleys, were starting to get fed up with the racket. Fiona and Henry had to move into their spare room on the other side of the house because it never stopped: thump, thump, thump all night, she said, like hobnail boots walking all over the walls. Our Elsie and her friends wouldn't walk past the Hartleys' house after dark anymore, just in case them two were lurking. It was all silliness really. All thanks to Robbie and Danny's behaviour, it had everyone up a height.

It was when they started vandalising things that enough was enough, something should have been done, really.

—*Vandalism in the village? Robbie and Danny?*

—Oh yes. It was daft things as well, done to upset people. Just like they done to Laurence Graham. Other people began to see them at night; like little shadows they were, flitting in and out of doorways, quiet as mice. Reverend Little had a nasty fall off a ladder, trying to undo those boys' mischief.

—*What had they done?*

—It was mindless really, just silly. They'd got onto the church roof somehow, swarmed up there like little monkeys. It's an old building as well, been there since the twelfth century. They'd hung a rope off the edge to make a swing.

—*Really? A swing?*

—Well that's what the vicar, Ben Little, said. He said it was a big, thick rope; God only knows where they'd got it from. They'd tied a loop and thrown it over the stone cross that stands on top of the porch roof, over the entrance, the little beggars. There were scratch marks all over the church door, where they'd presumably been swinging and scuffing their feet. That door had not long been painted by the volunteer group as well, Sidney Parsons being one of them.

The poor vicar broke his collar bone falling off that ladder to cut the rope down; he never came back to the village. They got one of those African ones to take his place. I've got nowt against them, of course, but it never felt the same, you know?

—*Had anyone seen the boys do this?*

—Look, in a place as small as this, everyone knows what everyone else is doing. We didn't need to have caught them on camera to know it was them. They got rid of their teacher and then the vicar. Then they done the same thing to Terry Atkinson, didn't they? Hung a rope off his house. We should have known then. You're right, someone should have done something.

Just to pause for a moment; there is, believe it or not, rather unpleasant significance to this rope-hanging in Ussalthwaite, dating back to the 1600s. I promise we'll return to this, hopefully in the next episode. Now though, I want to return to 1995.

—And before Terry Atkinson, there was that poor dog up at the farm. By then it was too late.

It's about now that I need to warn you that where we're going is a dark place, a place of cruelty and violence. If this isn't for you, I suggest you stop here. Turn back, return to a place of light.

—I don't know who told me about poor Richard Greenwell's dog. Raised it from a pup, he had. Used to take it on the back of his little quad bike thing, checking the ewes, making sure they're ready for mating, you know? You'd see them up on the fields towards the end of summer. Word is that he got up one morning, and the dog's nowhere to be found. Him and Danny looked for it all day then that night, Richard goes looking in the barn, the one what had been locked ever since his poor wife took her life there.

—I'm not sure I want to know.

—Words can't do it justice. Apparently he found the poor thing all ripped up in the middle of the barn, like a wild animal had been at it. There's plenty of folk what say they've seen big cats out on the moors, but that's just rumours.

—And did people in the village think that Robbie and Danny were responsible?

—Well that's what we all thought. It stood to reason, especially after what happened with Sidney Parsons. One of the coldest parts of it was that Danny Greenwell helped his dad search for that poor creature all that day, knowing what he and his mate had done. Richard Greenwell never said nowt to no one, though, did he? Kept his business his business, no interest in the rest of us – stayed up on that farm with his sheep and his boy. No wonder Danny Greenwell turned out the way he did.

In retrospect, we can see the escalation of events in Ussalthwaite leading up to the murder of Sidney Parsons in the months after Robbie Hooper's arrival: the noises in the Hartley home, the deterioration of both boys' behaviour at school, the terrorising of the teacher and the death of the farm dog. The final event before Sidney's death was even more serious: an assault on a boy called Terry Atkinson, a friend of Sidney Parsons. I want Penny to talk me through this incident.

—So this was early September, a beautiful Sunday afternoon. I'd been at church that morning, listening to the kids singing. "*We plough the fields and scatter, the good seed on the land...*" – you know. It brought such a lovely feeling, hearing the little ones sing. I remember it from when I was a girl. I thought I'd take a walk in the fresh air down by Barrett's Pond, maybe feed the ducks on such a glorious day. I had a stale crust, and I know you're not supposed to feed them bread now, are you? Bad for them, isn't it? Well I didn't know back then, and I'm wandering up Wynburn Road, humming away, *"Come ye thankful people, come"* – at one with the world, you know? When I see something that's not right.

Well, now, when you get to the end of Wynburn Road, past the houses, there's a little copse where bluebells grow in the spring; some steps go down and then you're on the path round the pond. It's an old fishpond – very muddy with lots of bushes and reeds round the edge, a few trees. It feels secluded and quiet down there. Anyway, I see something on the path; some*one*. A young lad. He's crouched down where the bank of the pond meets the path, and there's a stretch of mud covered in logs and rocks. He looks up, and I stop dead in my tracks. My mouth falls open like a castle drawbridge, it does. His face. The poor lad's face. I didn't recognise him. It took me a few moments to work out who it was. It was young Terry Atkinson from down on Butterwell Court. Poor thing. I was only able to recognise him when I was a few feet away. He didn't have his glasses on, see? Those great thick things with the plastic frames. They were smashed, stamped into the path, both lenses broken and the arms snapped. It wasn't just that. He had blood all over his face and two great big shiners already swelling round his eyes.

I was ... I couldn't believe it. This young lad, twelve years old. I was in shock. There were tears through that blood on his face, and he was gasping, his shoulders shaking. He was crying, properly crying, like a little kid. He would have been in year seven at the high school, but he looked eight years old that day. I pulled out my hankie and started trying to clean him up, and he was shaking like a leaf, poor thing. I got him up on his feet and over to the bench. Of course there was no mobile phones in them days, but I knew his mam, cos she works in the chippy on Liddle Lane.

—*What had happened to him?*

—He must have been in shock or something, the way he was stammering and shaking. I wasn't naive enough to think that bad things don't happen, even in little villages like ours, but I was shocked myself. I thought it had to have been a grown man who done it, some druggie or something.

—*Who* had *done it?*

—He wouldn't say. Point blank refused to name names. I mean, the poor lad was clearly in shock, terrified, he wasn't thinking clearly…

—*What did he say happened? Did he tell you anything at all?*

—Not to me, no, but it was all over the village that he told his mam that there was suddenly two of them, one of them on the bank and one of them stood to the side of him, hidden in the bushes, like a shadow. He wouldn't say anything, not straight away. But we all knew who it was – Robbie Hooper and Danny Greenwell.

—*How can you be so sure?*

—That morning, Terry's mam, Kirsten Atkinson, she'd found a length of rope hanging down over their front door. Someone had tied it onto the satellite dish, and it was swinging back and forth in the breeze. Stands to reason, doesn't it?

—*Just like at the church.*

—Exactly. Anyway, at the pond Terry says he was scared and he turned to walk away when he felt hands on his back. They pushed him over and his glasses went flying. That's when they started stamping on him, see? And all the while, he said one of them was in the bushes, just watching.

—*That sounds more than just a random assault.*

—Sinister. That's how it sounded. Monstrous. I can still see poor Terry now, shaking and crying. What those two little monsters did to him. For no reason. No reason at all. Just for fun. He said his attacker only stopped because he ran out of puff, got tired. Terry said he laid down in the mud for what felt like hours until they were gone. He said that he thought he was going to die, that they would have had no problem killing him.

What I do know is that there was a police car parked outside the Hartleys' place that night. I tell you now, Terry Atkinson never took the bus to school ever again after that. His mam never came to any of the community events after, and they moved somewhere else a few months later. I don't know where, either, cos no one ever said.

—*And it was fairly obvious who attacked Terry?*

—I mean, folk round here all knew, but no one said, if you get what I mean? No one wanted to say owt outright, because no one was ever charged for it. Our Elsie says that Terry Atkinson was too scared and never told no one who it was, even his own mam and dad. She said that everyone knew it were Robbie and Danny what had done it, but the police said there was no evidence and Terry wouldn't say nothing to them. He wouldn't help. He wanted it over with, and you can't blame him, can you?

This was a highly significant incident and perhaps foreshadowed what happened to Sidney Parsons. Terry Atkinson's point blank refusal to name names or cooperate with the authorities helped the matter disappear relatively quickly. It was only a few weeks after this incident that the unspeakable crime that shocked the world took place. What happened to Terry would subsequently play a huge role in the fate of the two perpetrators.

When Robbie and Danny were initially questioned, both boys refused to give much detail. It is thought that they met, either by chance or pre-arrangement, at Ussal Top or the kilns at around nine in the morning, before walking down into Ussalthwaite together, where they met Sidney Parsons at approximately 10.30am.

Sidney Parsons was at home that day as he'd spent the morning complaining of a stomach pain. His mother had sent him not even five hundred metres from his front doorstep to pick up a loaf of bread.

He never returned home.

Robbie's and Danny's testimonies differ slightly, but in general terms, the two of them came across Sidney on his way home, carrying a shopping bag.

They asked him what was inside and were disappointed to find a loaf of bread. This is when Robbie, or Danny, depending on who you believe, asked Sidney if he wanted to come with them to the forbidden kilns.

—The worst thing about it for us what lived here was that Sidney would have gone with anyone. He wasn't quite right; he had a disability, didn't he? Not enough that he had to go to one of them special schools, but Sidney would do anything for anyone if they asked him, and those two little devils knew it.

Sidney, who like many of the boys in the village was in awe of the two troublemakers, said he'd go with them. It's been speculated that he was intrigued and flattered – these two 'bad lads' asking him to go somewhere he wasn't allowed will have pulled at his notion of adventure. We were all twelve once.

—Sidney didn't want to be 'bad' like them two, he just wanted to be accepted, bless his heart. I bet he thought that hanging about with those two would be a start.

The three boys walked through the village and up toward the kilns. There were several sightings of them by local business owners, but nothing that raised alarm. Strangely, there was not a single witness who could say with one hundred percent certainty that they saw Robbie and Danny. A shop owner who doesn't wish to be named said she swore she saw just one child – Sidney Parsons – carrying a plastic shopping bag, but this cannot be right. Others say they saw 'some kids walking through the village', or, in one case, a blurry, black shadow. But this is witness testimony – well known to be ragged and unreliable. What matters is the three went to the kilns and only two came back alive.

—Terrible, terrible business. It's lost none of its potency, even now. That poor boy, that poor, poor boy. My heart breaks, thinking of him, it really does. He always had a smile for everyone, did Sidney. He had all these problems, his epilepsy and … you know … but despite that, he had a little heart of gold. I hope that wherever he is now, he's warm and he's happy.

It wasn't until a few hours later, when Sidney's frantic parents began calling the authorities, that Sidney's body was found. North Yorkshire Police acted swiftly, setting up a perimeter around the crime scene. According to their statements, both Robbie and Danny were at this point sitting on top of the kilns, watching the police cars and ambulance wind their way through the moors and into Ussalthwaite.

It was several days before Robbie and Danny were brought in for another round of questioning at Pickering Police Station, not far from Ussalthwaite. After a forensic investigation and enquiries throughout the village, police felt they had enough evidence to charge both Robbie and Danny with murder. Sidney Parsons' blood was found on the boys' clothes, and dirt from the stream was under their fingernails.

—After what happened to Terry Atkinson, after everything with Laurence Graham at the school … everyone knew it was them. Everyone. No one had any doubt. It all added up. Terry Atkinson eventually told his parents that yes, it was those two who had attacked him that day. Everyone knew how brave he had to be to do that.

Robbie and Danny were subsequently arrested, questioned and charged with the murder of Sidney Parsons. Both boys initially denied committing the crime, making statements to that effect, each blaming the other for it, before taking advice from their legal counsels and admitting their guilt; recounting what had happened to the police. Their statements were read out during their hearings at York Crown Court in October 1995.

Many of the statements provided in this case are difficult to explain and ask more questions than they answer. There's one such question that stands as the key to this entire series. When asked, 'Why did you attack and murder Sidney Parsons?', at first both boys said that they didn't do it, but 'something else' did. When asked what this 'something else' was, both said they didn't know.

After another round of questioning, however, Danny Greenwell changed his story, saying that he'd been 'told' to do it – by Robbie, it was presumed. When Danny's claim was presented to Robbie, he said the same, so each boy implicated the other. Eventually, the police told the boys that they'd been identified as the two who had attacked Terry Atkinson. This is when their legal counsel intervened. Neither would be pushed any further at this point, both breaking down in tears.

North Yorkshire police officers reported some bizarre behaviour from the boys after this. Robbie apparently once began a whispered argument when left alone in the custody suite, while Danny would close his eyes, shake his head and mutter. Sometimes he would push his fingers into his ears. Eventually, in what was described as 'eerie', both boys called officers to their cells at exactly the same time and admitted what they had done.

Robbie said they were 'wandering around' Ussalthwaite when they met another child, presumably Sidney Parsons, who apparently 'wouldn't leave us alone'. Danny's account was slightly different, stating that the pair had been up at the kilns in the morning when 'the boy' had walked up to them and 'started messing about'.

This was roundly denied by every witness who knew Sidney, Robbie and Danny. Sidney, they said, was the last person to start any sort of trouble, especially with Robbie and Danny.

Regardless of this, mild irritation was, and would be, the only explanation ever given for the murder of Sidney Parsons.

There is a great deal more to this case. In this episode, I have looked to establish the background – a picture of the place where it happened and the events that led to the killing of a child by two other children. We've talked to someone who has lived in Ussalthwaite all her life, who knows the land, the area and its community.

Right now I am not looking to establish a clear reason why this atrocity happened. In fact, I don't believe there is a concise explanation. Like many of the cases I examine, there is no black and white here. Cases like this are like weeds – their roots are deep and complex; and long before the plants are visible, long before they produce flowers and thorns, those roots have become tangled knots in the dark beneath the earth. When we come to notice them, we are only seeing the results.

Twenty-six years later, we have the suicide of an unknown man at the same place where Sidney Parsons was apparently murdered.

—What happened here was awful, it went against everything, all of our values. It was something that we thought could never happen in Ussalthwaite. Not here. Not in this community, where we let flowers grow and our streets are clean. Not here, where we help out old folk, where we accept anyone and everyone, where kids leave toys out on front walls when they're done with them, for others to pick up and enjoy. Not here. But maybe that's why? Maybe it happened here because we're small and we're kind. I don't know?

What I do know is that everywhere has dark places; there's shadows everywhere and if you think there isn't then you're deluding yourself. You just have to burn brighter, that's all. You have to keep being kind, keep being good and outshine those shadows. Lots of folk have left since ninety-five, lots of the families that were here then are long gone. I don't blame them. But you know what I think? I think Ussalthwaite is bigger than what happened.

—*Why do you think they did it, those two?*

—Is that what you're trying to get to the bottom of with all this? Is that what you hope to find out? I think you'll be looking for a very long time. I've been on this earth many years, and I've learned that sometimes there are things you can't explain. Sometimes there's no clear answer. And sometimes I think it's best to let the dead lie – leave them with whatever things they've carried, you know? What I do know is that it wasn't human behaviour what them two done. It was demonic. They were born evil. Simple as that.

Maybe Penny's right. Maybe searching for answers around this case, raking the dirt from a child's grave, is futile. I wish I could leave that grave alone. But, as we'll come to find out, there's a great deal more to all the questions I'm asking.

I think this is a poignant place to leave Ussalthwaite and Penny, for now at least, and to carry on a little further from the point where Sidney Parsons' life was cut short.

In October 1995, both Danny Greenwell and Robbie Hooper were charged with grievous bodily harm with intent, and with murder. Terry Atkinson's eventual admission that it was Robbie and Danny who had assaulted him was the key reason the two retracted their denials and owned up to what they had done – most likely to avoid trial.

They were both sentenced to an 'indeterminate' time in custody, with a recommendation that their minimum detention period should last seven years. In 2002, Robbie and Danny, by now both eighteen, were granted lifelong anonymity by a senior judge at the high court. Sir Michael Oswald ruled in favour of the application by the official solicitor's office that the release of the two boys' true identities could lead to vigilante attacks. The ruling was not contested. Neither Robbie or Danny have ever given a clear reason why they did what they did.

The rights and wrongs of all this have been contested in the public eye. There are arguments on both sides about whether rehabilitation, the eventual release of Robbie and Danny back into society, and their anonymity, is a good thing or not. This is a debate that I'm not here to add my two penn'orth to. My opinion is inconsequential, as is yours, because both boys were released in 2002 with new identities after their time in young offenders institutions. Does this reflect a society that dispenses justice in a measured and balanced way? Should our society be measured by its ability to successfully rehabilitate criminals – even child ones?

Like I say, I'm not here to debate whether what has happened to Robbie and Danny is right or wrong; I'm here to discuss what happened to Sidney, and maybe find some peace in the case.

—I just want to say, Mr King, that Ussalthwaite is the best place in the entire world. Despite everything, despite all of what's gone on, it's the most beautiful village. We still hold fast to traditional values round here. Always have, always will. We're tough as nails up here, but we've got heart. Despite everything, despite all the stories, the tragedies. Another place, a less proud place, wouldn't hold its head up high like we do round here, you know. But our heads are still high.

I believe all of this has been sent to test us. Horrible things have happened here because of who we are, because of what we value. It's a test. It's the making of us and this poor man … well … it's just another one. Just another test. That's how I see it.

This has been our first step on a long, complicated and difficult road. I appreciate this road is not one that everyone would want to follow me down, so let me warn you now: nothing in this case will get any easier, and answers are not something I can promise.

If you're coming with me, I wish you respite for now.

I have been Scott King and this has been our first.

Until next time.

Dear Mum,

I spent most of the weekend there again, at the special place. I finished *William the Fourth* and I brought up some of the books you used to read to me when I was little. I've still got them. I proper laughed out loud reading the old Michael Rosen poems, 'Eddie and the Gerbils', and I only cried when I read *The Sad Book*.

You always told me it was OK to cry, that I had to cry when I needed to, that all the sadness wanted to come out, and if I left it in it would fester and ferment, you said. It would get poisonous and come out in other ways.

So I cried, Mum, right there in the special place, all on my own; I let it all out rather than keeping it in and my tears went all over the stone.

I don't know if anyone knows about the special place. Some people think it's scary there, you know. Actually, most people think it's scary, or they want to dare each other to do stupid things there. Not me. I go there when it's just getting dark, when everyone's gone in for their tea. I go there when it's quiet. Sometimes I go when I've finished helping Dad in the morning. The only scary bit is when you have to go through the gap in the dark, but it's not that bad, especially because I always bring our torch, the lantern one that Dad thought was broken.

I remember you told me you used to bring me there when I was a little baby. I wish I could remember. You said you used to put me in a special carrier thing on your front. You said it was a place of peace. You told me that if I was crying, when I was a little baby and I wouldn't go to sleep, you would take me there and I would always calm down. You said that there was a lot of 'female energy' there, and you said I'd understand when I was a bit older. I'm a bit older now, Mum, a whole year older, and I still don't really understand what you meant.

It doesn't matter, though. When I go there, I feel close to you, and that's what matters, isn't it? I won't tell anyone because they'll all think I'm off my head. You said that, sometimes, you've got to find the place that everyone thinks is bad and really look at it and decide for yourself. I've decided it's our place, Mum.

I don't think it's bad. Not at all. I find it peaceful too. I sit there and read, and I hear your voice, Mum, and sometimes I smell you and sometimes I doze off. I woke up once and my arm was warm, and I knew you'd been here, Mum. I could feel that you'd been here. With me.

You used to tell me that some places have power, that they are like blurry areas between two worlds. I think the special place is one of those. I think people are only scared of it cos some bad things happened there. That's not the special place's fault, that's what you always said. A place can't be bad, only people. That's why I like it at the special place, that's why I know you're with me when I go there. Me and you. No one else.

It's Monday and I want you to know that I made a new friend today at school. Dad's always on at me to go and 'make friends', but he doesn't get it, he doesn't understand like you did. It's not that easy. You always said not to try too hard, that I have to let my inner light shine, and people would be drawn to it. Well it worked. There's a lad my age who got on the school bus this morning. He didn't know anyone, and everyone was laughing at him cos he was wearing the St Catherine's blazer and a tie, when no one wears that, everyone just wears the polo shirt and the jumper. I remember when I wanted to wear the blazer too, on my first day, to look smart. They all laughed at me too.

Darren Robson shouted out at the new kid, 'Who's this knob-sack, then? Sloth?'

All the lads at the back laughed, and so did some of the girls. Darren Robson started shouting, 'Hey you *guys!*' in that 'spacker' voice he does, with his tongue under his bottom lip. I didn't think the new boy looked like Sloth at all; it was just because he had a few teeth missing, I guess.

The new boy sat down next to me, and he'd gone all red. I didn't think he looked like Sloth. He pulled off his tie and put it in his pocket. I told him to not worry about any of that lot, who sit at the back, cos Darren Robson's not even hard, he just pretends he is. Robbie, the new lad, pretended he wasn't listening at first, but then I whispered to him and told him in year six, back at Moorside Primary, Darren Robson got told off in front of the whole school for fiddling with himself in the girl's toilets. Robbie started giggling at that, and I knew he felt better. We started talking then. Robbie was dead quiet at first. He was whispering. He's got a funny accent, like a farmer from the telly, and I knew that was going to make Darren Robson and them laugh at him even more.

He told me he was here cos his dad was sick in the hospital, and he was staying with the Hartleys. Lucky him, I said. I thought that it might not be a good idea to talk to Robbie too much more, Mum, because Darren Robson and that lot have left me alone for the last year, and this might start them all off again. Then I remembered something you told me. You said that if there was someone new or someone different in the village, or even someone who had no friends, I should be the one to go and talk to them. You told me not to be like everyone else, you told me not to follow the herd.

At school, they put Robbie in my form, and Mr Eggers said he could sit on the seat next to me, cos no one sits there. We talked a bit in form time, and on the bus on the way home. He spoke a bit louder and told me that Darren Robson had called him a 'gaylord' in English, and Miss McCarthy heard him and made him explain to the whole class *exactly* what a 'gaylord' was, and everyone was laughing at Darren Robson for a change.

They left Robbie alone on the bus on the way home, and I think that's maybe because of Miss McCarthy, but more because Robbie was sitting next to me, and Darren Robson and that lot only pick on you when you're on your own. Cowards, like you said they were.

I think you would have been proud of me today, Mum. I

was the only one that talked to Robbie, and I think he liked me. I let my inner light shine and finally, someone came. Just like you said they would.

I'm going to stop now, and I'm going to remember our little talks about this sort of thing just before sleep. I'm going to try not to cry when I next go to the special place, Mum. I'm going to remember you and smile instead. I'm going to let my light shine.

Goodnight, Mum xx

DISPATCH*Online*

Home • News • Sport • TV & Showbiz • Money • Property

TELLING IT LIKE IT IS: Allan Davidson

DAVIDSON SAYS: We've paid for his board, food and entertainment for the last ten years of his life, now we're letting him walk free. Surely the woke brigade aren't happy protecting the identity of a cold-blooded child killer? Oh, it seems they are. No surprise there.

By Allan Davidson for DISPATCH*Online*

667 SHARES 1.4K COMMENTS

Today, of all days, on the anniversary of a child's brutal murder, there appears, instead of a sympathy for a grieving family, to be a sudden flurry of interest in protecting the identity of a killer. Not just any old killer either, instead, a killer who has been living anonymously in our society for the last nineteen years.

No one knows who he is. He might be your next-door neighbour. I doubt it; your next-door neighbour probably arrived yesterday by boat with no papers, and was immediately given a five-bedroom semi.

This killer of children might be the guy who scans your shopping at the supermarket or joins you for some banter at the pub on a Friday after work. You might even be friends with him; this man, who in 1995, at the age of a mere twelve years, played a part in the savage, unspeakable murder of a disabled boy his own age.

I think we have a right to know where this monster is, don't you?

DISPATCH*Online*

Home • News • Sport • TV & Showbiz • Money • Property

STILL NO CLUES TO IDENTIFY MYSTERY USSALTHWAITE SUICIDE

North Yorkshire Constabulary have admitted they are no further forward in identifying the body of a man found at a local ruin close to the village of Ussalthwaite.

The man, estimated to be between thirty and fifty, was found at the site of old iron smelting kilns on Ussal Bank on Monday, 20th September, and police believe he had been there since Sunday night.

Drawings of the man have been released, with descriptions of his clothes, and a profile has been created on the UK's missing persons' database.

Investigators have not released specific details of the cause of death, save to rule it as suicide and to confirm there are no suspicious circumstances. So far, no one has come forward to identify the man, who is not believed to be from the local area.

The site itself carries a dark reputation; the ruined iron-smelting kilns were the place where Robbie Hooper and Danny Greenwell killed vulnerable youngster Sidney Parsons in 1995.

Police will not confirm whether the body that was found has any connection to the Sidney Parsons murder.

Episode 2: The Witches' Rede

—Horrible things they are, we found one in our chimney when we had it redone about twenty years ago. 'Witch bottles' they call them. Apparently quite common round here. I honestly thought the place was cursed. I expected all sorts – the walls to start bleeding, things to start flying about, you know, like they do in the films? I never believed any of that sort of nonsense before I worked in Ussalthwaite.

Now … I wish I didn't believe in it.

That's my hand holding it, see. Can you see it there? On the phone? It was full of brambles and pins, from what we could make out. We were sure that we could see fingernails in there too, and at first I wanted rid of it. It brought it all back, you see, all that business up at the farm. My missus, she said no, told me they were for protection, those were. Some of them what were getting their houses done up round here have found other stuff: dead cats under their porches. Rusty horseshoes in the walls. We took a couple of pictures, and I asked the builder to put it back up there. You might think I'm daft, like, but I'm telling you, nothing bad's ever happened in this house. I reckon if we'd messed with it, gave it to a museum, things might have got dark.

I remember when I was working on the houses back up in Yorkshire, scraping all that old woodchip wallpaper off the walls and knocking through all them old fireplaces, we found a few of them patterns on the bricks, you know? Looked like flowers. Never knew what they were; thought they were old builders' marks. There's a load of them on that church wall and all, if you know where to look. They were supposed to be for protection, weren't they. All of these horrible things. The bottles, the cats, the marks what look like flowers. Protection against witchcraft and that.

Fat lot of good it did for that village.

I'm telling you now, there's places that are bad, that are evil. Just like people. You never know, do you, if a kiddie's going to turn out like one of them bastards. You can give them everything they want, you don't knock them about, and still, they are one of those that sits and pulls the wings off of flies or kicks the blind man's stick; picks on the little, unfortunate one at school. Sometimes people are just born with something missing, or worse than that, something else, some black mark on their soul. It's the same with places too. Take that Greenwell Farm, and the old Hartley place – both of them places should be torched, if you asked me, the land levelled and a memorial put in its place – to him, that boy, Sidney. That might even help things, you know. Burn some sage, sprinkle it with holy water, bless the land. I don't know.

There's summat not right – summat wrong with that whole village, because that rot, that evil what happened there didn't start with them two lads, and what happened with Sidney Parsons, that was just the most recent thing. And now look what's going on – the graffiti, the ropes; now this fella, dead up at the kilns. Whatever's going on there started a long, long time ago. And now it's stirring again and it isn't going away.

Where do I even start?

You talked to Penny Myers? Did she even tell you about the witch? Of course she didn't. There was load of them round there who just wanted to stick their heads in the sand and pretend everything was perfect. It's still the same, twenty-six years later. Disgraceful. You don't get rid of evil doing that, do you? Sometimes you have to look at what's gone wrong before you can even start to put things right.

Welcome to Six Stories.

I'm Scott King.

The voice you have just heard is forty-five year old Leo Corrin. Leo speaks to me on Zoom from his home in Falmouth. He was eighteen years old when he left his birthplace on the south coast and went north to 'start again'.

—I didn't know anything. You think you do, don't you, when you're that age? You think you know it all. I just drifted with the wind. I hadn't got no qualifications or nothing like that. I just drifted around, picking up work where I could. It was easier then; I was young and I was fit, and I'd just walk into a building site and talk to the gaffer.

Once he knew I wasn't a thief and I put in the work, grafted my balls off, he left me to it. Cash in hand. No worries. And I was off again when the job was done. What a life, eh? I was like a dandelion clock, just going with the wind. Eventually, I ended up in Yorkshire, didn't I? I did a few bits and bobs in Wakefield and Bradford on the houses, but I'm a country boy at heart, see, and I ended up there. On that farm in Ussalthwaite.

Leo is settled down now, back in his birthplace on the south coast, but we're taking him back twenty-six years and two hundred miles north. Ussalthwaite is where we're headed in this, episode two of our current series, which explores the murder of twelve-year-old Sidney Parsons in 1995 by two children of the same age: Danny Greenwell and Robbie Hooper. Those two names now carry a certain weight when you say them out loud. This is a difficult and emotive grave that we're raking over, and I promise you, we're proceeding with honesty, sensitivity and caution.

What are we looking for, in this series? What question are we trying to answer?

Alongside the mystery suicide at the kilns on Ussal Bank, rumours have circulated recently that one of Sidney Parsons' killers – both of whom were granted lifelong anonymity – is soon to be identified by an unofficial source. I wonder what the rights and wrongs of that are. For how long does someone need to pay for their past? Is it possible for someone to be born evil? Should adults still pay for the crimes they committed as children? If they have paid that price, are they worthy of redemption? These are not questions that I, personally, feel in a position to answer. These sorts of issues aren't black and white for me.

But maybe we'll have some answers to these questions if we find out more about this terrible event.

—Sheep? Nah, I didn't know the first thing about them, but he didn't seem to be bothered. I'd worked at a few farms on my travels, see? Mucking out, shovelling shit really. That's all I expected to be doing. So long it was cash in hand, it would do for me. He offered me somewhere to sleep and that. And he didn't ask too many questions neither. That was fine with me. I thought this would be a nice, easy stop-over, get my head down, get some cash together and move on.

Never in a million years did I expect what happened there.

Leo was a casual labourer at Greenwell Farm. He arrived in Ussalthwaite in the freezing January of 1995, a month before Robbie Hooper.

—I met Richard Greenwell in the pub. That's the best place for local gossip, isn't it? Not the one in the village, where they do the dinners for the tourists and that, but the one right up on the hill. The one the proper locals go to. The Cross Keys it was called. To be honest, I thought the guy was the town drunk at first. He was a mess – covered in shit and smelled like it five times over. I got told about his missus, didn't I? Poor soul. I got told he had a boy too, and I think I felt sorry for him more than anything. I know what it's like not to have your mum around, so I bought the bloke a cider and got chatting, didn't I? Easy as that.

Leo ended up lodging at Greenwell Farm while he worked there, sleeping in the old root cellar below the farmhouse. He was happy working all hours and doing whatever jobs Richard Greenwell asked him to.

—Sounds mad, doesn't it? It was alright down there though. I was on a camp bed, with all the junk they kept down there around me. Lucky I don't have arachnophobia cos I seen some of the biggest spiders I've ever seen in my life there. I was allowed to use the bathroom upstairs, and I got chips and that from the village to eat. I've stayed in worse houses, I'll tell you that right now.

I did the shit jobs, you know? Cleaning the barns and the equipment, and moving stuff about. Taking the sheep feed up into the hills. I didn't mind it back then, though. I just got on with it. Head down, money in my pocket. When I was working like that, I didn't have to think about nothing, did I? Fine by me.

—*What was it like, working on the farm?*

—The place was a mess, inside and out. Everything half falling down; great big puddles everywhere, mud. It didn't help that it was winter – dark and grim and cold. Richard had me patching up roofs and barns; getting it ship-shape for the March lambing. He had me shifting sugar beets and hay and that up into the fields. Sometimes looking at his tractors and that. There was always something to do.

—*Was he a good employer?*

—He never said much to be honest. One of those silent types. He was a man's man. Meat and two veg, whisky on a Sunday. Old school. He never spoke about his missus, never mentioned her once. I never asked neither. None of my business. I knew she was gone; I saw things around the place that didn't fit: a load of them dreamcatchers, or whatever you call them, hanging on the walls all covered in cobwebs. Sometimes I thought I could smell joss sticks in the house. I heard down the village that she was like that; she was one of them New-Age types, you know? Yoga and crystals and that. As for Richard, I don't think that was his sort of thing. The sheep was all Richard knew how to do. There was one place that he told me never to touch, though, never to go near. That barn; the one where the boy found her the year before.

As was mentioned last episode, Richard's wife and Danny's mother, Saffron Greenwell, was found hanging from the rafters of a barn on the farm in December 1994. Of course, there was an outpouring of support for Richard and Danny at the time, but the villagers say that the man, already a withdrawn and introverted type, disappeared almost completely from village society. Danny was only ever seen in school.

—Everyone does their grief different, don't they? When my mum finally died of the drink, I just ran, I kept running for years. Worked, bust my arse everywhere I went so's I didn't have to think about it. Too many feelings, all conflicting with each other. Love and hate, and all that. I didn't know how to handle them. That's what I was doing on Greenwell Farm, working so I didn't have to think about her. I never saw no visitors at the farm, no friends or relations or nothing like that, not the whole time I was there, and that were a few months short of a year. Richard spent his time in the fields with the sheep. That was his way of doing it.

—*What about Danny? Did you see much of him while you worked at the farm?*

—Yeah, I did. He was like his dad. Quiet at first. But where his dad was stern, the boy crept about like a little shadow. I'd be on my back under the tractor, unclogging the axles, and I got this feeling like I was being watched, so I'd slide out, dead quick, like, and he'd be off like a cat, round the side of the barn, I could hear his feet splashing in the mud. Shy as anything, that boy, but I felt for him, I did.

—*He and his father, were they close?*

—Hard to say really, if I'm honest. I think Richard found it hard, and who can blame him – raising a boy all alone, doing the cooking and the cleaning and the washing. It was all a foreign country, it really was. I don't think Richard was to blame for what happened with the boy in the end. He done his best. That's what I thought anyway. That boy … well, I felt sorry for him at first, I really did.

At first.

Not now. I need you to know that. No sympathy for that little freak.

Danny showed little of himself to Leo, and Leo didn't have much interest in Danny. If Danny was walking across the farmyard and met Leo en route, he would slip around a corner or behind something. But towards the end of January, 1995, after a few weeks of Leo working at Greenwell Farm, Danny began to get used to Leo's presence. Gradually, Danny began to trust him.

—I didn't really think about it at the time, cos I was so young and messed up and that, but the kid must have looked up to me a bit, you know? I thought he was younger than twelve; the boy looked about nine. His only friend seemed to be that farm dog, Jip. I've met loads of farm dogs on my travels; some of them are half wild, most of them sleep outside, do their jobs. They love their masters, and that's it. But I'm telling you, them two were best mates. Inseparable.

After a bit, the boy used to watch me. He used to just stand there and stare at me with those big eyes of his. I always asked him if he wanted to help, and he slunk off to find the dog or just shook his head. I don't think I heard him speak for my first two weeks. Then he got a bit braver. Sometimes he would pass me things – nails and that, when I was fixing the barn. Once he even helped me varnish the wood, the end of his tongue stuck between his lips, holding the brush with two hands. The dog, Jip, would just sit there in the corner, watching us. Watching *me.* It was as if it was always on guard, just in case. I knew what had happened to the poor kid's mother, but I didn't even know how to start talking about that, so I didn't. I just stayed quiet. Maybe he liked that.

Anyway, one Saturday morning, it was bitter and frosty, and I was about to go up to the hill, Ussal Top, they called it, to fill the troughs and check the water wasn't frozen over for the flock. I says, did he want to come, like? I had the sheep nuts loaded on the quad bike, and I expects him to say no, but the kid just nods and climbs on the back. Off we go.

That's where I first heard about the witch, up there on that freezing-cold morning in January. The kid, he tells me the whole thing. It's as if he'd had it all bottled up and could finally let it all go.

The pair were at the top of the bank where the Greenwells' flock grazed. The grass was tight with frost, and the wind up there was like a knife. The view is spectacular, particularly with the frost clinging to the fields and the sky a desolate blue. Danny Greenwell, apropos of nothing, pointed to the kilns in the distance.

—I'd never seen nothing like it; like tunnel entrances cut into the hills. Proper history there from decades ago. Stunning. I wanted to go and have a look at them for myself, when I feel this tug at my sleeve, and it's him, the boy, and he says that I shouldn't go, that he's not allowed to and that everyone says it's a 'bad place'. I starts laughing, and I says what's there? Goblins? Knockers? I says we've got plenty of that rot where I'm from, and he looks at me dead serious, and he tells me about the witch. What was her name again?

The name that we've yet to hear on this podcast so far is Awd Ma Spindle o' Ussal Moor — a 'moor witch' who terrorised Ussalthwaite and the surrounding area in the 1600s. I have pieced together her story from various sources:

Ma Spindle lived in a dilapidated shack somewhere on the moors and would provide healing potions and charms for those who came to her for advice. She was apparently also happy to 'confess' and flaunt her other powers, appalling and frightening the stuffy and God-fearing residents of the villages around, who shunned her when she came to ask for shelter or food in the winter months. Among other unpleasant deeds, she buried the head of an unchristened child in a farmer's haystack to ruin his crops, and chased a flock of sheep in her black carriage pulled by a fleet of toads, rendering the terrified animals barren and diseased. She could also turn into a hare.

Locals from the surrounding area would ward off Awd Ma Spindle by hanging lengths of rope from their own houses – Ma Spindle herself was accused of 'swinging from ropes'. It is thought that villages would hang these ropes from their houses as a message: 'We're already cursed, move on.'

—I asks the boy, what's that got to do with an old kiln, and he says right out of nowhere that his mum had told him about what happened to her – to the witch.

According to a book that I've referenced before on this show – Witch Covens in Northern England *– Awd Ma Spindle became the scourge of the parish of Ussalthwaite. Whatever slight was done to her is unclear, but her position of wise woman switched to that of a menace. Ma Spindle 'swung from a rope' from people's roofs, which brought 'a cursed mania' to people's children, making them 'emit strange cries, like the barking of hounds or the shriek of a furious boar' and 'to land blows upon any that tried to placate them with the savagery of many men'.*

Ma Spindle tried to recruit many of Ussalthwaite's women to her 'coven', at night, 'hag riding' them over the moor to 'a black furrow in the rock which no man can find lest he have been smeared with ointment; where the hag's diabolical coven did meet'.

Awd Ma Spindle used a set of 'stones' to 'entreat a long black fellow' to dwell 'like ice inside her'. At the time, a man in dark clothing with black hair was usually a euphemism for a devil, or some kind of demonic entity – not the devil himself but one of his minions – who would serve as the head of a witches 'coven'.

—I'd honestly never heard the lad speak so much. This whole story just came pouring out of him. I says, we'd best not go up there then, had we? And he puffs up his chest then and it was almost funny. I nearly laughed, but I seen his eyes; I seen something, a steel that I felt somewhere deep inside myself. He tells me he's been up there by himself before. He says his mum told him he didn't have to be scared.

So I asks him. I says, does he believe in the witch then, and he says 'sort of'.

—*What do you think he meant?*

—I asks him the same thing, I says, what's that mean then, and he says his mum told him that story, and she also told him it was a big old lie. Again, he was so serious, it was nearly funny. Danny says his mum told him that Ma Spindle probably did exist, and she wasn't a witch, but a wise woman, a healer or something like that. He says that Ma Spindle was an easy 'scrape goat' because she was a woman, and hell, I didn't have the heart to correct him. 'Scrape-goat' – bless him.

It's not like I'm smart or anything. He says he was learning about it in school, and his teacher laughed at him when he said that Ma Spindle wasn't a witch and that the village blamed her when things went wrong, when the crops failed or the animals died. It seemed a lot for such a young lad, but I still remember things my mum told me – life lessons. Treat others like you want to be treated yourself.

Could Danny's teacher 'laughing at him' for standing up for the name of the local witch be connected with the subsequent incidents with Mr Graham. Did it provide Danny with motivation for terrorising him?

According to Witch Covens in Northern England, *Ma Spindle apparently waved 'a white cloth three times' at a farmer who refused to give her alms. That very evening, his daughter became 'stiff and sullen' before 'raving and crowing like a bird'. She was placed in the barn with the flock, presumably to pass on the 'spirit' to one of them, but was found the next morning amidst a 'mess of blood and bone, cawing and pecking at the entrails of the animals she had killed'.*

There were several more incidents – including women in the village waking to find Ma Spindle standing beside their beds. It was decided enough was enough, and a local magistrate set out to get rid of her.

'The witch woman was driven into the hills like hunted quarry. The hounds followed her into a fissure in the rocks where no man could follow. All but the very bravest of the hunting pack were driven out, whimpering

and crying, great gouges ripped from them. The hunt masters waited, and eventually the hag emerged in the form of a great, black hare which was 'pierced by many bullets' before turning back into a human. Unharmed.

The accounts of what happened to Ma Spindle afterwards vary. The woman was either weighted down by rocks, or else chained and left to die in the place that would eventually become the Ussal Bank Kilns, two hundred years later. One last extract from the book:

'The bones of Ma Spindle were shattered by a blacksmith's hammer and buried amid a cairn of rock at the banks of Ussalthwaite Parish, her hovel burned to embers later that day. The churchmen raked the ashes and blessed the site with holy water.'

I ask Leo if that was the reason Danny gave for children not being allowed to play at the kilns.

—The boy said that everyone in Ussalthwaite said it was a 'bad place', but I wasn't to tell anyone that he'd told me the story. He said folk would laugh at me. Well, I said his secret was safe with me.

—*Danny told you he had visited the kilns, didn't he?*

—Yeah, I mean, at first I thought he was showing off, trying to impress me. And then he tells me his mum used to take him there when he was a little 'un.

—*Really?*

—Yeah. I didn't know what to say to that, so I just shut up. Danny says his mum said it wasn't a bad place at all. He said there was a hidden cave at the back, a special place, a *powerful* place. It had 'strong, female energy' or summat like that. For some reason, that gave me the heebie-jeebies a bit. More than anything to do with witches or any of that nonsense. I honestly didn't know why he was sharing so much. He didn't know me from Adam. Now I reckon it was because he had literally no one else. 'Cept that dog.

—*Did you ask him what he meant?*

—You know, I didn't. It was him talking about his mother that just did something to my insides. It was all such a long time ago. In hindsight I wish I had talked to him a bit more … Maybe it would have helped? I dunno.

Saffron Greenwell's body was discovered by Danny himself on the day after Boxing Day, 1994. That's a fact. The story of what exactly led to her suicide has never been made public, so speculation is all we have to go on.

Leo says that when he told people in the pubs and farms around Ussalthwaite where he was working, he was told a lot of stories concerning Saffron Greenwell. He says he won't speak ill of the dead, but the stories about her were 'mean'. Especially from the local men.

—It was like she didn't fit in nowhere. Some of them admired her, some of them thought she was evil. I tell you what, loads of the blokes said she was a bit of a goer, you know? None of them knew anyone what had gone with her though. That's what happens, isn't it? When there's a woman who's got a strong head on her, especially in small places like there.

There were claims made in the press after Sidney Parsons' death that Saffron Greenwell was a 'pagan witch'. I put this term in quotation marks as it is clearly not the correct one. These claims were often accompanied by photographs taken of her at various events in Ussalthwaite. The one that is most commonly used shows Saffron standing behind her stall at the village fete, smiling. She had curly brown hair that spilled over her shoulders. There are certainly no overt indications of witchcraft – just incense burners, golden Buddha statues and crystals laid out neatly before her. At the time, a stall like hers probably wasn't as common as those selling jams or farmers' meats, but selling incense and practising yoga is not synonymous with witchcraft. However, Saffron's services were very much in demand, and perhaps this put other business owners' noses out of joint, which led to the gossip about her.

As for the promiscuity rumour; all I have to go on is what Penny Myers told me about how she'd heard that a naked Saffron Greenwell had been seen returning from Ussal Top in the middle of the night one spring.

Whatever the circumstances of his mother's suicide, the trauma that Danny Greenwell, only eleven years old, experienced, must have been catastrophic. I want to add that trauma like this doesn't make somebody a killer, and also that it is OK both to feel sorry for eleven-year-old Danny Greenwell and to condemn his actions months later.

There are interesting parallels between the stories of Saffron Greenwell and Awd Ma Spindle. I ask Leo if anyone else in the village ever mentioned the older witch story.

—I just thought it was one of them daft local legends, you know? Then, after what happened to the Parsons boy, I heard about the other time that something happened there. So maybe it was a bad place after all? Cos it wasn't long after we'd been up there that Robbie arrived in the village and things went south, if you get what I'm saying. Things went badly wrong after that one turned up.

It is said that Ma Spindle cursed Ussalthwaite and its people before she died. Her screams as she was executed on Ussal Bank apparently 'sent the dogs and cats of the town cowering in fear, and when milked, the cattle produced blood, and a clergyman was called to bless that terrible place.'

What the curse actually was is not clear.

Leo refers to another unpleasant and significant incident that occurred at Ussal Bank Kilns. I assume it's the one in the seventies Penny has mentioned. That will have to wait until next episode. For now I want to stay with Leo's story. I ask him if he noticed any changes in Danny when Robbie Hooper arrived in Ussalthwaite.

—You know what? I did. Right off the bat as well. Now, don't get me wrong; I wasn't mates with a twelve-year-old kid, but I was there, on the farm, pretty much all the time, and after he'd told me that story about the kilns and his mum and that, we sort of had this bond. We never really spoke, but he would trail after me, him and that dog. Whatever I was doing, fixing stuff, moving stuff round, he was there. Like I say, I felt for him, this lonely little kid, you know? Maybe he thought I was his mate. I wanted to say to him, no, find a better mate, find a proper grown-up. I'm just this drifter bloke from down the South Coast, twenty years old and living in someone's cellar on a camp bed propped up on sheep nuts and weed killer. Find someone proper.

Well, when that Robbie came along. I didn't know who he was, anything about him really. I just noticed that Danny wasn't there anymore.

—*No longer following you around?*

—Yeah. He was just gone. It was night and day. One day he's

traipsing round after me while I'm sorting out that lambing shed, and next day he's just not there no more. I nearly asked Richard if he was OK. I only saw Robbie later. He never came up to the farm. I saw them a couple of times around the village. I also saw the pair of them on their way up to the kilns once or twice. but I said nothing to Richard about it. None of my business, was it? I was just glad the boy had found someone his own age to knock around with.

I want to skip forward in time a little bit now.

The lambing season on the farm began in late February and ran through March, finishing at the end of April. Richard hired a few more seasonal workers to help out.

—It was non-stop. All day, all night. I slept when I could, ate when I could. Just got on with it. The boy was literally the last thing on my mind. Those months passed quick. Summer came along after that.

Leo got casual work on other farms in the area, on the recommendation of Richard Greenwell, helping out with muck-spreading for a couple of months before going back to Greenwell Farm in June to help clean the lambing shed. By this time, he says, he'd almost forgotten about Danny and anything to do with the kilns.

—I'd met a girl as well. Nancy Hallowell, she was called. Lived in one of the villages and worked seasonal up in Whitby. Lovely, she was. Well I was head over heels, wasn't I? Didn't think much about much else at the time. Danny was hardly ever there. I never thought about him. Sometimes I'd hear him inside the house, the toilet flushing and stuff, but that was about it. Ships in the night, we were. But then I met Robbie.

This was a small but troubling incident. Leo isn't entirely sure when it happened.

—I was back in Ussalthwaite and it was hot, so I'll say summer ninety-five. I remember that plague of flies. Did you hear about that? Horrible it was.

—*Penny Myers told me about it.*

—They were everywhere. You couldn't even walk along the street without getting them in your gob. Disgusting it was. I've never seen anything like it in all my life. I was doing some job up on the fields near Ussal Top, fixing a wire fence. I remember cos I was burning up out there, sweating my bollocks off. It's a fiddly job, and I was out of water. I remember how my mouth felt, like a ruddy desert. I'm on one side of a dry-stone wall, half fallen down where the sheep could get through, when I hear voices coming up the track on the other side. Kids' voices. And I see it's Danny and another boy. Bigger than him. Well I'm parched, tired, and all I'm thinking of is getting off work, jumping on a bus and going to see Nancy. So I just gets on with it, wait for them boys to go past to wherever they was going. Anyhow, suddenly I hear a voice. ''Scuse me, mate, you got the time?' It wasn't Danny; it was a West Country accent, and that's what made me look up, and I see this bigger lad stood on the other side of the wall. First thing I notice is that he looked rough, you know? Big, thick forehead, a few missing teeth. I look down at my watch and give it a rub cos it's all covered in sweat, and when I look up again, the lad leans forward and gobs in my face – sprays me full on with spit. It fucking stank like fags and bubblegum, and off they go, sprinting up the path, away, laughing like little devils. I was so shocked that I just stood there like a lemon, with this boy's spit all over my face.

—*Was Danny there too?*

—He looked back, just before they turned the corner, and I caught his eye for a second. Little buggers. I swear I nearly went off after them to give that one a piece of my mind. Maybe cos I was all loved-up, hot, thirsty, I just couldn't be arsed. Kids are kids, aren't they? Horrible little bastards. It was the sort of thing I'd have done at that age. I wiped it off and finished the bloody fence. Word round the village was that them two were up to all sorts. I was surprised, I have to say. I never thought that shy little boy with his dog would be up to the things that folks said they were.

Similar incidents were reported by a few residents of Ussalthwaite in the months before Sidney Parsons' death. Robbie and Danny had become somewhat of a menace around the village. The pair were shoplifting, throwing stones and eggs, petty vandalism.

Then there was the terrorising of the teacher, which no one could prove but everyone knew about. Leo says he didn't really know much about it but he'd heard the gossip in the pub. He wasn't surprised that people were becoming scared of these two boys.

—It escalates, stuff like that, doesn't it? I was no angel when I was a nipper, and I done some bad stuff alright, but terrorising a bloke and his family? For no good reason? Out of order, that. Then there was that other boy, wasn't there? Beat him black and blue they did. Bad seeds, them two were. They didn't know when to stop. There was no one what tried to stop them.

—*What about you?*

—I wasn't spending much time in the village then, to be honest with you. I was back and forth across the moors, courting Nancy, wasn't I? I told her about it, actually. I remember cos she said something weird.

—*Really?*

—You know what it's like when you're in that stage of courting? You talk a load of old bollocks to each other. I was telling her that I saw a bit of me in Danny, how I used to be when I was his age … After my own mum passed, I went off the rails a bit. Turns out Nancy knew a bit more about his mum – Saffron was her name, wasn't it?

—*That's right.*

—Well, Nancy says to me that she was known all over. She was something of a … well … these were her words, not mine, but something of a witch, if you know what I mean? Nancy said that she did a lot of 'rituals' – stuff to do with the moon and that. She wore one of them devil's stars round her neck. Folk in the area wouldn't cross her.

—*Why was that?*

—Nancy said she heard that Saffron had 'powers'. I told her it was a load of old gossip.

—*Did Nancy elaborate any further?*

—I can't remember. Just silly stuff. People said Saffron was in a 'coven', and practised 'sex magic' and all that. To help her business, with the yoga and that. She was popular and expensive, and I think a lot of people in the area were jealous, that was all. Nancy said she knew some who'd had 'hexes' put on them by Saffron Greenwell, and they got ill the next day. It was all very silly, teenage stuff really. I don't think they even knew her. Just before she died, there was a rumour went round that she had done a deal with the devil or something.

Based on what we've heard about Saffron Greenwell so far, it's possible that she practised Wicca, a nature-based religion that is commonly mistaken for devil worship. This is why I objected to the term 'Pagan Witch' used in the newspapers. Wicca is a legitimate religion. I believe that it is certainly likely that Saffron's practice was misunderstood by the village, and I also think that Wicca itself needs a little explanation, as there are many misconceptions and unkind stereotypes floating around about it that Saffron Greenwell is no longer here to defend herself against.

Wicca was officially founded the year after the Witchcraft Act was repealed in 1951. There are many variations among those who practise Wicca; the majority observing solstices or equinoxes, and worshipping a male god and female goddess. Wiccans also practise ritual nudity, or as it's known, being 'skyclad'. However, there is nothing remotely sexual about it, so if Saffron was indeed seen naked it shouldn't be linked to the accusations of promiscuity levelled at her. Regarding the claims about 'hexes', I will point to the moral code of Wicca, known as the 'Wiccan Rede', or witches' commandment:

'Bide the Wiccan Rede ye must in perfect love, in perfect trust. Eight words the Wiccan rede fulfil, and harm ye none, do what you will. Ever mind the rule of three, what you send forth comes back to thee. Follow this in mind and heart, and merry we'll meet as merry we part.'

A fair take on this is that practising magic to hurt people is not permitted. Different witches interpret this in different ways, however, suggesting that stopping someone hurting others is in fact harming none. Many come back to the rule of three: if you put it out there, you'll pay for it.

When I think of this, I wonder about not just Saffron Greenwell but Awd Ma Spindle too, and whether the 'curse' she apparently put on Ussalthwaite was real. I also want to mention that there were never any concerns from schools or the authorities about Danny Greenwell's safety or wellbeing when his mother was alive.

Let's return with Leo to the farm and Ussalthwaite.

—So this was the beginning of summer 1995, a few months before Sidney Parsons' death.

—It was late June, shearing season, so I was back with a load of lads at Greenwell Farm, shearing, worming, all that. It never stopped. I was there a lot more, and there was definitely a different vibe, a different atmosphere up there than before.

—What do you mean?

—I spoke to the other workers, the seasonal lads, and they all said the same. There was just summat not right. The place was a mess, and it was getting worse, inside and out. There was old machinery just lying there in the yard like old bones, great puddles of oil and a pile of rubbish bags. The farmhouse itself was falling down anyway. It was old, you know. Great big place it was, whitewash on the outside, gone the colour of a winter sky. Slates all falling off the roof. It looked like Richard had almost given up. That's what the others said too, that something was wrong. We all knew about Saffron, but it felt like there was … something else. Something darker still.

—Did you have any idea what?

—Hard to say it really, hard to find the words. It was … *gloomy* … No one wanted to chat much, we just got on with it and got away. Nancy and me, we were pretty steady by then so when I wasn't at the farm I was with her. No more root cellar for me.

I tell you one thing I remember. All the lads knew what had gone on at that barn, the one behind the house, all dark metal and shadows. It made the place look grimmer than it was, I think. The windows were filled with cracks and cobwebs. As long as I'd been there, there'd been this great, old, rusty chain on the door, but at some point it either fell off or someone broke it.

—This was the barn where Saffron Greenwell had been found the previous year?

—The same one, yeah. Black walls, pointed roof. All the lads were scared of it. No one would go near. Now, one afternoon, the sun was out, and I was going by, and I stopped in the shade of that barn for a quick smoke, you know? Now maybe it was the wind or some animal, a cat maybe, but I swear I heard something low, something rumbling, like he's got a tiger in there.

—*Like a growl?*

—Like a growl. It sounds crazy, doesn't it, and of course I realised just how stupid I was being, how childish. Because, you see, my mind didn't go the place it should when I heard that noise. It was like something out of one of those old Hammer films, with Christopher Lee; Dracula ready to come lurking out of the fog with his fangs out, you know? I go sprinting off, away from there. Maybe it was the lads playing a joke. In fact, that's what it probably was, but I don't know. We all knew not to go in there; we were daft young lads, but respectful, you know. This guy was paying us, and by Christ I didn't want to go in there.

—*Did you ever find out what it was?*

—No, but there were other things, too.

—*What sorts of things?*

—Just … silly stuff. At first the other lads kept saying they could see someone in the windows of the farmhouse, a shadow watching us.

—*Richard perhaps?*

—I doubt it. He was always away up on the fields with the flock, or else up at the school, sorting out that boy of his, who was forever getting in bother. The lads said they saw it in the fields as well, or hiding behind the trees, just a shape of a person, a black shadow. Whenever anyone moved towards it, it would vanish. I think folk were getting paranoid if I'm honest. The farm was not a nice place; all that rubbish everywhere, shadows, rats running round. It was depressing. Maybe that's all it was, just a shadow.

It sounds like there had been a deterioration in Danny's home life that matched the start of his problems in school. As Leo says, Richard was often called to the school, and Danny spent a lot of time at the farm, in theory, grounded. Often though, Leo says he saw Danny sneaking off with the boy who had spat at him, Robbie. He saw them on their way up to Ussal Top and the kilns on Ussal Bank, or else on their way back.

—One afternoon, we were sitting having a bite to eat, in the shade of one of the old tractors in the farmyard, all our food out in a spread, you know, and one of the lads shouted out. We thought he'd been stung by summat, a bee or a wasp, but then I saw something come flying past, it made a *zip* noise in the air. Someone was chucking stones at us.

—*Who?*

—Well, we didn't see no one around, so we go off hunting round the farmyard. Once we get back, there's a load of stuff missing, butties and that all gone. Someone's missus done him a load of fruit cake, all wrapped up in wax paper, and it's disappeared too, all of it.

Well then I notice something out the corner of my eye. That old barn, the door's open just a crack. I don't say nowt, but I nod my head, and a few of the lads follow my gaze. They all start shaking their heads. No way, they're saying, no way are we going in there. I dunno what got into me, but I thought of them two lads, Danny and that Robbie, and I wondered if it was them two causing mischief. I thought it couldn't be. He wouldn't, would he – go into that barn? But I had to look, didn't I?

So I plucks up my courage and tells the lads to keep an eye out, and I walks over and pulls open that barn door. I swear to God, the noise it made was like a scream, like a cat when it's shrieking-angry, you know? This old smell comes wafting out; dust and rot. It's almost pitch-dark in there. I pull out my lighter and step in. The air's thick, and I can taste the warmth of it on my tongue. I only dared take one step, cos I can hear things, mice and that, rats maybe, all scuttling away. I wait till my eyes get used to it in there, and I take a quick look about. It was such a sad, horrible place, frozen in time, nothing there at all; just old, dried-up hay and cobwebs. It felt larger inside than it looked from the outside; it went back and back into blackness, it was like stepping into a mouth.

'Come out now, you little bastards,' I shout, and it was like the shadows, the darkness, just *swallowed* my voice. Silence for a couple of seconds, and I thought, no way are they in here, them two. Then I hear this noise, like a creak, but not a door this time; quieter. And I look up where there's this thick, black beam across the ceiling, and I swear to God, I swear on my life, there's a rope on there, an old bit of rope, fat and frayed at one end like it's been cut. And that rope was *swinging* back and forth, but there's no breeze, no wind in there. Well, I'm out of the barn quicker than a scolded cat, and I close the door behind me as tight as it'll go. I was shaking, I remember that, shaking like a leaf, wasn't I?

—*What did the other workers say? Did you tell them what you saw?*

—I would have done, but they weren't there.

—*They left you?*

—That's what I thought, then I turns round and see they've caught someone; this young lad. One of them has him by the ear, and he's wriggling like a pig, swinging, trying to punch us. At first I nearly tell them all to leave off, thinking it's Danny, but it's not. It's his mate Robbie. I recognise him after him spitting at me that time. The lads say they caught him round the side of the farmhouse with a stone clutched in his hand. Bang to rights. I was still shaken up by what I seen in the barn, and I'm looking about for Danny, cos if Richard comes along and finds the lads manhandling his boy and his mate, then we're in trouble.

I walks right up to this Robbie, and I smile and asks him if he remembers me. It's him alright; I remember that forehead and those missing teeth, poor little bugger. Not so little though, is he? I put my hand out and says give it to me, and he shakes his head like a little kid, and scrunches up his face and tells me to get fucked.

Well, I says, if you give it, you've got to learn how to take it, haven't you? I swear I only meant to scare him a bit, put the shits up him, you know, give him a bit of chat. But then there's this racket, and Jip, the farm dog, she comes running round the corner.

—*Where was Danny at this point?*

—If he was there, I never seen him, none of us did, we were all staring at the dog.

—*Why?*

—It was the way she was acting in front of this Robbie, wasn't it? Well, you know farm dogs, half wild, aren't they? But I knew she loved Danny, so I figured she was a bit of a softie. But as soon as she sees this Robbie, all her hackles go up, and she starts making this awful snarling noise. We don't know what to do, and the lad who has Robbie by the ear lets go. Well, what happened next was a bit of a blur. The dog is stood there, tense as a coiled spring, growling at the boy. None of us knew what to do. I puts out my hand and says, steady on my 'ansum, dead calm like. Robbie's glaring at the dog, and I swear he growls right back at her. Stupid thing to do, cos that dog, it jumps, it goes for him, and it's got him by the wrist, and we're all of us suddenly in a mad scramble to get the dog off him. I'd never seen it act that way before, not once. Robbie was screaming and swearing, and one of the lads chucks a pail of water over Jip, which seems to do the trick. She lets go and runs off behind us, into the barn. The door's open. I swear I'd closed it tight behind me when I came out before.

Anyway, we're all suddenly helping the lad, trying to make sure he's OK. But he's in a fury. 'Where *is it?*' he keeps shouting, and there's blood running down his arm. And we're talking about tetanus shots and all that, but he's not even arsed, he's scratching round on the yard looking for that stone of his. He's like that Tasmanian Devil, this little whirlwind of anger.

—And Danny didn't make an appearance amidst all this?

—I don't remember seeing him if I'm honest. I remember looking, because I thought if anyone could call off the dog, it would have been him.

—What happened next with Robbie? Did he find his stone?

—He's muttering and swearing to himself, not looking at any of us, just concentrating on the floor. Anyhow, after a minute or two, one of the lads found it, and he holds it out and says, 'Here you go, mate. Calm yourself down. Are you OK?' And Robbie, he just snatches the stone off the lad and off he goes, away, out of the farm and down the road, like he's being chased by the devil himself. I didn't know what to make of all that, none of us did. I seen a little dark figure catch up with him on the road, and figured that must be Danny. Probably been hiding away in the bushes.

—Did you tell Richard what had happened?

—We thought best not, eh? Seems Danny said nowt to him either, cos Richard never mentioned it, and we just got on with our work. But after that, we started noticing that barn door: sometimes it was open, and you'd look round and it'd be closed again. Unnerving, it was. None of us said nowt, but we started having our dinner over by the lambing shed on the other side of the yard. No one wanted to go near it.

—Did you or anyone else ever go back inside?

—Just once. One more time. Then I moved on after that. I'd had enough.

The following incident requires some listener discretion, I'll warn you now. Already feeling increasingly uncomfortable after what happened in the barn and with Robbie and Jip, Leo decided he'd leave Ussalthwaite and get some summer work in the seaside town of Whitby. He explained this to Richard Greenwell, without mentioning the strange incidents, and Richard accepted it and thanked him.

However, the night before he departed the farm, Leo was drinking late in The Cross Keys pub when Richard turned up and begged him to accompany him back home. At first Leo wondered if it was something to do with the ewes.

—It's dark, and Richard takes me around the side of the house, past the crumpled little wooden porch that's piled high with old flowerpots and piles of rotting firewood, and we get to the barn.

—*That barn?*

—*The* barn. I was a bit lathered up, and you would have thought that would have helped, wouldn't you? It was scary enough on a hot summer afternoon with all the lads there, but then, at nearly midnight, with Richard Greenwell stood next to me, his face all sunken in like a skull and smelling of sheep shit, and the summer sun gone behind the hills, I swear to you I wanted to turn tail and run out of there.

—*Had he told you what had happened by this point?*

—He just said there was a 'problem' and nothing more. His eyes were haunted, great bags underneath them like he'd not slept for weeks, his hair and beard like a bird's nest. Then he says he needs someone else to see what he's seen, just in case he was going mad. I felt for him then, I really did. My heart went out to the man. So he's got this great flashlight in his hand, and he pushes the barn door open. It makes that same noise as last time, like a scream, and we go inside. I was shaking by then, I really was. I thought those pints of ale and pork scratchings were going to come right back up again, I'm telling you now. I walk into that barn, and I can hear all those scurryings and creakings like before. I look straight up at the beam, and it's gone…

—*What's gone?*

—The rope. The rope what I seen only the other week, it's gone. But there's a new smell in there. An empty smell, a smell of hopelessness. A lonely smell. Sweet and rotten. And then I hear this buzzing noise, and Richard shines his torch on a pile of rags that's in the middle of the floor, right underneath that beam, and I feel my heart catch in my throat.

'Please,' he says to me, and I can see that there's tears on his face. 'Please can you look...'

So I get closer to the pile of rags, and I realise what's lying there, in the middle of the barn. It's moving a bit, and then this great cloud of flies rises up, and I'm nearly sick all over myself. I take a breath, and I whisper that I'm sorry. I tell Richard Greenwell how sorry I am, and was it a fox or something? Did the poor thing get attacked?

He tells me him and the boy, they've been all day in the fields looking for the dog. He kept going after Danny was in bed, and he says the barn was the final place he went before he turned in himself.

We stop there in front of a mess of bones and fur and dried blood. Maggots were already working away in there like some terrible heartbeat. We stop and we stare at the yellow bones and the bruise-covered innards of that poor dog, Jip, and he turns and he says to me in a voice that's like it hasn't been used, a rusty old instrument, he says, 'No fox has done this.'

I don't want to go much further in describing the horrific scene that met Leo's eyes. Whether Jip had been killed there or somewhere else, and then brought into the barn and torn open, was not clear. What was more worrisome was when the men got a closer look.

—I says to Richard, it was a fox. It has to have been. Or else the poor girl got into a fight with something out on the moor, surely? What about another dog? Some hiker or a bad lad with one of those Staffies? He just looks back at me then with those sad eyes of his, and all we can hear is the rustle of rats and the hum of those flies. It was such a sad scene, like something off of a painting. It'll stay with me, that night, it still does. Sometimes I see it as if I'm far away, like I'm up in the rafters of the barn, looking down.

I thought about Robbie. I swear to you, I nearly said to Richard, what if ... what if it was that boy? The bad one what spat in my face and was chucking stones at me and the lads. What if it was him?

But then I thought of Danny, about how Jip was his only friend before that Robbie came along, and if he lost Robbie too … well … who would he have left?

Then we get a closer look and I see that rope. That rope what was hanging off that beam. It's tied round the poor dog's neck, and I can see where it looks like it's been cut, all frayed on the ends. Horrible, it was. Proved that this was no fox.

It's Leo's belief that Jip the farm dog had been cut open then strangled with the rope before being placed in the middle of the barn, beneath the beam, for maximum effect. What troubles him most is the idea that the dog could have actually been hung. The thought that it could have been one or both of the boys chilled him.

—Next, the both of us started. Up there in one of those dark corners of the barn ceiling, something moved. I see Richard jump, then he points the torch upward into the rafters, and whatever's there has gone. I says it's a bird or a bat or whatnot, isn't it? Just a starling or a sparrow, roosting for the night. He looks at me and tries to smile, shrugs, tries to laugh. But there's no humour in it. He nods, and he says aye, just a bird, and he shakes his head. But I swear to you now, on my mum's ashes, I seen something bigger up there, some shadow that slunk back from the torchlight. It was bigger than any bird or any bat I've ever seen.

Well I got a spade, and I took the body of that poor dog and got it out of there, flies all buzzing around my head, and the maggots writhing inside it.

—Did Richard report it? What happened?

—No. None of that. He said he wanted it gone, burned. He said we could do it right there and then, take the dog up onto the moor and burn it.

I says, what about Danny? I says, what about your boy. Wasn't that dog his best friend? Well, Richard just looks at me and says that Danny's got a new friend now. He never said more than that, and I felt a shiver go through me, and that's when I decided I'd never come back here, to Ussalthwaite, to this sad farm and this broken man. I never wanted nothing more to do with the place as long as I lived.

Leo helped Richard place Jip's body into a sack and laid it across the back of the quad bike before making his excuses and preparing to leave.

—He just nodded, tears falling down his cheeks, just silent. I said to him that there's a boy in there what needs his dad. Now I don't know much about anything – my dad wasn't exactly a model parent, was he? But I thought of that boy, Danny, all alone in his bed, and his dog dead like this, and I says, do this with the boy, do it in the morning cos if that boy wakes up, you're the one he'll call for.

Richard nods and that, and he looks back to the house, then to the barn, and he says something to me.

'If she was still here, on this day of the year she would have had him up in a few hours; taken him off over the moors in her car to watch the sun rise over the Ramsdale Stones. Maybe we'll do that too … Maybe we'll remember her.'

Well I hadn't the foggiest what that meant, but I says yes. I says, why don't you do that, because if they needed anything them two, it was to be together right now. And then off he went, without so much as a goodbye. I stood and I watched the torchlight bobbing away toward the farmhouse before I set off myself.

The Ramsdale Stones are a Bronze Age stone circle on the aptly named Standing Stones Rigg, not far from Ussalthwaite. The idea that Saffron Greenwell was Wiccan makes sense if Leo's got his timings right. If this occurred in late June, then it would have been close to the summer solstice, which pagans often celebrate watching the sun rise over stone circles. In fact a few local pagan groups make regular pilgrimages to the Ramsdale Stones.

I think our interview is coming to an end, but Leo has one more thing to tell me.

—It's such a sad tale, isn't it? Such a tragedy. I wish I could tell you I seen something in that boy, in either of those boys, that could explain why they did what they did. But I can't. I've got my life together a bit more since them days, but the whole thing still haunts me, you know. Sometimes in my dreams, I'm back there. That night. In that barn. Sometimes I can still hear the buzz of them flies and the rustling of the rats. So I want to tell you summat I never told no one before. I don't know, maybe it'll help? Maybe it'll help me.

—You're free to say what you want, Leo. I'm grateful for how much you've shared.

—Maybe I haven't told anyone cos no one ever thought to ask me about any of this before. And why would they? I wasn't there when they killed that boy. I'd been out on the boats in Whitby for two months when I heard about it. And when I did, I went back there, to that farm, in the dead of night. Put them back in that barn and then left, I never wanted to think of that farm again, not as long as I lived.

—I'm sorry. What did you put back in the barn?

Leo takes a deep breath and puts his fingers to his mouth, as if smoking the ghost of the roll-ups he gave up ten years ago.

—So, when I said goodbye to Richard Greenwell that night, it wasn't quite the end. You see, after that, I was walking through the farmyard when I saw something. I see the barn door. It's open again. I thought, no way, that's it, that's me out of here. But something stops me leaving. I can't just leave that door open. I have to have it closed behind me. I don't want nothing that's in there coming out and seeing where I'm going. I'll just push it closed, and then I'm gone.

So I step up and of course, I can't resist, can I? I can't resist one more look, even though everything inside me's screaming at me to leave it alone.

So I look.

I pull out my lighter and I look.

It's not what I seen that still scares me, that wakes me up in a cold sweat to this very day, twenty-six years later. It's that noise. That creaking. Not the door, but higher, *thinner* if you know what I mean. And there it is, back on the beam.

—The rope?

—The rope. Thick, old, frayed rope, all covered in cobwebs, swinging back and forth, creaking like there's something heavy hanging from the end. But there isn't. And I swear to God, I thought my heart would stop, and I'm about to turn and get the hell out of there, when I see something else. There's something on the floor, just next to where the body of poor Jip was. I can't believe neither Richard nor me saw it.

—*What was it?*

—It was a shoebox – cardboard. It looked weird sat there, on the floor next to the stain of a dead dog, in the dried-up hay and dust.

I know what you're gonna say. I knew it myself. I should have left it. I should have just left well alone, because there was something not right going on. That box and that rope were definitely not there when we found the dog. Suddenly all the creaking and pattering in the barn all seemed to go quiet, and I found myself stepping forward and opening the lid. Stupid, stupid thing to do, but I *was* stupid back then. There was something inside me that thought it had been put there for me to see. I was expecting a cat's head or summat, but it wasn't anything like that.

It was a load of paper. A stack of paper with a little black stone placed on top. I don't know what that was all about, but it made me think of Robbie and Danny chucking stones at me and the lads. I wondered if Danny'd put it there for me to find.

—*What was on the paper?*

—It was letters.

Dear Mum, the top one said, in a messy child's writing.

I stood there, staring at them, and I felt my heart break right there and then.

Don't ask me why I took them. I don't know to this day. They made me think of Christmas, when I was little and I used to leave a letter for Father Christmas. I used to leave it at the foot of my bed, and I always asked for just one thing, something small. When I woke up on Christmas morning it was always still there. Once I thought it had gone, and I remember my belly filling up with excitement. When I looked under my bed, there it was; it had just fallen on the floor. I never got no presents for Christmas, not once, not ever. Mum and Dad just got out of their heads and watched telly all day, before knocking seven shades out of each other while I wandered round the streets trying to keep warm. I dunno how old I was – eight, nine – when I made a promise. I promised that if I ever had kids, I'd always take their Father Christmas letters. I'd always let them have that little belief on Christmas morning, cos it doesn't take much, does it?

Well that's what I thought when I found that box, sat there in the place where that boy's mum hung herself on the day after Boxing Day. I thought of magic, and I thought of that sad little boy, and I wondered if taking them might help him believe that the world was on his side, just for a moment. That she was listening from wherever she'd gone.

I can't never forgive myself. Especially after what he done. I can't believe I ever felt sorry for him.

—Whatever the rights and wrongs are of what you did, it sounds like it came from the heart. From a good place.

—Maybe so. I don't even know why I'm telling you. But maybe it'll help them, that family that have lost their kid. Maybe it'll help them understand why.

—Did you read them?

—I did, and I swear to you, I've never read anything so sad in all my life.

—Can you remember what the letters said?

—There were loads of them, so many of them. The last one was dated the day before; it was that recent. It felt bad, like I was prying into the poor boy's private thoughts. Which I was. They were just letters to his mum, telling her things what he'd done and that. Now I look back, they all seemed … like … It's hard to say, to find the words. He had written them to her like she was still here somehow. That's what was saddest about them. Maybe that's what was wrong with the boy. Maybe he did think that somehow she was still here. Maybe it played some part in what he did.

But they'll never leave me, those letters. The words of that poor boy. Then after what he done, I don't know what I'm supposed to feel anymore. Sorry for him? Hate the very bones of him. Inside me is that question, that conflict. Sometimes I can't bear it. Maybe that's my punishment for reading them?

Just like the Wiccan Rede says: 'What you send forth comes back to thee. Follow this in mind and heart.'

Leo says that nowhere in those letters were there any homicidal thoughts. He says they were just about what the boy was doing, how lonely he was at school, how much Danny missed his mother, really.

Leo seems tired and emotional, but I can see that he's grateful to have shifted his burden slightly. He says he feels guilty about never mentioning the letters to anyone before, but if he had, would it have stopped Danny and Robbie committing their terrible crime? I'm not sure. We come to my final question.

—Do you have a theory about why Robbie and Danny did what they did?

—I'm not clever. I don't know much about psychology and all that. But I know what I know, and there are folk what'll tell you that there was something haunting Greenwell Farm, and maybe even those boys. I know that he changed for the worse, did Danny, while I was there.

—Why do you think it was that Danny changed?

—Grief. That's what haunted the Greenwell place. There was a shadow where a mother had been, a wife. Grief's a funny thing; it clings to you like oil does to a seabird; however much you try and flap and escape it, it just keeps clinging on, soaking deeper and deeper. Their grief had swallowed them, and the way to get rid of grief is like that oil slick. You have to sometimes accept you can't get through it on your own – let others clean it from you, like. I learned that. I learned that when I grew up. For them, though, it was too late. That black cloud of grief had suffocated Richard and the boy.

—Could that perhaps be an explanation? Why Danny played a part in the killing of Sidney Parsons?

—Grief? I don't think it's as simple as that. There are some who'll tell you that whatever his circumstances, there was no excuse for what he did, and I think they'd be right. There are many who'll tell you the boys had to be born evil, to do something like that; that there was no helping them, that it was only a matter of time. But I tell you now, whatever he went on to do, I felt sorry for Danny Greenwell. I did then and I do now. Despite what he done. Do I think it was grief that made him do what he done? Drove him to it? No. I certainly don't. But I don't think it was evil either.

I agree in part with Leo. The answer to this case lies somewhere in the strange hinterland between pity and condemnation. It's a rocky and treacherous place to stand, so I understand Leo's conflict when he talks about Danny Greenwell. Certainly, it is possible to feel for the young boy, lost and alone in that remote farmhouse, with a father who did not have the emotional apparatus with which to discuss their loss. Of course, Danny Greenwell may have had other issues, and the death of his mother may have been the final blow for an already disturbed boy. We're not privy to what went on behind the walls of Greenwell Farm, so we'll never know what dwelled there.

Leo wasn't in Ussalthwaite on that fateful day, nor is he able to provide any clear explanation for what would drive two twelve-year-old boys to commit such a terrible crime. All Leo can tell me here is what he observed during his brief stay at Greenwell Farm.

The growling, the missing food and the open barn door: were these the pranks of two lost boys, desperate for attention, or was something really haunting Greenwell Farm? I can't say, but Leo's been able to give us some interesting insights into the psyche of Danny Greenwell.

—Like I said, that farm, it needs burning down, levelling and getting rid of. Nothing left. Just memories. But is there anyone left to remember it? Richard Greenwell is long gone, vanished like a shadow in the dawn. Who do you blame when something like this happens?

I don't think we can find the answer to why Sidney Parsons was murdered in 1995 within the crime itself. The murder was a tragic and horrifying event, a vicious act committed by children who were the same age as their victim. Sadly, this is not the first time this has happened, nor will it be the last. Each time such an incident occurs, we look at ourselves as a society and try to decide what causes something so unimaginable and ask how we prevent it happening again. Video games, music, gun laws have all been suggested as scapegoats when it comes to this kind of crime. But it's almost impossible, like Leo says, to pin the blame on something so corporeal. So what other answers could there be? What other explanations might we find here in Ussalthwaite, a place hacked out of the rock, shaken by its many losses: of industry, of people – maybe, as some would tell you, of its very soul?

I think it's important that we look at the events leading up to the murder, that we turn over every stone we can. I believe it's there that we may be able to find the reasoning, the motivation for the senseless murder of Sidney Parsons. It is a very real possibility that the identities of one or both of Robbie or Danny will become public, and in light of that, we must decide where we stand as a society when we've placed our blame and our idea of justice has been served.

What if we don't get a concise answer, though? What if we have to default to old stories and rumour to placate the anger and the sadness that saturates this tragic case? It feels like the rumours and witchcraft stories have long, embedded roots in the hills and the deep places in and around the ancient lands of Ussalthwaite. I wonder how much the whispered rumours and stories that surrounded Saffron Greenwell drove her to her death and what impact this had upon a young boy. Was murder a way that Danny Greenwell and Robbie Hooper expressed their grief?

In the next episode we have to do what Leo did when he pushed open the door of the barn on Greenwell Farm; we have to take another step deeper into the darkness that passed over this small, forgotten village.

Until then, I have been Scott King.

And this has been our second.

Dear Mum,

I'm sorry I haven't written for a little while. I was worried that it was pointless, writing these letters, because I didn't even know if you'd get them.

But now I know you do, so this is why I've started writing again.

I have some really good news, Mum. I can almost see that proud look on your face, like when I'd brought home one of my daft drawings from school when I was in year four. The boy I met has turned into a really good friend.

I know what you would say next – you would tell me to be cautious. I was, Mum. I was careful and I didn't let him in straight away. You always told me to be careful of people, and I was.

But Mum, I know Robbie's my friend now. You know how I know for sure? Because when Darren Robson called us 'bum chums' when we were walking around together on the field at break, Robbie turned round and hit him. Right in the face. Darren Robson's nose started bleeding and he ran off, and I swear he was crying. It was *amazing*. Everyone was standing around with their mouths open, and Robbie just shrugged and said, 'Come on mucker.' And we walked off, and I swear down, I felt six feet tall.

I know you said violence doesn't solve anything, Mum, but this time it did, because Darren Robson hasn't come near us since. No one's bothered us at all. And we're friends, definitely friends now. Robbie told me about his mum and dad back in Gloucester when I asked him why he was staying with Mr and Mrs Hartley; he said they were 'bad people'. He told me that they fought a lot. Not arguments like you and Dad sometimes had, but proper fights. Robbie said that his dad taught him how to fight when he was little, and sometimes he would get him to fight his mates' kids. Imagine that? He said he didn't care that his dad is in hospital, because he hates him, but he feels so sad about his mum. He hates his dad because his dad used to hit them both when he got drunk. Not anymore, Robbie said, and laughed! I wondered if that was a bit too far, but then Robbie told me he once broke his ankle, and his dad never even took him to hospital for a week. He said that when his dad crashed their car it was because he were drunk or 'stoned', but I'm not really sure what that means. Robbie says they smoke 'wacky baccy', and his dad used to let him have it too. I don't know what that is, Mum, but I don't suppose it matters, not really.

I wanted to ask him about his teeth, because he's got loads of them missing, and his breath smells like rotting hay, and everyone laughs at him behind his back about it. Not me though.

Not them anymore, now.

Robbie says he thinks it's boring here and everyone is stupid – except me, that is. So we've started making things a bit more fun round here. You always used to say that everyone round here is boring and scared of everything, and we're not being *bad,* not really, just getting up to mischief, like in *Just William,* when Aunt Emily was asleep and snoring and they put up all those signs calling her the 'Fat Wild Woman', and charged people to come and look at her. Even William's dad gave him a half-crown at the end. I lent Robbie that book, and he was chuffed because he'd never been lent a book before, and he read it all that night and asked if I had any more.

Me and Robbie have started our own Society of Outlaws, even though there's just two of us. We even have our very own 'old barn', like in the Just William books – it's the half fallen-down bothy right up at the edge of top field, you know? Robbie was well impressed, even though it's half-collapsed, old, burned stone, and not even a barn, not really. He likes the tree roots in the floor that sit up like seats. That's where we sit, in there. But no one else in the village knows that it's there, even when they're up at the kilns, cos of the big tree that hangs over it. The sheep won't even go in it, so we have it all to ourselves. Robbie brought some candles the other day, and I think he stole them, but he said he didn't. We're going to build a roof over the top with old sticks and stuff we can find, and we might even stay in there overnight. It's brilliant, Mum.

The old barn's our place now, Mum. It's where we make plans and hide from people and eat sweets. Robbie says we need to get bows and arrows and shoot things next.

Robbie's sometimes not in school every day, because he gets sent home or suspended, and the teachers say we have to be 'kind' and 'think about what he's going through'. Sometimes he's not suspended and he's still not in school, and I know he's up at the old barn. What would you think if I went there too on a school day? I know you always said that going to school is really important, but so's being a friend. I think Robbie needs a friend, and I promise I'll do double homework if I do bunk off one day and go to the old barn with Robbie. We're only doing boring stuff at school anyway, and when Robbie's not there, I have to sit on my own and no one speaks to me all day, and at break I just have to wander around by myself, like before.

I wonder if I should tell him about the special place? I'm really sorry I haven't been up there for a while, Mum. It's just that I've been busy with Robbie. We've been near it. The old barn is so close that I can almost feel you watching us, Mum, and I know you wouldn't have minded. I haven't shown him the special place because that's ours. Yours and mine. If you are reading these, Mum, can you show me somehow that it's OK to tell Robbie about the special place, because he's so sad and I think he wants his mum too. Then we'd have two places. The old barn and the special place for our Society of Outlaws to meet.

I'm going to bring more Just William books up to the old barn at the weekend, and maybe I'll take him up to the special place then, and we can read, and maybe he'll hear his mum's voice too.

I miss you.

Xxx

DISPATCH*Online*

Home • News • Sport • TV & Showbiz • Money • Property

MYSTERY USSALTHWAITE SUICIDE SOLVED?

Police tight-lipped about identity of Ussal Bank body

The identity of a man found at the ruined kilns of Ussal Bank near Ussalthwaite, North Yorkshire, the site of the Sidney Parsons killing in 1995, will not be disclosed to the public, North Yorkshire Police have confirmed.

It has come to the attention of the press that a person who wishes to remain anonymous has positively identified the man, yet no details have been released for either the deceased or their identifier, leading to speculation from many that the suicide has a link to the murder of Sidney Parsons in 1995.

It is thought that the body is that of one of the Parsons killers – Danny Greenwell or Robbie Hooper – but police will not comment further on the legal implications of an anonymity order granted to the pair in 2002.

It is not known whether fingerprinting or DNA has played a part in the identification of the man.

A senior detective provided this short statement: 'The body of a male found at Ussal Bank has now been identified. North Yorkshire Police would like to thank everyone who assisted in this investigation, which is now closed.'

To: scott@sixstories.com
From: <sixstories website contact form>
Name: [blank]
Subject: WTF are you doing??

I can't actually BELIEVE you're doing this. Shame on you.

What's all this rubbish about witches and spells. This is NONSENSE. A little disabled boy DIED, he was MURDERED and you want clicks and advertisers on your podcast off the back of his death.

YOU'RE A DISGRACE. STOP THIS NOW. You'll have blood on your hands. Mark my words.

DISPATCH*Online*

Home • News • Sport • TV & Showbiz • Money • Property

DEMONIC DUO PODCAST REVELATIONS
Amid rumours that one of the callous Sidney Parsons killers are set to be named, new revelations are exposed in popular podcast.

- The two boys formerly known as Robbie Hooper and Danny Greenwell, brutally tortured and killed a well-loved disabled boy.
- TWELVE-YEAR-OLD Sidney Parsons was found face down in a stream with 'catastrophic' injuries that 'sickened' police officers.
- Broken bones and skull 'caved in' with a rock.
- Both killers granted lifelong anonymity when judge ruled they had committed themselves to rehabilitation.
- FURIOUS Ussalthwaite residents call for justice as village vandalised on anniversary of boy's death.
- True-crime podcast exposes new revelations about killers.
- Questions remain about identity of man at Parsons murder spot – who identified the body?

In a twist of fate that some are calling 'karma' and others calling 'justice' – the two murderers of twelve-year-old Sidney Parsons in 1995 are set to have their anonymity shattered when their identities are revealed.

Despite a massive public outcry, the savage pair, known as the 'demonic duo', were sentenced to a paltry EIGHT YEARS after terrorising the small North Yorkshire village of Ussalthwaite and eventually killing a popular disabled boy.

The thugs are said to have broken windows, thrown rocks and hung nooses from buildings in a vile wave of terror that drove their history teacher to LEAVE the area amid fears for his pregnant partner.

There was also a disturbing and sustained assault on another local child that left him too frightened to reveal who had attacked him until the demonic duo were in police custody for the savage torture and murder of twelve-year-old epileptic Sidney Parsons.

Now, the crimes of the pair, which are being documented on popular true-crime podcast *Six Stories*, are sparking unspeakably cruel pranks in the village, which is still trying to recover. Witches hats being hung on walls, statues and gravestones, and occult symbols spray painted on the ruins of the farm where Danny Greenwell grew up.

The anonymity of the duo will continue to be protected, at a cost of at least £500,000 each to the taxpayer.

The investigation by popular true-crime podcast *Six Stories* is uncovering more about the circumstances leading to the brutal murder, including a farm-hand claiming that Greenwell Farm is 'haunted'.

Questions remain about the identity of the man found at the site of the Sidney Parsons murder and why *Six Stories* is not investigating that.

Scott King has been approached for comment.

Episode 3: Claws That Won't Let Go

—She was seventeen years old or thereabouts when it happened. Julia Hill was her name. It's important that she's remembered, that what happened to her should never have happened. Not then, not now, not ever.

I listened to a podcast about the Julia Hill case, actually. *The Nope-Cast*. It's good – American. Two women. True crime-slash-paranormal. It's not like yours though. Not at all. It's funny … Sorry, that's not supposed to be a dig.

Anyway, Julia Hill. She and her family came to visit Ussalthwaite in the 1970s; just a day trip, apparently. They were from somewhere in the Midlands – and they were holidaying in Scarborough. Anyway, they were odd, the Hills; full-on evangelical Christians; fire and brimstone types. They came to Yorkshire for fresh air and long walks on the moors. After the death of the mother's mother I think it was. Apparently they stumbled across Ussalthwaite by accident and were charmed by the place. The little bridges and the sheep on the hills. They visited the little church and then went up to look at the kilns on Ussal Bank.

Apparently, that's when it happened.

They were standing at the bottom, looking up under those arches, into the row of black mouths all lined up on the side of the hill like that. I've been up there myself and it is pretty spectacular, all the moors and the heather in bloom, purple, like a big bruise, spreading across the hills. Nothing for miles, just little dots of sheep. Sorry, where was I? Yes, that's when the daughter, Julia, says she can hear a voice coming from inside. Well, Mum and Dad Hill, they thought she must be mistaken, but Julia climbs up the bank on her hands and knees and vanishes into one of the kilns.

After a few minutes, she comes out again. Mum and Dad said she looked 'confused' and 'dreamy', and she said she was wrong, no one was there. And that was the end of it.

It was when they got home that Julia kept saying that an 'old lady' was visiting her bedroom at night. Now, maybe it was grief about her grandma or something like that. The Hills though, they didn't like it. And then Julia started having seizures – her body would go rigid for hours at a time. We all know what they should have done, don't we? A hospital? A therapist? Nope, Mum and Dad got in a priest, just to make sure that Julia wasn't harbouring any demons or anything, you know how it is with kids these days? Sorry, that's what they said on *The Nope-Cast*, and I thought it was funny.

Anyway, yeah, so the priest searches Julia's bedroom, because that's normal, isn't it? He finds a stone buried under her underwear in a drawer, and as soon as it's in his hands, Julia goes *nuts*, screaming and thrashing around, calling him all sorts of names. I mean, yeah, some old man is going through a seventeen-year-old's underwear drawer – she's not going to be happy. But that's it for the priest. Demon possession 101. No other possible explanation. Julia tells him that someone 'gave' her the stone on holiday in Yorkshire, but it's thought she took it from the kilns at Ussal Bank.

From the moment the priest got involved, Julia's behaviour became increasingly bizarre. She spat and growled at the sight of him, and laughed in a horrible way whenever he and her parents tried to pray with her. If they removed the stone from the house, she would lie rigid on her bed or on the floor, and under the kitchen table, apparently, growling and cursing until it was returned.

So at this point, any other family would have taken their child to the hospital, right? Not the Hills, no, they decided to call in … you guessed it, another priest. Julia seemed to take even more exception to this one. His rosary went missing and was found hanging from the roof of the Hill's house – no one knew how it could have got there. Julia stopped eating, refused to sleep, and after apparently exhausting all other possibilities – read that as *bullshit* – the priests attempted an exorcism. I mean, they go into much more detail on that podcast, but that's the long and the short of it.

So, there you go – ill-informed, insular religious zealots getting it wrong?

Or … something else?

Now, those two priests left the house and refused to return. Neither of them would ever say what had happened during the attempted exorcism of Julia Hill, and apparently both took the details to their graves. All that they would say was that Ussalthwaite was an 'unholy' place and swore that they would never return there as long as they lived.

As for Julia Hill, she was committed to St Crispin's Hospital, a mental-health facility in Northampton, in 1976. Not too much is known about her after that, and her parents apparently became fixated with the idea that 'something' had called them to Ussalthwaite and the 'devil' had led them astray.

I'd love to have known what happened when they tried to exorcise her, though. I guess we never will.

So you've got the witch story from like the seventeenth century; you've got Julia Hill in the seventies, and then Sidney Parsons in the nineties.

Now there's this guy … this suicide. Why won't the police say who it is? Who identified him?

There's definitely something wrong up there, isn't there? I mean, you wouldn't exactly want to go and visit, would you? Yeah, that's what I thought too.

Welcome to Six Stories.

I'm Scott King.

We're approaching the halfway point in our look back at the shocking and brutal killing of twelve-year-old Sidney Parsons in 1995. As is widely known, the two perpetrators were boys of the same age, and since their conviction, their identities have been legally protected. It is rumoured that at least one of the two killers' names is to be revealed to the public. When this will be, exactly or by whom, I am not certain. All I know is as much as you, that it is supposed to be imminent.

I'm no legal expert, I'm not qualified to make an informed judgement on the rights and the wrongs of these matters. What we do here, on this podcast is rake up old graves. I talk to six people involved with each cold case that will be the focus of the series, and with these stories, try to give a fair and balanced telling of what has occurred.

So far we have heard from a stalwart of the Ussalthwaite community and from someone who was on the outside, looking in. Both are looking for answers – as are you, the listeners to this podcast.

We've also had an insight into the dynamics of life at Greenwell Farm.

In this episode, though, Danny Greenwell must take a complete backseat as we move on to his cohort, Robbie Hooper.

There is a definite and unsettling supernatural atmosphere to this case that cannot be ignored, and the voice you heard at the beginning of this episode is all too familiar with the esoteric bend in the road that we have taken.

Will Campbell is an affable, self-described 'old nerd' in his early sixties. He joins me on the Zoom call from his home in the town of Ipswich in the east of England. His bookshelves are covered in ornaments – mainly superhero themed with a range of Funko-Pops and Bobble-heads of various film and comic characters. Will is also a passionate member of the Warren Heath Investigators of the Paranormal, or WHIP. We'll come to that later.

He is also a long-term friend of Ken and Jennifer Hartley.

—Those two met when we were all at Lancaster Uni together. She was one floor below him in their halls of residence – Bowland Tower, this great big tower block that's on the campus up there. They met in freshers' week in some bar and were inseparable from that moment. A proper love story.

I met Ken Hartley in lectures. First year psychology, 9am, walking across campus in the driving rain to sit and puzzle over statistics for three solid hours. I still remember the smells of the lecture halls all these years later. I'll never forget those days. Hangovers and hot tea.

—Were you friends with Jennifer back then too?

—Jennifer was Jennifer Butcher back then. She studied English, and we'd all get together, the three of us, at the Nelson Mandela Coffee Bar, for a drink and some lunch and to put the world to rights. Wonderful days they were. Wonderful days. Sometimes I'll get a smell of something, hear a song on the radio, and I'm straight back. Those were my happiest times. With Ken and Jennifer. No more wonderful people could you ever meet. They were my closest friends. I like to think they still are.

—After university, the three of you went your separate ways, is that right?

—That's right. Jennifer always wanted to be a teacher – one of those inspirational English teachers that everyone remembers, you know? And she was good at it, really good. Ken never really got on with the psychology and ended up in finance eventually. Fair play to him though, he earns decent money.

—*And you?*

—I have to say I floundered a little bit once uni was over. I got myself a Desmond in PPR – sorry, that's a 2:2 in Politics, Philosophy and Religion. I didn't really know what to do next or where to plant myself. I was single, young. I felt I had to travel a bit, you know? See the world. Ken encouraged me – he said it would be the making of me. Of course, I thought we could all do it together, the three of us; go inter-railing or something, it would be an adventure. Alas, those two had their jobs, their home and were just so wrapped up in each other, which made sense I suppose. So I took Ken's advice. I took the plunge, did it on my own.

Will, now a graduate, took two years out to travel, first through China and then into Eastern Europe via Russia.

—I like to think I found myself out there, but really, I didn't. That was disappointing. I went to experience things, see things and … well, I saw them and I experienced them, and then I came home again. That was it. I think I was more than likely just trying to delay the inevitable – having to settle down, find someone, all that sort of thing. I was never very good, socially, and I guess I sort of clung to Ken and Jennifer when we were students, rode on Ken's coattails in a way. He was always so nice, so gentle and charismatic, whereas I was this awkward little chap. When I came back from my travels, I hoped that something inside me would have changed, that I had matured or become more confident perhaps. Sadly not. Sadly I've always found other people to be just … too complicated I suppose.

Social situations are hard work – like flat-pack furniture; it feels like all the bits and pieces are splayed out on the floor and everyone else has the instructions except me.

I've never really felt like I ever belonged anywhere else, except when I was with my best friends. I just wanted to belong somewhere. Now, with the ghost group, with people who've experienced the things I have, who've seen the things I've seen, I feel like I've finally found my tribe. It's taken long enough!

When Will returned to England, his best friends were building their lives together in the North Yorkshire spa town of Harrogate. Ken and Jennifer were trying for a baby. Will, with no job and nowhere to live, returned to his parents' house in Ipswich and began work as a teaching assistant in a local primary school.

—It wasn't the best-paid job, and in the interview they asked me, with my degree, did I not want to go into teacher training. I remember thinking that I just wouldn't be able to hack it, not like Jennifer could. I just never really had the confidence on my own, without them. But working at that school, with those kids, was great. It did wonders for my confidence, and after a couple of years, I applied to work in a children's home. It was the making of me, it really was.

I'm sorry, this isn't my life story, is it? I think I just wanted to give some context about Ken and Jennifer. It just seems like everyone's quick to blame them for what happened with Robbie Hooper. They did everything, gave everything. They were really great people – really good at what they did. They were well off, educated and they'd earned it. They were like mentors to me. I would have been at a total loss without them in my formative years.

—*You were still in touch?*

—Yes. Ken was always at the end of the phone and he has a lot of patience, I must say. Even now. Even after everything that happened at their house in the nineties. I know Ken doesn't believe, that he's burying his head in the sand, but that's his way of coping and I respect that. Me, though, I know the truth now about what was happening in Ussalthwaite. I know how people will think of me – some old madman, some old crank – but I honestly don't care. I was there when it happened. And what happened in Ussalthwaite has opened my eyes, allowed me to see things that perhaps a certain degree of scepticism kept me closed to before.

Will is keen to tell me much more about the experiences he and his paranormal group claim to have had only recently at the reportedly haunted Nutshell Pub in Bury St Edmunds. However, I want to keep Will on track, as he wasn't always so convinced by the esoteric. I ask him to return to the years before the murder of Sidney Parsons and his relationship with the Hartleys.

—Ken was always on the end of the phone and up for a chat, to help with my CV. We did visit each other. I mainly came up to Yorkshire to visit them, and they were always the hosts with the most. They had a really lovely little flat in Harrogate and were doing well. I always slept on a blow-up bed in their living room. We would stay up late, chatting about the old days, as old friends do. It was just so sad about them, that they could never get what they wanted.

—What was that?

—All they ever wanted was a child of their own, and they would have made the best parents, they really would. But they couldn't. It was something to do with Ken. He told me over a few ales – in about 1989 I think. Stuff like that always happens to the best people, doesn't it? I wonder why that is. Fate can be really bloody cruel sometimes.

This was the end of the 1980s. As the decade turned, the couple seemed to throw themselves into their work. Jennifer landed a head-of-department role at a prestigious grammar school in the North Yorkshire Moors, which prompted the pair to move to the more remote location of Ussalthwaite.

—Ken commuted to Leeds for work. Add Jennifer's wage and they had more than enough. They bought that old house in Ussalthwaite and did it up inside and out. It was beautiful – inspirational. It was the jewel in the crown of that village.

—Were you working at this time?

—Yes. I had a job in a residential children's home, back in Ipswich. I think I finally found what I was really good at. I loved that job. I was there for nearly fifteen years in the end. As much as I loved working with the kids, it was hard going, especially when you're working alongside trauma and damage; it can wear you down.

—Did you believe in any way at this time – in ghosts and the like?

—Actually not at all. It never really crossed my mind. I'd never been interested in it. Not even as a boy. It's that funny thing, isn't it? The people who actually experience ghosts and the paranormal are the ones who stumble upon it by chance.

—And your experience was in Ussalthwaite?

—Correct. I was one hundred percent a sceptic until I went to Ken and Jennifer's place in 1995. I think when I went there, to Ussalthwaite, that was a warning.

—*Really?*

—Well – I've now experienced things that put me in a place of no doubt. None at all. To some, they'll sound fanciful. Even to myself they can sound ludicrous. It's like I'm looking back on someone else's memories – like an old television show or something like that. Maybe it's my brain trying to protect me. Maybe I just can't fully conceive of what happened there, at that house. That day. But it was enough to change my entire way of seeing the known world.

Fast forward to the summer of 1995, and Robbie Hooper had been staying with the Hartleys for almost half a year. Will tells me that it was an unexpected placing but he understood it.

—These two were well off, but they'd give you the shirts off their backs. They weren't tight. They were always doing things for local charities, giving as much as they could. The press don't like to report it, but that's how they got to know Robbie's family.

The details of Robbie Hooper in the press tend to focus on one thing: what he and Danny did to the village of Ussalthwaite and Sidney Parsons. A few reports talk of his 'toxic' home life, which they've taken, in error, to mean the Hartleys.

—That's why they had to move. They had to disappear, give up their jobs. Robbie Hooper was in their care when it happened, so everyone blamed them for it. No one bothered to really dig below the surface. These were good people. They did their best. I'll defend them to the death.

—*What did you know about Robbie's actual parents?*

—Not a great deal, if I'm honest. I think Jennifer met his mum through working with a women's charity back in Lancaster. I think she was vulnerable, and she and Jennifer had struck up quite a close friendship. She ended up marrying some alcoholic piece of shit and moved across the country to Gloucester with him. He knocked her and their son about. And more. Much more.

This is similar to what I've been able to piece together: Robbie's late mother, Mildred Humboldt, married Sonny Hooper in the early eighties before they moved two hundred miles from the north-west town of Lancaster to the city of Gloucester.

—I think he was a classic piece-of-shit abuser, from what I know. He isolated his young wife from her friends and family before using her and the boy as punching bags. It was all over the papers at the time – and is again now, of course.

Robbie Hooper's early childhood has been described as 'abominable'. He came from a chaotic and unpredictable household. His mother and father, both alcoholics, provided no boundaries or structure for the young boy growing up, and this was reflected in Robbie's extreme behaviour. By the time he was eight years old, his father would allegedly give Robbie cannabis to make him sleep at night. It is claimed he encouraged Robbie to fight other small boys, and as a punishment, young Robbie was made to sleep on a dog bed in a corner of the kitchen. If any aspects of this are true, I cannot confirm. What is true is that Robbie Hooper's parents both drank heavily and smoked cannabis. By eleven years old, Robbie was out of control – smoking, sometimes drinking, and committing petty acts of vandalism. Expelled from every school he attended, he was eventually placed in a PRU – a pupil referral unit.

—You wonder what that did to him, in those early years, with his brain still growing. The violence, the drugs. If anyone could have helped him though, it was the Hartleys.

I am not exactly sure of the circumstances of Robbie being sent to live with well-off Ken and Jennifer Hartley in Ussalthwaite, but it was only a matter of days after the car accident that claimed the life of Mildred Humboldt and put Sonny Hooper in a coma.

It seems that it was Jennifer's friendship with Robbie's mother that was the catalyst. Again, from assumptions and from what I can piece together – official records being confidential – a year or so before the car accident that would claim Mildred's life, Sonny Hooper ended up in custody for a GBH charge. It seems Mildred took her opportunity and contacted Jennifer Hartley, so perhaps it was then that the Hartleys offered to take care of Robbie should the need arise, which it subsequently did. In legal terms, according to the Children's Act of 1989, Robbie was entitled to be accommodated with the Hartleys with the agreement of his parents. Sonny Hooper was in a coma, and Mildred was dead, so there was an intermediate period when Robbie was placed in the care of the local authority, before the Hartleys took him in. According to the 'family and friends' clause of the Children's Act, 'The local authority does not have a duty to assess informal family and friends care arrangements, unless it appears to the authority that services may be necessary to safeguard or promote the welfare of a child in need in their area.'

The Hartleys became Robbie's temporary guardians as the agencies working with the family began to discuss what to do. It was clear that the Hartleys were able to provide a caring environment for Robbie, and he was enrolled in St Catherine's High School, half an hour drive from Ussalthwaite. Whatever the legal ins and out were, it was certainly an unconventional arrangement, but it seemed that everyone was happy with it. Most importantly, Robbie.

—When Ken asked me if I wanted to come and stay for a weekend that summer, I have to say I was intrigued, as well as overjoyed to see them both again.

—*Had Ken told you all about Robbie?*

—Precious little, actually. I knew he was going to stay there, and I knew that he was from quite a troubled background, but that was about it. Honestly, I wonder now if Ken asked me to come because of my background, working with young people. Maybe they'd realised they'd bitten off a bit more than they could chew.

Will arrived in Ussalthwaite in late July, 1995.

—'Can you smell that?' That was the first thing Ken said to me when he opened the door. I was about to lean in for a hug, but Ken was talking to me like he only saw me yesterday.

I wish I'd known what I know now, because it's one of the first signs that there's something wrong.

—*What sort of 'wrong'?*

—Spiritually, that's what I'm talking about. And there *was* a smell. At the time I just thought they had a bin that'd been full for too long or perhaps it was the cat litter. Eggy. Honestly, I expected more of a welcome. It was late and I'd come a really long way. It's a long drive to anywhere from Suffolk. This was supposed to be a bit of a reunion, you know, a few ales and a pie down the local – a good catch-up. At least, that's what I'd thought.

'Come in,' he says, and he's got his nose in the air. 'You can smell that, right?'

To be fair to him, it was quite strong, and I was worried in case I'd stood in something nasty, so I checked my shoes. Nothing.

'We just can't get to the bottom of it,' Ken said. He was utterly baffled.

Further into the house the smell got a bit worse. It was weird. Not overpowering, just this undercurrent of rotten eggs. I was about to ask Ken where Jennifer was. I hadn't seen either of them for ages, but he's stood at the bottom of the stairs, staring upward and sniffing.

'You have to see this. You have to,' he says, and starts haring up the stairs. I asked him how he is and everything, but he wasn't listening. So I followed. I only caught a glimpse of their house: coats hung up; trainers and wellies all piled up in the porch. I don't know if Jennifer was even there. I just assumed she was.

'Come on!' Ken says, and I tried to ask him what we were doing, but all I could hear is his feet clumping one floor above me. But that's Ken. The guy will never change. If I hadn't known him, I'd have probably been annoyed.

When we get to the top of about a hundred staircases, we're standing outside the attic door and I'm sweating like a pig. Ken's got that look in his eyes, the one I remember so fondly, and, like I say, I should have been annoyed, but you can't get mad with someone like Ken. Heart over head every time, but that heart is gold; I swear it's ruddy gold. That's why everyone will do anything for him. Including me.

So yeah, we're stood there, puffing and panting, these two middle-aged men outside a closed attic door, and I want to laugh, I really do, but it's like … there's a shadow over everything. He's turned the lights on, of course, but it's still dark up there, and … quiet. Ken looks at me and says, 'You can smell that, can't you? I'm not going mad, am I?'

I remember smiling; all that old excitement flooding back. But Ken's face … he looked *wild*. His hair, thin on top last time, almost bald now, was all sticking up at the sides like some kind of mad professor. I noticed a big blob of something on his jumper; tomato sauce at the corner of his mouth. His eyes frightened me – they were huge and intense. Ken's always been intense but this was … different.

To be honest I began to feel uncomfortable. I'd just spent four hours on the M1, for God's sake, and I wanted to get my coat off at least. That weird, rotten, eggy smell was stronger up here, but still just on the edge of the air. I got this weird feeling in my belly. Instinct, something primal telling me to get out of there, to leave well alone, to get in my car and go back down the M1 again and get under the duvet.

Nowadays I trust that instinct, it's a very old and very important one.

—*What happened next?*

—'Look at this,' Ken says. He was pointing to the bottom panel of the closed door. Now, obviously, I know it was Robbie's bedroom, but right then I had no idea what was going on. When I saw what he was pointing to, I almost laughed.

—*What was it?*

—Scratch marks, all over the bottom of the door panel. Like a cat's been at it, but great big ones, great gouges out of the wood. I said, 'Where do you keep the tiger?' expecting a laugh, but he just looks at me.

'Let's go inside,' he says and he looks at the floor. 'I know it's … private, it's his bedroom and I should really respect that, but right now…' And then he pushes open the door.

I don't know what I was expecting really. At the time though … I was a little … underwhelmed, you could say. It was just a bedroom, a kid's bedroom. The bed wasn't made; there were posters on the wall, and there was *that* smell, you know the one – a mixture of deodorant and feet. Not that strong, the lad was only twelve. But the eggy odour was there too, stronger in that bedroom. Another layer. The room was big, pretty much the whole top floor of the house, and there was just nothing in there really. There was two slanted windows on each side, the bed was a double, shoved against one wall. A polished wooden beam, just over our heads, a desk at one end, a bookshelf. All pretty new-looking. I knew Ken and Jennifer were looking after the boy, and I knew that, obviously, he wouldn't have much, but from what little Ken had told me on the phone about him, I guess I was expecting something else. A pentagram carved into the desk perhaps? Sorry, I'm being silly. It was just … normal. Apart from the smell, I didn't know what Ken was on about really.

There was one thing. One thing that stood out in that bedroom. It was on the desk actually, something that didn't fit.

—What was it?

—On the desk there was a pile of what I think were school textbooks, and an exercise book, all in the corner. An angle poise lamp. The lamp was on, I remember that, a little pool of yellow light on the wood. It was what was in the middle of that pool of light – I remember it being slap bang in the middle, as if someone had taken the time to place it there.

A black stone.

It looked wrong somehow, like it shouldn't be there. I walked over and took a closer look; Ken was behind me and I could almost feel that nervous energy of his, humming and crackling. I looked down at that stone – the size of a tiny fist; it would fit in your palm – and, I don't know, something inside me, some instinct told me not to touch it. Was it a lump of coal? Maybe jet? You get that a lot around North Yorkshire. It looked, to me at least, as if it had been carved; some old ornament.

—Did Ken know what it was?

—No, and I reached out for it. I don't know why. Everything inside me was telling me not to but it was like I suddenly lost control. I felt Ken go suddenly all tense. 'Don't,' he says, and I looked round, and for a second, he looked scared. Then he hid that face away, turned it into a smile. 'It's not right,' he says, 'to go through his stuff.'

It was weird. I still don't know what exactly it was he wanted to show me. It was definitely a really awkward moment, the two of us up there. I asked Ken where Robbie was, and he said he was at school but no doubt he'd end up getting a phone call and have to go pick him up. This was happening nearly every other day, Ken said. I said, let's go get a cup of tea, maybe even a pint in the local. I could tell Ken wanted to talk it all through, whatever was going on.

And talk it through he did. So did Jennifer. The three old friends walked through Ussalthwaite together from the house, through the village, over the stone bridge where the River Fent rushes by, past the community centre and the old scout hut, where twenty years later, a 4G football pitch would be built with Sidney Parsons' name engraved on a plaque over the changing-room door.

While Will was keen to reminisce, it was clear that Ken and Jennifer were concerned about Robbie.

—Ken said that when he first arrived, they tried to get him involved in the football team – Ussalthwaite Juniors U13 Kites. Robbie had said he liked football, but after a couple of weeks, the coach called Ken and Jennifer in for a meeting; he said that Robbie's behaviour was becoming an issue. They tried to explain a little bit, asked for some understanding, but after a few more weeks of training, he was told to find another club to train with. Apparently, his play was 'too violent', and the other kids on the team weren't happy with him being there. Nor were their parents.

Ken and Jennifer called it 'snobbery'. They were angry – really pissed off about it. Sorry, am I allowed to swear? Anyway, they were furious with the coach and the other parents. They thought that Robbie hadn't been given a fair chance. He'd been written off straight away, and that angered them.

I remember we got to the pub – it's a nice one, one of those faux country pubs, but in the country; you know the sort, with wallpaper that looks like bookshelves and taxidermy all over the walls. Portraits of dogs in bowler hats. Well, I remember Ken and Jennifer getting a few looks from people, and I wondered if this was because of Robbie too. I didn't say anything, God bless them.

—What was your take on all this? You must have worked with quite challenging young people in your career. Is that why you think the Hartleys invited you to stay?

—I think so. I mean, we were friends, and I was happy to help them. It was only when they really started explaining what was going on that I began to worry for them.

A lot of troubled young people, those from challenging backgrounds, start off by testing. I'm generalising, of course, but often they'll push and they'll push, their behaviour escalating, like they're testing your limits. It's terribly sad. It comes from a place of pain, of hurt; they believe themselves to be utterly unlovable, and when someone shows them love, they sometimes can't handle it and almost want to prove that person wrong. They've spent their early years being abused and neglected, and come to expect that from the adults in their lives – *How could these people love me when I'm inherently so unlovable?* It takes real understanding, real compassion, to understand this kind of behaviour. I think Ken and Jennifer were prepared, but maybe not enough.

—*It must have affected them.*

—It takes its toll. Ken and Jennifer were good people but they weren't immune to the pressure. There's no magic bullet, no *right way* of understanding and helping. Each young person is different. But those two were the type of people with enough compassion to help. I've listened to some of your earlier series, and … I'm sorry but … I mean, you had some similar experiences, didn't you?

—*I think it's best we stick to what was going on with Robbie and the Hartleys.*

—Sorry, yes, of course. Well, Robbie sounded different. Ken told me that a few strange things happened after he arrived. Jennifer went upstairs to check on him on the second evening he was there. She heard things go tumbling down the attic stairs and the two of them had strategically ignored it, thought it best to let him settle in and address the behaviour later.

Eventually, she knocked at his bedroom door and there was no answer. She tried to turn the handle and was met with resistance, as if he was on the other side, holding it closed. Jennifer backed off for a few moments and tried to speak to him. No answer. Eventually she tried again and this time was able to open the door. When she entered, she found the room empty. Not so strange, she thought, he might be in the bathroom. But Robbie was not in the house. They couldn't find him anywhere. They were about to call the police when he just showed up again, as if he'd never been gone. It was weird.

—*Where had Robbie gone?*

—Who knows? Then there were the next-door neighbours – always complaining about noise from Robbie's room. Ken and Jennifer had talked to a few people in the village, forewarned them a bit, just made them aware of Robbie's situation. Asked for a bit of compassion. But this backfired, Jennifer said. They had it in for the boy from the start.

What sort of noises were they complaining about?

—Nonsense really. They said that Robbie was 'kicking' the walls all night long. I mean, really? I'm sorry, but I've met the Browns next door, and they were both deaf as doornails. I just think they didn't want the boy in the village, messing up the place, you know? It felt like no one did.

—*Then he met Danny Greenwell?*

—Yeah … that's right. That's when things, shall we say … escalated? When those two met.

As we know, the pair met on the bus that took the children of the village to the high school when both were in year seven. Robbie arrived in February 1995. Robbie, apparently, wasn't much of a talker at school, but he said he was happy and with no real issues reported from the school, it seemed that he had settled quite well.

—They were worried Robbie might not fit in – but when he and Danny Greenwell started hanging around together, they were happy, at first.

It took a few months for the boys' tentative friendship to blossom into the 'reign of terror' that has been described by many. So far, very little is known about those early days of their relationship.

—Ken and Jennifer didn't want to push it; they wanted him to feel 'normal' – they wanted to give him his own space. It seemed like things were going well for Robbie until word reached the Hartleys that the boys had been seen at the kilns together.

—*No one was allowed to play there, right?*

—The Hartleys weren't daft – they knew that the place was a bit of a beacon for the local kids, and yes, they discouraged it, but they didn't want to ground him, not straight away. That's what conflicted them, really: how hard should they clamp down?

I think this is a tough call for most parents. Robbie and Danny had not been causing any problems, as such, going up to the kilns together at the weekends, and it seems Ken and Jennifer Hartley were reluctant to tighten any restrictions. However, they noticed a change in Robbie at home, and then his behaviour at school quickly became unmanageable.

—Robbie started having these blackouts. He'd be getting on with things as normal and then just … He would stop. He'd go rigid, his face and his hands would go claw-like, stiff. A few minutes would go by, and he'd *wake up* with no memory of what just happened. It was frightening.

—*I presume they took him to the doctor?*

—Yes. There was little in his medical records, and the doctor made Robbie an appointment with a neurologist.

—*Epilepsy? Like Sidney Parsons?*

—That's what they thought at first. But an EEG showed nothing. There were other things too. Robbie would get up in the middle of the night and come into Ken and Jennifer's bedroom and tell them there was 'something' in the house.

—*'Something'?*

—He never said what and seemed to be half asleep, or sleepwalking. Ken or Jennifer would take him back to bed, and he'd be quiet. The next day, at breakfast, he would be sullen, he didn't want to mention it. Ken told me once it was as if he wanted to but something inside him 'wouldn't allow it'.

—*Did they ever find out what Robbie thought was in their house?*

—They asked him, and he couldn't or wouldn't say. They thought it was for attention. Jennifer told me that she had an idea one morning – she brought Robbie a pad of paper and some pens, and asked him to try to draw his dreams. She said he looked relieved at this and was eager to start. She said she was getting ready for work, sorting out Robbie's packed lunch and watching him out of the corner of her eye. He was holding the black felt-tip in his fist and … well, she said it looked like something was jogging his arm. He was drawing these odd shapes that didn't look like anything. He'd do one then crumple the paper up and start again. He kept going, again and again, and she could see his face getting redder and redder – he was getting angrier and angrier. Finally he threw the pen across the kitchen and slammed his fist down on the table.

'I can't do it!' he screamed, and then burst into tears. Jennifer took him in her arms as he cried; he wouldn't explain what he was trying to draw, and the pens never came out again.

Trauma can take many, many forms. That's what I thought at first anyway. With hindsight I know better.

—*Robbie sounds deeply troubled.*

—Yeah … and it sounds like it only got worse as time went on. Things began going missing or being moved around in the house. Odd things – the telephone for example just disappeared from the table in the hall and ended up in the fridge. Ken and Jennifer put it down to Robbie, of course. I mean, who else would be doing this sort of thing? But he denied it every time. In fact, they said he started getting quite distressed about it. Whenever these things happened, it was Robbie who was often the first to notice or the first to point them out. Once, Ken went upstairs to find Robbie curled up on the landing, crying. He was holding a wedding photograph of Ken and Jennifer that had come down from the wall. The glass was covered in scratches, like something sharp had been rubbed across it. Robbie was terrified that they thought he'd done it. He was almost inconsolable.

—*This does seem like odd behaviour. What do you think was going on?*

—At the time I thought I knew. It can be odd, from my limited experience, with children who carry trauma. They're often quick to blame themselves, even if whatever's happened is clearly not their fault. But with this … it just seemed there was something more.

Will tells me the story you heard at the start of the episode – the troubling account of Julia Hill in 1974. The parallels between her and Robbie are unsettling. Will thinks so too.

—I only realised what was going on afterwards, when I joined the ghost club, WHIP, back in Ipswich. I'd never heard of Julia Hill until then, but when I did it all began to make sense. I was like you at first,

I was sceptical. Back before I know what I know now, I thought it was trauma, a messed-up kid. I mean, from that background – the poor lad didn't have a chance, did he? But then I met him. Then Ken and I had the experience in Robbie's bedroom. And it all added up. It wasn't a jump to something ridiculous, I promise you.

—Experience? Was this what you mentioned earlier, with the stone?

—No. God, I wish it was just that. No, this was far, far worse. We'll get there, I promise.

Ken and Jennifer explained to Will about recently catching Robbie and Danny up at the kilns when they both should have been in school. Ken had taken Danny back to Greenwell Farm and grounded Robbie. He was no longer allowed to associate with Danny Greenwell after school, and Ken would drive him to school and pick him up instead of letting him get the bus. Until his behaviour improved.

I have to note here that this was the Hartleys' one and only interaction with Richard Greenwell. The man was not interested in speaking to anyone in the village.

After this, the deterioration in Robbie's behaviour in school only got worse. Now came the disruption in the classrooms, throwing things around, as well as the claims that Robbie and Danny were supposedly eating insects. I put these to Will.

—Yeah, that was true, I think. Ken and Jennifer were being called in for meetings, but this was late July, remember. I know after I left, it got much worse. There was that poor teacher, wasn't there? Mr Graham. They drove him out, didn't they? Terrorised him and his family. And I'm just so glad I wasn't there when they assaulted that poor boy down by the pond for no reason, beat him black and blue. I'm just glad I was well away from Ussalthwaite by then.

I ask Will about what he thought of Robbie, once he'd met him.

—That's what I wanted you to know before I … Well, look, there *was* an incident, while I was there, that started me off, that made me think this was more than just…

Robbie was grounded by Ken and Jennifer while Will was staying. There had been too many detentions, too many meetings at the school. Will says he didn't see much of Robbie, as he spent most of his time in his bedroom. One Sunday morning, Will says, they were all on their way to the church. Will says that Ken and Jennifer weren't churchgoing types, but they were doing their best to repair relations in the village, and the church was something of a community hub.

—That morning, Robbie was sullen, almost catatonic. He just sat, slumped at the breakfast table with that nasty eggy smell coming off him. The same one from in his bedroom. Ken told him to go and have a shower and get dressed, and he just drifted off back upstairs like a ghost. He hadn't touched his bacon sandwich. This was very out of character, apparently. You know what boys are like at that age – human dustbins. I think we all put it down to having to get up early.

Well, he stayed up in that bathroom for what felt like hours, and we could hear the shower running. When he eventually emerged, he looked tired, big bags under his eyes, his clothes pulled on, all skew-whiff and creased. I remember he asked, 'Where we going again?' and there was something in his voice. I wish I had the words to articulate what it was; something strange … That doesn't do it justice. It didn't feel like it was *his* voice. That's the best way I can describe it. There was something … *crafty* to it, a sneer underlying it. Ken told him, church, of course, and I saw fear in his face; the colour seemed to just run out of it. 'Oh no,' he says, 'not me. I'm busy.'

Well by that point I think Ken had had enough, and he says, tough luck, he's coming and that's that. I sat in the back of the car with Robbie – he was like a little cloud of black smoke, sulking and staring out of the window. We had to all have the windows down, the smell coming off him was that bad, but no one wanted to say anything.

—Did you try and speak to him?

—I had no idea what to say, really. I hadn't really interacted with him much since I'd been there. On the way to the church he was whispering to himself, barely audible, hissing away like a little snake. It was … unnerving. If Ken and Jennifer heard him, they were doing their best to ignore him. I have to say, I was … Was I scared? Yes, I'm old enough and ugly enough to admit it, I suppose.

—*Did you catch any of what he was saying? What was the tone?*

—I just thought he was attention-seeking, trying to frighten us, something like that. To be fair, it was working, at least on me.

When we actually got to the church, that's when things really escalated.

The church was the twelfth-century building Penny Myers described in episode one; the same church which Robbie and Danny hung a rope from. That morning, however, the Hartleys barely even made it to the church door.

—I was shocked. More because of the *scene* Robbie was making. This wasn't the first time he'd been taken to church with Ken and Jennifer, and you could tell that this had totally thrown them. They were doing their best to put a brave face on it but Robbie was … I don't even know.

You can imagine, can't you, early Sunday morning in this sleepy little village in the middle of nowhere, just the birds chirping away, a family on their way to the church – extraordinarily idyllic. We were the first there, thank God. We got out of the car and the second the shadow of the steeple touched Robbie's feet, he stopped dead. Refused to go any further. I think Ken was at the end of his tether by that point; he will tell you himself that he didn't handle the situation as well as he could have done. He told Robbie to get moving, to stop messing about. Robbie had that sneer in his voice and he tells Ken no way, he's not going in there.

—*What did they do?*

—Oh, it wasn't nice. It was a little bit of a Mexican standoff. Robbie all tensed up, standing a foot outside the shadow of the church, Ken and Jennifer stood there doing their best not to look impressed or scared. Me in the middle. When the other car pulled up into the car park, we all looked round.

Out of the car, stepped, in a savage little twist to the tale, Sidney Parsons and his family: mother, father and grandma. Little has been said about the victim of this terrible crime, but this is Will's story, and this is the first time he had ever encountered the boy.

—The significance of this … I mean, there wasn't any, not really, at least not at the time. They got out, this little family. *I* was embarrassed, let alone Ken and Jennifer. They were mortified. Because then, of course, Robbie starts playing to the gallery.

—*What did he do?*

—I actually wonder now if he'd seen *The Exorcist* or something like that, because he was doing that *voice* – you know the one? 'Your mother sucks cocks in hell!'

—*Is that what he said?*

—Something like that … something horrible, something offensive. I heard that poor old lady gasp, it must have been the grandmother. But I also heard something else. The boy. Sidney Parsons. He was laughing, giggling away with his eyes wide and his hands over his mouth. I was shocked, I have to say, because there was nothing funny going on, not at all. It was excruciating. Everyone's just stood, frozen in shock, as Robbie's cursing and Sidney's laughing. And then off he goes.

—*Robbie?*

—Robbie. It reminded me of a cat, you know, when something spooks it? Off he went in a flash, scrambling over the car-park wall and away into the fields. Ken went to give chase, but Jennifer stopped him. She said to let him go. The Parsons family were giving Ken and Jennifer daggers, and they pull Sidney away. He's staring after Robbie like he's the best thing since sliced bread. It was horrible. Awful. Really awful. I felt for Ken and Jennifer, I really did.

—*What did they do next? Surely they had to find Robbie?*

—Jennifer walked off. She knew where she'd find him. Me and Ken went back to the house. I was going to just pack my stuff and get home. It spoiled the visit, it really did. We were in near silence in the car. I honestly thought Ken was going to cry. I had no idea what to say to him.

Back at the house, we just sat there in the kitchen together, not speaking. I didn't know how to help him, what I was supposed to do.

That's when we heard it; a noise from upstairs. It sounded like running, it sounded like someone was up there. Ken's face went scarlet, I mean he just looked *furious*, and without a word, he got to his feet. I have to say I was frightened too. I'd never seen Ken like this before. He began slowly making his way up the stairs, and I got this terrible sense that he was at the end of his tether. All of it, the humiliation in front of everyone, Robbie's behaviour at school – I felt like Ken had finally had enough.

We go up the stairs, and I swear on my life I can hear the footsteps too, running about up there as if Robbie's going from one end of the room to the other. Ken's still silent and very slowly, very calmly he opens Robbie's door.

Nothing. No one there.

I'm guessing many of your listeners will be able to explain all that away though, won't they? I wonder if what happened next will be so easy to explain? I wonder, I really do. Because for me…

At first I think there's been a technical hitch with our Zoom call. He sits very still, staring past me. Eventually, he shakes his head and turns back to me.

—I haven't spoken this out loud for a very, very long time, Mr King. I can't remember if I've even told anyone to be fair. I wouldn't tell the papers, that's for sure.

—I can assure you, Will, there's no judgement here. I just want to know what happened.

—Good thing too, I say. I think that any sort of reporting on the more … esoteric events that led up to the terrible murder of that poor boy would have been taken as trivialising the whole thing. I just … I don't want to be seen to be doing that, it's not me. Do you understand how important that is?

—I think I do, yes.

—OK, well, suddenly those gouges in Robbie's open bedroom door, they unsettled me – much more than before – and I wondered if this was a good idea at all. To be in here.

Ken just … All the fight goes out of him, and he sits down on Robbie's bed, his head in his hands. I don't know what to do. Comfort him? I sit down beside him and that's when I hear Ken say, 'Oh no…' 'What's happening, Ken?' I said, and I went to get to my feet but he grabs hold of me and pulls me back down onto the bed, and he's smiling, but I can hear his breath is suddenly quick, and he just tells me to *sit tight*. Those were his words: 'Sit tight till it's over.'

—*Until what was over?*

—It was odd. Ken told me to close my eyes and then started talking, just really quickly in this little breathy voice about some party back at Lancaster all these years ago, some night in Bowland Bar, and his voice was shaking, and he was laughing too loudly. I could see beads of sweat on his top lip and along his hairline. I went to stand up again, and Ken catches my eye and just says, 'Don't.' He puts his arm around my shoulder then, pulls me toward him so we're forehead to forehead.

—*What was happening?*

—There's a huge part of me that wished I'd just pulled away, gone against Ken's wishes and did what I wanted to do right then. He was holding on to my collar tight, and I could feel this awful cold, like a window had been suddenly opened.

Ken was doing his best to rail against it but it was no good. I could feel the ends of my fingers and weirdly my toes starting to nip. We were both shivering and then … It's hard to explain exactly, but there was suddenly a *presence* in the room. Something dark. I didn't want to look up then. I closed my eyes. I admit it, I was scared. I was really scared, and I could feel my instincts pulling at me to look, to glance up and over my shoulder to the doorway where the hiss of the door on the carpet and the draught from the stairs had trickled inside. Ken dropped his voice then, and said, 'Don't *look*, it's better if you don't look.' There was something there, I swear it, something in the room with us. I could *feel* it.

—*Did you see anything at any point?*

—There was a moment where I nearly did it; I nearly looked. It was almost like it was daring me to, like it *wanted* me to. That was the most horrible moment of my entire life. I'm not exaggerating, and I've never spoken about it until now. In fact, I've done my best to try and forget about it. But I can't. Sometimes I'll wake at some ungodly time in the morning with the sun creeping into the window and I'll remember it. That feeling. Then I'll remember what we heard next. The laughter.

It sounded like it was coming from far away, as if the voice had come floating in through the open window. Horrible, sent a chill up my spine.

—*What was it?*

—Honestly, I don't know. Thought I was going to cry. I wanted my mum. It was laughter, but like no sound a human could make. I've never heard anything like it, and never want to ever again. Not as long as I live. I remember Ken and I just holding on to each other, our eyes shut tight while that laughter danced all around us, this terrible, mocking sound.

It felt like it had looked *inside* me and could see every shameful moment, every fear, every insecurity laid bare, and it was laughing at it. That's when I knew we'd got a glimpse of something beyond our comprehension.

—What was it? Can you put a name to it?

—In all these years I've not wanted to – to give a name, the term for what was going on there. Ironically, to combat a demon, one of the things you have to do is name it.

—A demon?

—There's no other way to describe it other than what it was. I'm sure of it now. It was the same something that got inside those boys, both of those boys. It had to be. Everything began to add up. All the signs were there. The case of Julia Hill suddenly began to look different too. Suddenly everything began to fall into place. What if there was something up at the kilns? Something old? Something powerful? What if the boys had found it?

Then it was gone. Just gone, like that. The cold as well. It was like a dream, a shared hallucination.

—And Ken?

—He starts laughing himself; laughing like nothing had happened. Like it was all a big joke. Come on, he says, let's get you packed up. I felt like even more of a failure then, like even this was futile. It was like no one could help them.

—What help did they need?

—All the signs were there. It was textbook demon possession. I know how that sounds. But it's *true.* Believe me, it took me a long time and a lot of research to come to this conclusion.

—Really? You're sure?

—The smell – eggy, brimstone. The abrupt change in personality; the growling and the seizures. The bad behaviour, the eating of insects, all of it…

—*Will…*

—Robbie's aversion to holy objects – I saw that with my own eyes; the way he behaved at the church, like an *animal.* Then the laughter, the presence in that bedroom. I've never been more frightened of anything before in my entire life.

—*Do you have any real evidence that any of this took place?*

Another long and painful silence. Will sighs.

—Of course not. But I know what I felt, what I heard. That moment, that experience changed me. It's difficult to articulate the horror of it; to have something look into your very soul like that – something so terrible, so cold and uncaring stare into you and just laugh like that. In that moment I realised that we are not alone here, that there's so much more to this world.

—*Will, I have to ask, could this possibly have been a set-up? We know that Robbie and Danny were causing trouble in the village, they even drove that teacher to leave. Is it not beyond the realms of possibility they did this too?*

—Like I say, it's hard to explain, that sudden cold, that laughter. The feeling it left me with. There was no way. No way in hell it could have been twelve-year-old boys doing this.

—*Could it have been Ken and Jennifer?*

—Are you joking? No way at all. Not to me. No. They were my best friends, they would never, *never* do something like this to me. I would say how? And why? What would be the point? For what purpose?

—*Have you ever talked about it with them?*

—I've tried, once or twice. Got nowhere; they change the subject or else roll their eyes as if I'm some kind of lunatic – *on no, this again.* They simply won't entertain it. It baffles me. Ken was there, he must have felt it too. All I can say is that now I believe, now I know what's out there, I'm determined to prove it.

—*For the Hartleys or for yourself?*

—I imagine both.

What we certainly cannot prove is that either Robbie Hooper or Danny

Greenwell was possessed. That is something we're going to have to decide for ourselves.

It feels like we've reached the end of the discussion with Will. He apologises for being so, as he puts it, 'dramatic', but he clings fastidiously to his belief in demon possession.

—The way I see it is this: Ken and Jennifer Hartley were, and still are, amazing people – compassionate, understanding, nurturing. But whatever they tried to do with Robbie was futile – it didn't even scratch the surface of that boy. Why couldn't they reach him? There had to be something else going on; there had to be something stronger than them. Otherwise those two would have been able to help. And there was so much darkness, so many strange events while I was there, and then that laughter. It was when I returned home that I became involved in WHIP and began to see that possession was the only explanation, perhaps not the most logical one, but the only one that made sense to me.

Especially after what he and Danny did just two months later.

—Robbie's behaviour feels like it was building to something. What did Ken and Jennifer think was going on?

—This is what surprised me so much. I mean, I know I do the ghost-hunting stuff, and it's something I know that they're sceptical about, but I'll use Ken's words here, because I'll never forget them. He said, 'Something's got its claws into the lad and won't let go.' I wish we'd been able to talk more about it. I wish I had the bravery back then to say what I thought was happening.

The term 'demon' was thrown around rather a lot at the time when referring to Robbie and Danny. 'The Demonic Duo' phrase was coined by one tabloid when it became clear the identities of the boys were not forthcoming. The term stuck. I ask Will if there is, in his mind, the possibility that Ken and Jennifer Hartley were simply ill-equipped to deal with behaviour as extreme as Robbie's.

—I have to say, I've lain awake at night, tossing and turning and asking myself the same thing. I think that, maybe, Robbie *was* too much for Ken and Jennifer, that he was someone they simply couldn't reach, his wounds were so deep. That was the thing with those two – I think they often felt a sense of responsibility, that they had to be able to do it all, you know? To right all the wrongs, to save everyone. Perhaps Robbie was someone that they simply couldn't save.

The Hartleys have been silent since the murder of Sidney Parsons. Despite the best efforts of the tabloid press, they've maintained a very low profile, only appearing at the sentencing of the two boys and making no statements. And as they won't discuss the issue with Will, it's hard to say whether they believed this idea of possession or not.

—Horrible business, it really was. Awful, absolutely awful, and the worst thing about it was that, as strange as his behaviour was, no one could have known Robbie was capable of doing what he did to that poor boy. There's been many who've condemned Ken and Jennifer for not seeing the signs. But can you really jump from poor behaviour to killing someone? Another child at that? I don't think so. I really don't.

—There was the terrorising of their teacher, then the assault on Terry Atkinson not long before, wasn't there?

—That's true. Yes, that's very true.

—Can we talk about afterwards? What do you remember about the immediate aftermath?

—Well I was back in Ipswich by then, wasn't I? I had plenty of regrets – maybe I should have stayed longer? Talked to the boy myself? Been there a bit more for my friends? Hindsight is a wonderful thing, isn't it? I did what I could though, when I was there, which, granted wasn't much.

To tell you the truth, I saw it on the news before I heard from Ken and Jennifer. I felt a bit disappointed. I wished they'd been able to tell me straight away. When I saw that there'd been a murder in Ussalthwaite and the victim was a child, I got this terrible feeling. I actually thought it was Robbie, that something had happened to him.

Will was to drive from Suffolk to North Yorkshire one last time. When Robbie and Danny were sentenced at York Crown Court in October, 1995, Will was waiting nearby in his car, packed with as many of Ken and Jennifer's possessions as he could fit in the boot.

—The press were going crazy. I was genuinely scared. Scared for me, scared for them. Luckily, we got a huge head start, and I was able to get them both here. They were terrified, paranoid, scared of every sound, every movement, and rightly so. There were people out for their blood. Many people, and I have to say, the majority of them, who didn't even live in Ussalthwaite, placed the blame squarely at the feet of Ken, Jennifer and Richard Greenwell, Danny's father. Of course, there was the usual nonsense about horror films and video games, but most people blamed the parents and the carers.

Ken and Jennifer Hartley now live in an undisclosed location. They have done since the two boys were sentenced. Will still sees them occasionally.

—They don't have many friends anymore. For such community-spirited people, they've changed a great deal. They've got insular. The lockdowns didn't help. I wouldn't go so far as to say what happened broke them, but it certainly came close. They live in relative isolation, they keep themselves to themselves, and they're still haunted by what happened. Whatever your opinion of their guilt is, they feel it. Those two feel responsible for what happened to Sidney Parsons. They always will. I know that because they've told me. Many, many times.

—*Is it something you often talk about with them?*

—I would say about half the time. Even all these years on. Around the end of summer, harvest, that's the hardest time – the anniversary. And recently, of course, it's got even harder for them.

Will is aware of the threats that have appeared on social media and in the press – to expose either Robbie's or Danny's true identity. We still don't know which of the two is to be identified or whether this threat is genuine.

—What those boys did will never leave them. I wonder if that's the real sentence. I hit a pheasant with my car the other day. I didn't mean to, didn't want to, and I took no pleasure from it. That night, the guilt stopped me sleeping. But there's people whose idea of a lovely day out is to kill living, breathing, sentient creatures that are capable of feeling pain and fear. Morality is a murky place, a boggy swamp, and all of us stand somewhere in it. I don't know whether these grown-up men need to be exposed for what they did as kids, so the general public can pass judgement on them. Maybe everyone having their say in public isn't the right thing.

—*What do you think will happen if Robbie, Danny or both of them, have their identity revealed?*

—Well I think we all know, don't we? At best, all those years of rehabilitation will be lost. At worst, they'll be attacked, maybe even killed. Is that right? An eye for an eye? I wonder what the only people whose opinions really matter think.

—*The Parsons?*

—Correct.

I imagine, with the recent controversy, that the Parsons have been inundated with requests from journalists and social commentators. So I don't feel I can press them for a reply to my own request to talk.

All I know is that Audrey and Arthur Parsons were a quiet and God-fearing couple from Ussalthwaite. The pair, much like the Hartleys were community-spirited and Sidney was a well-liked boy who was very involved in church activities. Audrey and Arthur were quick to show compassion for their son's murderers, rather than openly condemning them. The couple, who have, to the best of my knowledge, now split up, live in different parts of the country. As I've said, while their opinion has been sought about the exposure of Robbie and Danny, neither has spoken out publicly.

So what about us? Where do we go next.

Maybe with a case like this, it's best just to listen rather than to seek answers. Maybe Will's new-found belief in demonic possession is explained as simply that – a belief? Or was the idea of possession, or else another other-worldly explanation, genuinely part of what happened in Ussalthwaite in 1995? Were two innocent boys in thrall to some terrible power?

I think about the black stone that has appeared on the periphery of this story. In Robbie's bedroom. In other places. I think about the boys' shared trauma – the deaths of Saffron Greenwell and Mildred. I think of the two boys – outcasts from the village and united in their shared grief. I think of the pull of the kilns, a place surrounded by terrible stories and rumour.

Ultimately what has stuck with me is what Will thought he heard in Robbie's bedroom. Was it demonic laughter or auditory pareidolia –

hearing patterns that don't exist? Perhaps the latter is an apt metaphor for the entire case. What we think about it all depends on what we want to think.

So far we've looked in depth at Robbie and Danny, but I think we're still missing one key element to the killing of Sidney Parsons: motive. Even if Will's belief that demonic possession was behind the murder, does that stop the killing being mindless savagery? And perhaps that's exactly what the killing was, a mindless act?

But why Sidney Parsons? Why Ussalthwaite?

In our next episode, I want to get closer to the Parsons family. Maybe I need to know, ultimately, what they think those two deserve.

And maybe we'll find out more about what drove two children to commit such a terrible crime.

This has been our third.

Until next time…

Dear Mum,

I did it. I hope you're not angry. I know I haven't been up in a little while. Maybe I should have come. Just so it could have been me and you, one last time.

I honestly think you would have understood, Mum. You see, Robbie got pulled out of class yesterday morning, and everyone went *ooh* really loud – you know, when someone's in trouble? Mr Eggers went proper mental though and shouted at everyone to shut up. That was weird cos Mr Eggers *never* shouts like that. Robbie never came back, and after lunch, we sat down in form time, and Mr Eggers told us all what had happened.

Before Robbie came here, there was a car crash and Robbie's mum got killed and his dad was in a coma for a bit, but now he's died too so Robbie's an orphan. Everyone looked at me when Mr Eggers said that, and I just stared at that plant that sits on Mr Eggers' desk that Memoona Bangari got for him. I could feel their eyes, but I wouldn't look back, I wouldn't cry. And I didn't.

I was proud of that, and when we were walking to maths, Rhiannon Storey asked me if I was OK, and I told her to go and play in the traffic, and she started crying because her cat had got killed by a car yesterday, but how was I supposed to know that?

After that, I didn't think Robbie was coming back and things would go back to being the way they were. They didn't though; people still didn't speak to me, but not in an ignoring way like they used to. They did it in a nervous way that they do now, which is well better because it means that no one trips me up in the corridor anymore, and if I want to sit at the window at lunchtime, I just go and sit there, and everyone moves away like I've got the plague. It's brilliant, Mum. No one ever dares say anything about you anymore. Everyone's scared. Except Sidney Parsons. He kept trying to talk to me, Mum, and I know you have to be nice, but he was being really annoying and kept asking where Robbie was.

I got in more trouble that day for pushing my desk over in Mr Firth's French lesson. We have those stupid old individual desks with inkwells in that always remind me of *Just William*. Me and Robbie pushed our desks over last week when he wasn't looking, to make him jump, but I didn't do that today.

The minute I came in the classroom, Mr Firth said, 'Not so clever now without your little partner in crime?' I hadn't even done anything. Everyone was sniggering at me. But I didn't push it, Mum, it just fell over, probably cos it's a hundred years old, and Mr Firth sent me out of the room.

Today, Dad was supposed to come into school for a meeting with Mr Eggers and Mrs Armstrong about my behaviour, because Rhiannon Storey grassed me up and Mr Firth is a pure wazzock. But Dad never showed up, and I heard Mrs Armstrong whisper to Mr Eggers when they thought I had gone that Dad 'cared more about his f–ing sheep than he does for that boy.' You would have come, and you would have stood up for me and told them that I didn't do anything. You would have believed me. I know that, Mum.

It's shearing time, anyway, so Dad's got other things to do than sit around and watch Mrs Armstrong's hairy mole wobble on her cheek when she gets angry. When I hadn't even done anything anyway. Besides, when Rhiannon Storey called me a 'little weirdo freak' in science on the very first day, I could tell Mr Faber was trying not to laugh with everyone else, and her mum and dad didn't get called into school, did they?

What about when Sheldon Griffin put my hat and my bag in the bin next to the dining room that stinks like a tip, and everyone called me a tramp? He didn't even get an after-school detention, and that was because he's striker for the school team and they had a match that night. It was really unfair.

Anyway, Mum, this morning, I was walking to the bus stop and Robbie was waiting for me at the front gate. He looked different, Mum, and I thought he'd been crying. His eyes were all shadowy, and his hair was messier than usual, and he had this funny smell on him that was like eggs. He said that we shouldn't go into school and we should just go to the old barn. That's when I told him about our place, Mum, the special place.

I didn't tell him everything, not about us, but just that there was a place. A special place where special things can happen.

I wondered if it would work for him there too?

At first he said he liked the old barn better and that we should go there instead. But then I showed him how to ask for a charm, and, Mum, you won't believe this: it worked! Seriously, it worked. No joke. We went back to the old barn then, and Robbie was well happy, so that's when I told him about everything, I told him about how it worked in the special place, and I said he had to bring a book.

He asked if he could bring *William the Bad,* which I lent him last week, and I nearly said no, Mum, because I didn't know if it would work or whether you might get cross. But then I thought of the charm, and thought that must have been you, Mum. That must have been you again, telling me that it's OK. Just like the letters I left in the barn. It's you, Mum.

Robbie's got the charm though, he keeps it one week and me the next.

So I said yes.

He says he's going to go up there tonight and try it, and I said you have to go on your own, and Robbie's not scared of anything, so he said he will.

I hope it works for him too, Mum, especially after what happened to his mum and now his dad too.

I hope it's not too soon.

I miss you, Mum, and I think about you every second of every day.

xxx

CrystalMania: Is it Finally Over? Not for me. Meet those still clinging to the legacy of Zach Crystal.
A few years on since the death of the biggest pop star in the world, there are still those out there who believe he was innocent...

THIS is what wholemeal bread does to your insides.
We all know that it's supposed to be good for us but doctors are going wild with these new revelations.

Ussalthwaite suicide theory that is gaining traction across the country
While North Yorkshire Police stay silent over the suicide at the Parsons murder site, the identity of the mystery man may already be staring us in the face...

How to fall (and stay) asleep using this ancient Aztec technique
It turns out the appreciation of chocolate wasn't even the best thing to come from the ancient world...

To: scott@sixstories.com
From: <sixstories website contact form>
Name: [blank]
Subject: Thin Ice

I know you think you're being oh-so clever and edgy with this series. I mean, it's pretty bad taste on the twenty-sixth anniversary of Sidney Parson's death tbf, but whatever gets you that sweet, sweet advertising revenue, right?

I, for one, was actually a bit fucking disgusted with the last episode. Demon possession? Really? Out of all the people you could have talked to, you chose this whack job?

It feels to me, and many more listeners, that all this witch bullshit is kinda trivialising an important issue. It's bringing more and more attention to Robbie Hooper and Danny Greenwell, and now all the papers are looking for them. Those two have served their time and whether you agree or not, in the eyes of the law, they've been ready to live back in society for the last twenty years. All you're doing is stoking the flames against them. You're no better than the tabloids and clickbait online. I'd advise you to show a bit more respect to the Parsons family and their loss rather than helping a torch-wielding angry mob. What's going to be the last episode – a big reveal of Robbie and Danny's assumed names? Their addresses? Their workplaces?

You're on thin ice in your desperate attempt to get more listeners. One day that ice is going to break, Scott, and the water's cold. Believe me.

Someone else is going to get hurt and it's going to be YOUR FAULT.

DISPATCH*Online*

Home • News • Sport • TV & Showbiz • Money • Property

PODCASTER ALLEGES 'POSSESSION' IN DEMONIC DUO CASE

Spurious claims by *Six Stories* fuel village outrage
Speculation about identity of mystery suicide at Parsons murder spot

On the twenty-sixth anniversary of a much-loved child's death, a day that had already been sullied by heartless acts of vandalism and speculation over the suicide of a mystery man, residents of Ussalthwaite in North Yorkshire are facing another round of assault.

True-crime podcast *Six Stories* now alleges that one or both of the 'demonic duo' – Robbie Hooper and Danny Greenwell – were 'possessed' in 1995 when they tortured and killed twelve-year-old Sidney Parsons in cold blood.

This is not the first time evil spirits have been blamed for strange occurrences in Ussalthwaite; seventeen-year-old Julia Hill apparently was 'possessed' in 1975 after visiting the village. She was subsequently 'exorcised' before ending up in a psychiatric institution.

Presenter Scott King interviewed a supposed 'friend' of Ken and Jennifer Hartley, who were acting as guardians to twelve-year-old Robbie Hooper in 1995. This friend claims that the pair were possessed by a dark power that caused them to carry out their horrific deed. This is only increasing the anger against the podcast and its presenter, who, it has been alleged, has knowledge of the new identities of Hooper and Greenwell.

Residents of Ussalthwaite and fans of the long-running true-crime podcast are 'disgusted' and 'disappointed' with the content of the latest series. Many have accused the brains behind the one-man operation, elusive journalist Scott King, of 'going too far'.

Armchair detectives the world over believe they may have cracked the mystery of the Ussalthwaite kilns suicide. A theory spreading like wildfire online is that the man whose identity is being kept top secret by police may be either Robbie Hooper or Danny Greenwell.

Both were granted lifelong anonymity in 2002 by a senior judge, and this could be why police have refused to disclose any details, including who has identified the body.

The attention the *Six Stories* podcast has brought to the case could have been a deciding factor for the child killer's suicide, it has been speculated.

Scott King has been approached for comment.

Episode 4: Two's the Charm

—It was one of those hot summer's nights. You remember, when you were a kid? When it's past 10pm but it's not properly dark, and all you can smell is the grass outside. You're covered in a layer of sweat, and the duvet's wrapped round you like a massive snake. There's no sleeping going on, and the air's close. You can hear everything, cos there's no wind when it's like that. All the cats howling. Nowt seems to sleep when it's like that.

We were having a sleepover, at his house. I never wanted to, but Mum always said it was my 'Christian duty', and I had to be kind. To be honest it was decent over at his place; his room was bigger than mine, and I liked sleeping on the air bed on the floor, next to his chest of drawers. I would lie and look at his goldfish going round and round the tank, and it used to get me off to sleep every time.

Not this night though. I had this feeling that I just wasn't going back to sleep. There were copies of his *2000AD* comics all over his bedroom floor, and I think I read all of them – until it got dark. I didn't want to put the light on in case we got in trouble, you know? We'd watched the quarter-finals of *Gladiators* with our tea, and then we'd been messing on in his room, fighting with pillows, pretending we had those pugil sticks and trying to knock each other onto the floor. I was always good at doing the voice of that referee, that Scottish one: 'Contender … ready? Gladiator … READY?'

I think his mum come in at about eleven and told us to pack it in, said it was like there was a herd of elephants in her house. She was smiling though. I know she didn't mind *that* much. I knew she liked me staying over, him being the way he was and that, you know? No one else would have gone there to play, let alone a sleepover.

I found out afterwards that Sidney lived for those sleepovers. That gutted me, it really did. Still keeps me up sometimes at night, you know? I could have done it more – *should* have done it more, for him. But I was a kid. I was a kid too. I have to remember that.

So that night we'd been staying up way too late, chatting on, and I remember Sidney asked me if I wanted to see something secret. I says, yeah of course, and he goes burrowing away into the back of his wardrobe and comes out with this little bag made out of that sack stuff, hessian or whatever.

He says look at this, and he drops something into his hand. It's this little bit of stone, black like it was jet or coal or something.

Now, the thing about me and Sid, we were both mad into WWF – that's the wrestling, not the wildlife charity. It was huge back in the early nineties. I can still remember almost the whole of the commentary of Big Boss Man vs The Mountie by heart, we watched it that many times. That's the other thing I liked about going to Sidney's house; he had Sky TV, which was rare in those days, and he recorded all the big wrestling events on tape – Summerslam, Wrestlemania, Royal Rumble. We would sit and watch them over and over again, and of course, we would play it ourselves.

We created our own characters, our own wrestlers. I was Secret Agent, which I thought was a sort of James Bond and Brett 'Hitman' Heart crossover, but it was just me in my school shirt and my hair combed back. Sid's character was The Gravedigger, who was basically The Undertaker – Sidney striding round the living room wearing his grandma's black overcoat, his mum's summer sun hat and his dad's leather driving gloves. It looked ridiculous, and the lads at school would have had a field day if they saw us. But looking back, I reckon they were all at it too. Everyone was obsessed with wrestling back then.

Now a lot of these wrestlers had some sort of gimmick that would give them 'power' – remember The Undertaker's urn and Jake Robert's snake? We kind of all knew that the wrestling was fake back then, a bit of a pantomime; but you suspended your disbelief, you invested in it because it was fun.

Well, Sidney pulls this black pebble out of this bag, held it up in the floppy fingers of the driving gloves, and he was so serious, I nearly laughed. He said it was his 'demon stone'. I know how that sounds now, after everything, but at the time, I just thought it was part of the drama, you know, part of the game. He said he didn't want to show his mum and dad, and I wasn't to tell them because it had 'powers'. I mean, it was a pebble, and we were two twelve-year-old boys, but I think with Sidney, the way he was, the wrestling and all of it was real for him. I just went along with it.

Doing that – just going along with it – that's why I'm as much to blame as those two for what happened. People tell me that there's no way it could be my fault; but I know that I could have stopped it all by doing one thing. If I'd done that one thing, Sidney might be still alive today.

No matter what anyone says to me, that thought will never leave me, that guilt.

Welcome to Six Stories.

I'm Scott King.

Over the last three weeks, we've been examining one of the most tragic cases of murder in the last century: the seemingly unprovoked killing of twelve-year-old Sidney Parsons by two boys of the same age. This tragic event occurred in the small, ex-mining village of Ussalthwaite, deep in the North Yorkshire Moors National Park. The two responsible for the killing, Robbie Hooper and Danny Greenwell, have never given a reason for committing such an unspeakable act and both were handed indefinite sentences before being released at eighteen years old in 2002 and granted lifelong anonymity by a senior judge at the high court.

Recently, there have been rumours that one or perhaps even both of the identities of Robbie and Danny are about to be revealed. Speculation is also rife about the identity of the man recently found dead at the kilns on Ussal Bank, the site of the terrible event in 1995, as well as about who it was that identified him.

There is a great deal to unpack and I am not going to offer anything here, besides six accounts of six people involved.

It's old graves we're raking over; we're not speculating on unsubstantiated stories.

So far we've heard that there was a distinct change in the behaviour of both Danny Greenwell and Robbie Hooper before they committed their awful crime, and we've heard that this was matched by strange occurrences at the houses where the boys were living at the time. So far, we've talked to three people who were part of the community of Ussalthwaite and knew the families of the killers. The families themselves are much more reluctant to speak, especially now. Robbie was in the temporary care of Ken and Jennifer Hartley, whose whereabouts are unknown, and Richard

Greenwell, the father of Danny, has also slipped away into anonymity. This is understandable in both cases.

The Parsons have made it publicly clear they are not interested and never will be interested in speaking to the press about the case; they keep their own counsel, and I am going to respect that.

However, there is someone else who was, and still is, close to the Parsons. I track down Terry Atkinson in the town of Berwick-upon-Tweed, close to the Scottish Borders. He goes by a different name at work. Terry says he will never shake the guilt of what happened in Ussalthwaite in 1995.

Maybe, he says to me, now's the right time to speak about it.

—Everyone says I was his best friend. That's the story, isn't it? But I wasn't, not really. That's what's so hard. I just hung about with him because his mum and dad were friends with my mum and dad, and he was … different. I didn't get a choice in the matter. I know how that sounds. They know it too, Audrey and Arthur. It's not like they're under some delusion.

I did it for them. For him. I'm glad I did, because it meant that when he was alive, at least he had someone.

Terry's a clean-shaven, slightly nervy man in his late thirties with a head of brown curls. He lives on a new-build estate and keeps a large snake in a vivarium in his living room. As we talk he pours green tea from a large pot that sits in the middle of the table. The area is quiet, as most people are at work and the children at school. Terry has no children of his own and does not mention a partner.

Terry Atkinson was assaulted by Robbie and Danny in the week that led up to the killing of his best friend, Sidney Parsons. This assault was pivotal in that it prompted Robbie and Danny to admit their guilt and stopped their case going to trial. We'll come to this and the events leading up to Sidney's murder later, but I want to start by asking him to explain, in his own words, the friendship he had with Sidney Parsons in 1995 and how it played out.

—The thing is, after Sidney was murdered, I was approached by a number of journalists, all of them saying they wanted me to tell my story. I was offered silly money. Honestly, it was ridiculous. But I couldn't. I wouldn't tell them any story.

—*Why was that? Out of respect for your friend?*

—No. Not at all. It was purely selfish. Two selfish reasons: the first because Sidney wasn't actually my friend, not really. How could I say that to the press? I'd be public enemy number one. Secondly, because of what happened to me before he died; if I discussed it, then I'd be in the spotlight, I'd be part of his death. I'd be blamed, and what would that do to his parents, Audrey and Arthur? They were always so grateful to me, so loving, such wonderful people … I just … I'm sorry, I can't…

Terry chokes up at this point and asks for a break. There is a weight that has clearly been hanging from him for the last twenty-six years. So far, he's avoided all press, all interviews, anything to do with the death of Sidney Parsons. I wonder if now, on the twenty-sixth anniversary, with the vandalism of the buildings in Ussalthwaite and the very real threat that one or both of Sidney's killers might be named, it's all become too much.

When Terry manages to compose himself, we resume. I ask him why is it that he's decided to break his silence for me.

—I mean, selfish reasons again. Audrey and Arthur Parsons are old people. They certainly won't listen to a podcast. It means I'll be able to get this out, get my mind sorted, and talk to them before they read something in the fucking *Daily Express* about it.

—*You're still in contact with them?*

—Yes. I have been all my life. And even after Sidney was murdered, I didn't move too far away. So I could keep visiting, so I could show them that I still care.

Terry chokes again and wipes his eyes. Like he says, Audrey and Arthur are old now, and the loss of their son must never have left them. What is interesting is this duty that Terry feels towards the couple.

—Like I say, it was like that from being a kid. My mum and dad were friends with Audrey and Arthur before either of us were born, I think they met at antenatal. It doesn't matter. Sidney and I were together since we were babies.

—*Do you have snapshots, memories of the pair of you, growing up?*

—It's the daft little things. I remember sitting at the kitchen table at our house, after going swimming, eating cheese sandwiches with the crusts cut off. Sidney used to eat a whole apple. I remember that; the core and the pips and everything. It used to blow me away. I thought it was amazing and disgusting at the same time. We were about six. He always handed me the stalk afterwards, brushed his hands together, like 'that's done'. It had the grown-ups in stitches.

It was only when the pair reached their last year at Moorside Primary School in Ussalthwaite, that Terry began to really appreciate that there was something different about his friend.

—He was just … it's hard to say now, but he was *naughty* at first. Not bad though, just … It was like, when everyone else was sitting down, and writing or drawing or whatever, Sidney would be up out of his seat, distracted all the time. He eventually had to have a classroom assistant sit with him at all times to keep him on track. By year six, he needed help with everything.

In the playground as well, kids are dickheads, and as soon as they see difference or weakness, they pounce. Sid was like … he'd do anything you told him to. He'd do it to please, to make people laugh, even if it meant he hurt himself or humiliated himself. Pretty soon, at playtime, kids were asking him to fall off things, to roll in mud, that sort of thing. He couldn't play football. He didn't get it – kept trying to pick the ball up with his hands, that sort of thing. Like I say, kids are dickheads, and Sidney didn't really have anyone to play with.

Except for me.

As has been mentioned before, Sidney Parsons was diagnosed with epilepsy and a learning disability. It is pertinent to mention that there has been a much more significant understanding of these kinds of needs since the mid-1990s.

Sidney wasn't required to attend a special school, but he was entitled to help at all times in lessons from a teaching assistant. Terry says that in the world of school, this made Sidney stand out, it made him different.

—My mum and dad sat me down when I was in year six and explained it all to me in a way I could understand. We'd come home after church – we always went to church with the Parsons – and we sat on my bed. I remember I was still in my shirt – the one I used for wrestling – it was ironed though and smelled of Daz washing powder. There'd been an incident in school when I'd been off with a tummy bug on the Friday. Some lads had been mean to Sidney, calling him … well, derogatory things about the way he was. I didn't get it, why they'd do that to him.

Mum explained that Sid was 'different', his brain was different, and that he might need me to look out for him a bit. Honestly, it was a relief, because I knew that there was something that I just couldn't put my finger on. That's where the guilt comes in. I remember feeling it then, and even worse now.

—What made you feel so guilty?

—It was because … I was looking for a way out.

—A way out? Of what?

—Away from him, Sidney. A way out of the friendship. As I got older, I kind of didn't want to be his friend anymore, not really. I was growing up, we were both growing up, but he wasn't, if that makes sense? He could barely write, he had the teaching assistant sat next to him in lessons, he still wanted to play, like, little-kid games, and I felt like … he was cramping my style. How awful is that to say? We had no other friends; it was me and him, and I knew I needed to get out of that, get some other friends, 'normal' friends. What a little arsehole I was.

—Terry, you were, what, ten, eleven years old?

—I wanted to … not be seen to be like him, if you know what I mean? It felt like his … his problem was tainting me in a way.

—Almost like it would rub off on you?

—Yeah, and I knew, even then, that in a year's time, we'd be going up to high school. There were plenty of older kids who played out in Ussalthwaite, and I'd heard all the stories. We'd also been reading *Year of the Worm* by Ann Pilling in school, about the kid, Peter Wrigley, who gets bullied. They call him 'Worm', and his mum works in a chippy like mine did, so I was scared it was going to happen to me. Bullying. I was scared Sidney would get picked on, that I would too, and there'd be nothing I could do about it. I wasn't a hero. I knew I couldn't protect him.

The first time I saw him have a fit, it was horrible. He was laid down in the living room, jerking and frothing and it was … I was scared. I just stood there. I didn't know what to do. His mum and dad rushed in. After, my mum told me it wasn't my fault but I knew I should have helped him.

I did manage to actually help him when he had a fit once, though, not long before he was killed. That's one thing I can take with me I suppose. But really, at the heart of it, I wasn't thinking about him at all, I wasn't thinking about Sidney. I was thinking about myself. At least I can admit that now. I can admit I was a shit friend, an awful person. I kept saying to myself that one day I'd tell Audrey and Arthur Parsons all of this, that I'd beg for their forgiveness.

Terry's carried this guilt for the last twenty six years and it's hard to hear, yet I can understand where he's coming from. School can be a stark and brutal, dog-eat-dog environment. Bullies and victims can become quickly established and stigma is hard to shake: too fat, too small, too tall, too pale. A birthmark, odd parents. It's better nowadays, of course, there's a lot less inequality, but one thing will never change – there'll always be bullies and there will always be victims.

—Sidney was a victim. There's no other way of saying it. Always was – even in primary school. Last picked, slower, weaker. That's where I learned to look out for him, that's why we always made sure I was there for him: same table, same group. Our parents did that behind the scenes. Was it the right thing to do? I don't know now. It's hard to say, because they believed it was right, they thought they were doing the best for him. Maybe they should have let him stand on his own two feet a bit? They did their best, that's all I know. I was always told to look out for him. I did. But I wish I'd done it more; I wish I'd been more attentive, stronger.

At the same time, I wish I'd never been given that responsibility for him. It was too much for me.

However we feel about Terry Atkinson now, he is his own harshest critic. I am interested in the lead-up to Sidney Parsons' murder but first I have one more question.

—Terry, I want to ask you first about Danny Greenwell. You grew up in Ussalthwaite alongside Danny, is that right?

—Yeah. Ussalthwaite's a small village, so everyone knows everyone. I remember Danny from school. I think Sidney and I were in a different nursery to him, a church one, but Danny was in primary school with us. And high school.

—What did you make of him at the time?

—He was just … normal really. I wasn't his friend, wasn't his enemy. He was just another kid, I suppose. Then his mum died. He was different after that.

—There are a lot of stories about Saffron Greenwell.

—There certainly are – and there certainly were. It was a funny one; his dad was up on the hills with the sheep, and his mum was a … well…

—What were you going to say?

—Nothing. I wasn't going to say it. It's just what everyone else said. Look, she didn't make it easy for herself – she always stood out. When she came into school, came to the nativity plays and the concerts, she stood out because of the way she dressed. Us kids didn't really give a shit, but she was like 'a sore thumb', people said.

—Which people?

—My mum. His mum – Sidney's, that is. They weren't exactly fans of Saffron Greenwell.

—Why was that?

—You know what small places are like – anyone who doesn't fit the mould, anyone who stands out. All that new-age stuff she was into – yoga and crystals and that – it sounds stupid now but in the late eighties, early nineties, that wasn't as mainstream as it is now, and people like my mum, like Audrey Parsons, who went to church on a Sunday, who believed in traditional values – they couldn't understand it and didn't like it. There were rumours, even back in primary, as long as I can remember, that Danny's mum was a witch.

—A witch? That exact word?

—Yep. Kids are dickheads. Danny though, it was what he used to say back – he didn't help himself. He would say, 'Yes she is, what of it?' He never denied it, never got upset by it. That freaked people out a bit, I think. Looking back, she was like that too – defiant. Then there was the incident with the fire…

—*What happened?*

—I'm not actually sure how much of it is true. It was in spring 1994, the spring before she … killed herself. The word in the village was that there was a bit more going on than just Saffron's beliefs. I was a kid at the time so didn't really get it, but we'd all heard things.

In episode one, Penny Myers told me a friend of hers saw Saffron Greenwell returning from Ussal Bank, naked at one o'clock in the morning, accompanied by 'someone else'. Terry nods his head at that.

—Yeah, and the rest. There was a load of fuss made after that about a fire. Apparently, Saffron had been up at the kilns that night and people had seen her naked, dancing round a fire. Others said she was in the fields as well, at Ussal Top, and was burning her husband, Richard Greenwell's, sheep.

—*That sounds like a silly rumour to be honest.*

—Yeah, it does, but according to my and Sidney's mums, a few of them from the church had been up there and found a load of blackened wood and burned earth. Some of the sheep's coats were scorched. I saw where the fire was myself, in fact. Saffron had been conducting some kind of ritual they said. All the kids at school said she was talking to the devil, summoning demons to curse the village, and the priest had to actually come and bless the ground with holy water. It was after that that everyone turned on Saffron Greenwell.

According to Terry, the rumours about Saffron Greenwell went into overdrive. She was accused of vandalising an area of historic interest at one end of the spectrum, because her fire had been close to the kilns; and at the other end, conducting some kind of Satanic animal sacrifice amid sex with random strangers or demons. I ask if Saffron was ever allowed her say on the matter.

—According to Mum, she didn't help herself. In fact she admitted it, called it her 'sabbat' and said she was perfectly within her rights to do it. After that, no one would speak to her. She sometimes couldn't even get served in the shops, and poor Danny became a bit of an outcast. Kids would laugh at him. This lad called Darren Robson shouted 'Greenwell! Yer ma shagged the devil!' on the bus, and all the year nines and tens were cracking up about it. It was either that or they were frightened of him – of *her* really. Danny became lost, this little loner. Everyone said his mum was a witch and a prostitute, so when she died, no one knew what to say or do.

—Do you think this ostracising of Saffron in the village had anything to do with her suicide?

—I mean, probably. But like I say, she didn't help herself, did she? She never tried to get along with anyone. She was much more about upsetting people like mine and Sidney's mums.

This begs the question, was Sidney Parsons' death some kind of revenge on Danny Greenwell's part? I think it's a stretch for a twelve-year-old, but it certainly may have influenced the killing of Sidney Parsons. We'll never know. What we do know is that this incident with Saffron Greenwell has been expertly kept from the story until now, even though the press rumours about her continue to this day. It feels a little bit like Ussalthwaite closed ranks when Saffron Greenwell committed suicide. I put this to Terry.

—Yeah. It's certainly possible. We already had enough witch stories, thank you very much. We didn't need another one. I'm guessing that played its part. I'm guessing Penny Myers told you everything about the things she said about Saffron, about seeing her with 'strange folk' up on the hills at night. It was horrible.

Saffron Greenwell may well have been conducting a fire ritual for the festival of Beltane, which takes place on 1 May, halfway between the spring equinox and summer solstice. Beltane is a fire festival, celebrating the coming of summer, and, ironically, it brought communities together in the past. As for the sheep – the fires of Beltane are seen as purifying and protective, and historically, farmers drove their livestock between bonfires to protect and cleanse them. Beltane was also a fertility festival, which may explain Saffron Greenwell being naked or 'skyclad', although just a small amount of research shows that the ritual and festival is not sexual. It's sad that such an ancient custom could now be seen in such a terrible light.

I feel for the young Danny, caught in the midst of these rumours, and I can now see perhaps some of what drove Saffron to her death. If indeed suicide was actually what happened. I have to say I admire her stubbornness but wonder if there was a way she could have explained herself instead. Then I think, why should she?

I imagine there's a large rabbit warren we could explore regarding Saffron Greenwell and the village's attitude towards her, but I want us to return to Sidney Parsons and his eventual murder. I direct Terry to talk about his memories of Robbie Hooper's arrival in Ussalthwaite.

—One day he was just there. This weird-looking kid. He looked like a thug, all these missing teeth and a sloping forehead. I remember on the bus everyone shouted 'Hey you guys!' at him. Kids are dickheads. They really are.

Terry's story follows the path we've already traced. In February 1995, Robbie Hooper and Danny Greenwell became friends. Terry says that it seemed 'natural' for the two to come together. He said, for Danny, it was some respite from the taunts thrown at him about his mother, which had just begun to resurface. For Robbie, he was new, he had a different accent and it wasn't long until people knew about his past.

—'Yer ma shagged the devil' for Danny became 'Yer da's a smackhead' for Robbie. The thing about Robbie though, he fought back, he stood up for himself. I'll never forget the time he broke Darren Robson's nose. We were all a bit in awe of that. For those of us like me and Sidney, the quiet ones, the ones who were a bit different, Robbie was our hero.

For a little while.

In Sidney's eyes though, he was some kind of god.

That never stopped.

Again, as we already know from our previous episodes, Robbie and Danny's friendship led to incidents of strange and disruptive behaviour. Terry is able to confirm many of the rumours we've heard so far.

—The pair of them were just little shits really. They would push their desks over when the teacher turned his back, hard, make them slam on the floor. I thought poor Mr Firth, the French teacher, was going to collapse with a heart attack. They would chuck things about, and Robbie was always getting into fights. He looked hard, you see, plus all the kids had seen him pop Darren Robson's nose. He'd fight anyone, it didn't matter if they were year seven or year ten. He usually won. Danny Greenwell was always there next to him, this little shadow. So they'd made rods for their own backs. When something happened – when something went missing, when something got smashed, when there was a fight, everyone blamed them for it. Rightly so if you ask me.

—Terry, I'm very interested in you and Sidney, your social standing in the school. You've not actually said so much about the pair of you at this point.

—I was your run-of-the-mill little loser, really. I have contacts now, but back then I had to wear these ridiculous glasses. My mum didn't make massive money working in Liddle Lane Chippy.

And Sidney … when we got into year seven, he was in bottom set for everything. Like in primary, he had to have a TA sat next to him, and I only ever saw him after school or on the bus.

—What about break time? Lunch time?

—Yeah … I'm a shit person, I know. I managed to avoid him then, I had other friends, I started playing football. I was by no means in with the popular kids, but I just wasn't a loser anymore, do you see?

—It makes sense, it really does. Don't forget you were a child. What about Sidney?

—It was getting harder and harder with him. He still wanted to play wrestling, and I was starting to get interested in girls. My mum, his mum, they didn't get it. They didn't get that a gap was starting to open up between us. So I still had to hang about with him at church and on weekends. He was starting to notice too.

—What? That you two were drifting apart?

—No. It was more like … He knew that there was something wrong with him but he just couldn't really *get* what it was. He knew he was different.

Terry runs his fingers through his hair and the pain he's feeling is plain in his eyes. He tells me that Sidney told him he'd been asking God to help him find a 'cure'.

—*What did that mean, do you think?*

—I think it was the way he saw things. It was simplistic: if you were ill you could be cured. Oh man, I wish I could go back and tell him that there was no need, that he was fine as he was. He was *him* and that was OK. But Sidney wanted to be like everyone else. He didn't want to have the TA sat next to him, he wanted other friends. I could have helped him with all that, it was so easy. But I didn't.

Maybe if I had, he wouldn't have become utterly fixated on Robbie and Danny.

Robbie Hooper and Danny Greenwell were in most of Sidney's classes. They spent a lot of time disrupting and acting out, which Sidney thought was brilliant.

—He would never shut up about them. When he wasn't talking about wrestling. I wasn't even interested in wrestling that much anymore. Sidney was always going on about The Undertaker and how he had all these 'powers' from this golden urn his manager used to bring to the ring with him. I was more interested in football by then, and wrestling was just this silly sort of kids' show. I never had the heart to say that to Sid, though, I just humoured him. He was getting older though, and stronger and taller, and when he wanted to 'wrestle' with me, the kid was hitting *hard*.

I know everyone loved Sid, everyone thought he was a little angel, but Sid was starting to play up himself. Maybe it was his own frustrations, or watching too much wrestling. But actually I think he was copying Robbie and Danny. He saw how people looked at them and he wanted to be like them. It was then I realised I was really starting to go off Sidney. The next few times his mum asked me to go round, I pretended I had homework.

Terry tells me the story you heard at the start of the episode, about the sleepover and Sidney's 'demon stone'.

—That made me realise something. We all knew that Robbie and

Danny were bunking off. We all knew they were hanging round the kilns at Ussal Bank. I asked Sidney where he'd got that stone, and he said it was there. He said he'd gone up to the kilns after school and 'asked for a charm' to 'make him better', and my heart just sank.

—*What did he mean?*

—Look, there was definitely a pull to the place. It was horrible – dark and desolate, right out on the moor. When you're a kid it seems even bigger, these great gouges in the rock and all those ancient arches looming above you. It's cold, there's this freezing wind that blows through there. And there's this feeling of being watched. It's hard to explain. But everyone went there. The kids dared each other to go into the kilns, everyone, including Sidney, did it because they didn't want to be the scared one. But no one went right to the back. Including Sidney.

But everyone wanted to ask for a charm.

—*A what?*

—That's what everyone called it. A charm. It meant a few things. It basically meant something weird that happened at the kilns.

—*Something weird?*

—The story was that you had to go up there alone, you had to sit on the rocks at the front, right under the opening of the middle arch with your back to the kiln and you asked for a charm. You'd sit and wait, and maybe there'd be a noise behind you or a pebble would come flying past your head, and you'd go shooting out of there like a bullet.

Terry smiles and shakes his head as he describes this, as if it sounds too silly to be true. I ask him how he first heard about this practice.

—We all knew at first that we weren't supposed to play there, and that's what brought us there in the first place, see. Not a lot else to do in Ussalthwaite, unless you like bothering sheep or walking through the moors in the rain. I guess it all died out when the internet came along. But yeah, a lad from school told me about it. The lad, I forget his name now, said that when he did it, a glass bottle smashed behind him and he took off running out of there.

—*Who was there with them? In the kilns?*

—No one. That was the thing. That was the charm.

According to Terry, this odd little ritual was commonplace among the children of Ussalthwaite. Everyone had a story about what had happened to an older sibling, a cousin, a mate. The incidents are small but unnerving. Most common were noises – often laughter that came from below the ground; or else stones would be thrown, clattering and echoing against the inside of the kiln. Like any story such as this – a passed-down ritual, a little piece of childhood folklore – there were rules.

—Everyone knew that if it offered you summat, you didn't take it. No way.

—*What do you mean, offered?*

—Like if it threw a stone or whatever. You had to leave it, you couldn't take it with you, you had to leave it there. And it was always gone by the next day.

—*Why? What would happen if you took it?*

—Well … I guess then you were in its pocket, weren't you? You owed it something.

This is the first I've heard of this odd little piece of folklore, and it sends a chill through me as I think of Julia Hill and her experience in the 1970s. I ask Terry if the children of Ussalthwaite knew about her.

—Oh yeah. Everyone did. We knew that she must have taken it – the charm. That's why … Horrible, eh?

—*Did you know anyone who'd taken a charm?*

—Again, it was one of those stories, a friend of a friend, someone's sister, someone's cousin.

I wonder whether this mythology played some part in the tragedy. Time and time again, we come back to these kilns. It was where Sidney met with Robbie and Danny before he was killed, and it's only now that we might to be starting to understand why.

It's also becoming clear why Terry has sat on this story all these years.

—Charms, witches, demons; no one wants to hear all this, not when a kid's been killed. The way I see it, it was like the wrestling.

You sort of know it's fake, but you also suspend that disbelief because you're enjoying the show. Does that make sense?

—Perfect sense. And when something very real and terrible happens, all that pantomime has to fold away.

—Exactly. We have to stick with facts. But back then everyone was scared of the place and drawn to it too. The kilns, they were like our little bit of magic there, in the hill. Asking for a charm, it was ours.

—What I don't understand is who were you asking? Who was performing these 'charms'?

—More like *what* to be honest. Most people said it was the witch. Others said it was the devil. We'd all heard about Saffron Greenwell and her rituals up at the kilns. Summoning demons. There were still the scorch marks from her fires on the ground. That added to it all. Then there was that plague of flies that summer, in the village. It was awful, like something out of a horror film. I'll never forget that feeling of them on my face, in my mouth. Those tiny legs squirming.

—Apparently there was a logical explanation.

—Of course there was, looking back. These things don't just 'happen'. Back then though, everyone said it was a curse. Ussalthwaite was cursed.

—Who … or what … had cursed the village?

—It sounds so awful, but all the kids were saying at the time that it was Danny's mother's fault, they all said she'd done a deal with a demon.

—There was an incident with Sidney on the school bus, wasn't there? Someone was picking on Robbie and Danny and the bus just stopped, then Sidney had a fit. That must have only exacerbated—

—Hang about, what? No; I remember that, the flies, and I remember Sidney having a fit. But the two things happened separately, on different days. This is what I mean, everyone's got a different story; the facts, what actually happened, it gets all jumbled up. Of *course* the village wasn't cursed. At the time though, lots of us had seen those fires up on Ussal Top. There was a degree of … what would you call it? Belief? Belief among us kids that there was something … something 'other' – some old shadow, I don't know. It was all so long ago.

I feel Terry's holding something back so I let a silence fall between us. Eventually he takes a long, deep breath.

—Look, there was something else in all of this, all of those stories and rumours. For someone like Sidney, it was even harder for him to work out what was real, what was rumour, what was gossip and … well, Sidney had asked the kilns for help; he'd asked for something to make him 'better', make him 'normal', like everyone else. Whether he picked the stone up from the kilns and thought it had been thrown out for him, I don't know. But it didn't matter. It was magic. For him.

Terry takes a deep breath, holding it in and letting it out slowly.

—Whether he really went up there or not, I don't know. Maybe it was just in his head. But I would bet my life he'd have never gone up there on his own. That's why I thought he must have been copying those two again.

—Robbie and Danny?

Terry drops his head, hair falling over his face.

—That's the line I put out, that he was copying them, but maybe he was looking for me.

Terry takes another long, deep breath, and when he looks up his face is resigned. He won't meet my eye, and when he speaks, I can see the muscles in his jaw tightening.

—I'm just going to tell the truth. I've come this far. It's going to come out. Maybe that's just the right thing to do. If there's consequences, I'll take them.

So, I was hanging about with other kids, a new group, and I was doing my best to fit in with them. Sometimes that meant doing stupid things. Daft things. Like when we went up to the kilns.

This was the beginning of summer, 1995, when Danny and Robbie had begun bunking off from school, and after Robbie's father, Sonny, had died, joining Robbie's mother and making the boy an orphan. Terry tells me that their deaths were common knowledge. The details, of course, were surrounded by rumours and hearsay. According to Terry, this gave both Robbie and Danny a kind of mystique.

—These terrible things had happened to both of them, and it was like they were … tainted somehow. No one could imagine how horrible it was for them, but no one wanted to talk to them about it either. No one knew how. We were kids. Everyone knew they were going up to the kilns, though. So me and my mates, we decided to play a little trick on them. You would have thought we would have been nicer to them, considering their circumstances, right? Of course not.

One afternoon in July, when the sun still bathed the village in a slow warmth, Terry and two of his friends walked up through the fields, past Greenwell Farm, and took the track to the kilns. He tells me they were excited and nervous, hatching their plan as they walked. It was never supposed to be anything other than a prank, a silly bit of fun prompted by the good weather and the approach of the end of the school year.

—Everyone was half scared, half in awe of Robbie and Danny by then, and we just thought we'd mess with them a bit, maybe even climb one rung on that social ladder. Like when you dare each other to prod the grumpy dog, or go in the field with the bull. For me, doing stuff like that would stop people associating me with Sidney.

When we get there, we start creeping, hiding behind the bushes and rocks, cos we can hear them, hear their voices. So we don't get seen, we go over the top of the kilns to the other side, dead quiet so they can't see us. We hide behind a load of gorse bushes, which are all flowering yellow, and we can see them, Robbie and Danny. It was weird; they both had books in their hands.

—Books?

—Yeah, like, old ones, with those leather covers, and of course, we thought they must have belonged to Danny's mum. They must be doing spells or something.

Terry's two friends distracted Robbie and Danny, asking them what they were doing while Terry crept into the darkness of the kiln behind them.

—I was a bit scared and thought maybe this was a stupid idea. I'd never been back this far – it was grim and smelled funny, sort of this eggy odour. I heard my friends running off, Robbie shouting something at them, and I just thought, what am I doing, just sat here in the dark like a pillock? What will I say if they find me here? It was stupid, but I couldn't just walk out. There was two of them and one of me. It's cold in those kilns, and damp, and I was just crouched there. My legs started to ache, and I swear I could hear something, all these little hissing, squeaking noises behind me. I nearly bottled it, nearly ran out screaming, but managed to hold it in. I shuffled back as far as I could until my back touched rock. I nearly jumped out of my skin.

—*You'd reached the back of the kiln?*

—I thought so, but there was ... it was like I could feel a draught, like a breeze, cool air coming from back there. It was round my feet, like there was a gap under there, a space *behind* if you see what I mean?

—*Did you have time to explore it?*

—I had no time; it was just then that they came into the kiln, Robbie and Danny, and I'm shitting myself. They've got a box of matches and keep lighting them, and I can hear them talking, but it's not making any sense.

—*What were they saying?*

—It was something about magic, I swear, something about this being a 'special place' and they were going to 'talk to her'.

—*Her?*

—Yeah. I think they meant the witch. That's what I thought at the time – the witch. Or worse.

Terry stayed hidden, holding his breath as Robbie and Danny moved further into the gloom of the kiln when something stopped them.

—They stopped dead and looked around, and that was when I heard this voice and my heart sank.

—*Who was it?*

—Sidney.

Sidney Parsons had made his way up to Ussal Bank and was standing at the mouth of the kiln, holding his 'demon stone'.

—I just wish then that I had done something, jumped out, pretended it was all a joke. But in the moment, I think I was wondering why Sidney was there, and what they would do about it.

Those two went mad, telling him to get lost, calling him all sorts of names, calling him a spacker and a retard. I just got so angry. I guess I was still protective of Sidney, even though I wanted to keep away from him. So I decided those two needed a bit of a lesson, and I thought a scare would do it. So I started making a noise. I could never make it again. It was like laughter – horrible, loud, cackling laughter – and it was echoing off the walls of the kiln. I saw Robbie and Danny staring, mouths open, eyes wide. Both went white. Then I picked up a handful of stones and hurled it at them. That sent them running off as fast as they could, down the bank. I'll never forget how that felt. It was fucking brilliant. I thought, I'm going to tell everyone about this, I'll be a hero. These days, I would have filmed it on a phone. It would have gone viral.

—*What about Sidney?*

—I was a bit worried actually. I thought he'd be off, faster than them, but he wasn't, he was just standing there, staring, smiling…

You want to know my biggest mistake, my biggest regret? That moment, right then.

—*Throwing the stones?*

—No. I regret not walking out and telling him it was me, that it was all a joke. If I'd have done that, he might be alive today. If I'd told him that his 'demon stone' was just a stone, if I'd told him that wrestling was fake, if I'd told him it was just me playing a stupid joke in the kilns, Sidney would be alive. But instead, I just watched him clutch that demon stone of his to his chest and walk away.

Why didn't I say anything? I just didn't want to speak to him, didn't want to be seen with him. What if my mates had come back and were there, hiding? What if he told them about us being wrestlers and stuff? What if he told them about the demon stone and our sleepovers. No way.

—*But remember, those two had hounded a grown man and his*

partner, and they assaulted you before they killed Sidney. How were you to—?

—Stop them? Listen, I haven't finished this story. Far from it. There's going to be social-media backlash against me for this, I know it. But I don't care, not anymore, because I'm doing it for him. I'm telling this story for him, and if it turns out it was my fault that Sidney died, then I deserve everything I get.

The thing is, see, I *did* try to tell him. I did. The week before those two killed him.

It was another Sunday after church, and he wanted to play fucking wrestling again, and I was so fed up with it all, I said let's not, let's go have a walk or something, just get out of the house. I tried to think of somewhere that no one would be, where I wouldn't be seen with him by my friends.

Terry walked Sidney down Wynburn Road to Barrett's Pond, a deserted, shaded place. It was here that Terry tried to talk to him.

—I said to him, look, none of it is real, the kilns, the demon stone. It's not going to help you; it's not going to cure you. I'd like to think I told him he was fine as he was, that there was nothing wrong with him. I tell myself when my brain replays it over and over again and I can't sleep, that I told him people liked him, that he was a good lad, that there was no need for him to change.

—*How did he respond?*

—At first I thought he didn't understand. He was laughing as if I was joking. But I pressed the issue. I looked into his eyes and told him again, none of it was real.

He said that Robbie and Danny believed in magic, that they had found some kind of magic up there at those kilns. I explained to him that no they hadn't. They'd just said that to him, they'd made it up. That's when he lost his rag.

—*Sidney?*

—I told you he was strong. That summer he had grown taller, and when he pushed me, I don't think he knew his own strength.

After a struggle in which Terry's glasses were knocked off onto the path,

Terry skidded on a patch of mud and toppled backward into Barrett's Pond. Soaked in stagnant water, covered in mud and algae, he stood up, furious.

—I regret my words. I regret what I called him. Worse things than what those two said, I was so angry. I didn't mean it. But I saw what it had done to him, I saw his face. I remember it sort of in slow motion: he looked down at my glasses and stamped on them. And then I didn't know what came over me. I just picked up a rock from the pond and launched it at him.

The rock missed and landed at Sidney's feet.

—I saw him look down at the rock, then at me, and I saw this … hurt on his face. He just hadn't understood in the same way that someone else would, and I was too young to really understand that. I knew I wanted to say sorry, but the words wouldn't come out. Then I saw something else, something in the bushes behind him. This shadow, this shape, like someone was hiding there. I was looking at that when the rock hit me, nearly knocked me out.

Sidney had thrown the slimy rock, black with weed, back at Terry, and it caught him on the bridge of his nose.

—I heard him scream. It was … I'd never heard him do that before. It was a horrible sound, like a sort of creaking noise coming out of his mouth, and he began picking up more rocks and chucking them at me. He was throwing them hard. They hit me in the arm, the end of my finger and right in the middle of my knee. And all the time he was throwing them at me, I saw that figure, that shadow moving about in the bushes.

Eventually, spent, Sidney stopped throwing rocks at his friend and ran off in the direction of home. Terry pulled his bleeding, bruised form out of the pond and collapsed on the path.

—I was getting to my feet when I felt someone kick me, stamp down on my back. I couldn't see anything, cos I didn't have my glasses, and my eyes were already swelling shut. It must have been him, Sidney, but something just … It didn't feel like Sidney. We'd had plenty of pretend wrestling matches so I'd have known. All I could see was this black shadow, and all I could hear was this noise, like rope creaking in the wind.

I must have passed out then, cos when I woke up, Penny Myers was there, stood over me, wringing her hands.

Terry says he was half delirious when Penny found him. His injuries weren't bad enough to warrant a trip to hospital, and he managed to walk home, where his parents cleaned him up.

Terry knew this would be all over the village by the next day. The humiliation at school for being beaten so badly by Sidney Parsons, of all people, would be too much to live down.

—I wouldn't speak. Wouldn't tell anyone what happened. But of course my mum and dad immediately thought it must be Danny and Robbie – after what had happened with Mr Graham and his partner, and the other rumours about those two. But I just refused to say anything. Said I'd not seen who'd done it.

Terry spent the next week off school, and the reason why soon got round the village. He says the tension and bad feeling in Ussalthwaite at the time was palpable; mutterings in the shops and people crossing the roads to avoid each other. There was talk of fires on Ussal Top in the middle of the night, word of the dead dog in the barn at Greenwell Farm. And in the midst of it all – Sidney Parsons.

—Oh yeah, it was horrible. Kids were kept indoors that week, there were all sorts of stories going round – daft stuff, you know: Saffron Greenwell back from the dead, all that sort of nonsense. I know that Sidney's parents were having problems with him – he was acting out, acting up in school, showing off, wanting to be like those two, Robbie and Danny. I couldn't forget what Sidney had said – that there was some kind of magic up there at the kilns. I couldn't stop seeing that shadow in the bushes. How could I have told anyone about any of it?

I'll admit it, I was scared. I was having nightmares about it: the pond, the kilns, Sidney, those two. I kept seeing that black shadow in the bushes. In my dreams it danced all the way to Ussal Top and around a huge, burning pyre. It was awful. Because that wasn't him, that wasn't Sidney who'd attacked me. I'd known Sidney all my life, all his life, and that wasn't him. That's what scared me, more than anything.

After talking to Leo in episode two, I think it's certainly possible that the fires seen on Ussal Top could have been Richard Greenwell in his top field, burning the body of his faithful sheepdog.

As tension in the village reached a crescendo, the day came that Sidney Parsons was killed.

I ask Terry when he became aware of what happened.

—I knew it was them, immediately. As soon as I got in from school, after he was found. Sidney had been off, hadn't he? Stomach problems was the official line. I know that Audrey and Arthur had kept him off to try and talk some sense into him. I know they were looking to send him to a different school, a special school, at that point. It was all…

No one knew what happened that day, not really. We were all at school, Sid had been sent to the shop – I think that was true – but then some people say that those two were waiting for him and lured him up to the kilns to kill him.

—And you?

—People have said all sorts – that they lured Sid up to the kilns, or else he met them in the village by chance and that's where they took him. Me? I think he went up there, looking for them. He went up there because there was something about that place and those two that he got fixated on. I knew Sidney. I knew what he was like, and I knew sort of how his mind worked. It was like the wrestling: he would just hook on to something and be completely obsessed by it, and for whatever reason at that point it was those two and the kilns. He believed that there was power up there, and I believe that he thought it could help him somehow.

—You were probably the closest to Sidney at the time. What could have driven those two to kill him, do you think?

—If only I'd been a bit more understanding of who he was, then maybe I would know, maybe this whole thing wouldn't be hanging over me still. If I'd only been there and listened, then, yeah … maybe I would have known what drove him up there and why they killed him.

But I never will, and that's all my fault. After all these years, I can only, logically, put it down to one thing. After what happened at Barrett's Pond, everyone basically assumed Danny and Robbie had attacked me. It was spoken about around the village as if it was fact. And my mum and dad didn't stop trying to get me to talk, to say it was them so we could go to the police and get something done about them – for the whole village really.

I think somehow Danny and Robbie found out it was Sidney who'd attacked me, and thought he was spreading lies about them to cover his tracks. They killed him for that, I reckon. Because I wouldn't tell the truth.

Terry's explanation is speculative at best. It feels like a lot of things in his story add up, save for these final, crucial moments before Sidney was killed. So the question that has loomed over this whole series remains:

Why?

What was it that drove Robbie Hooper and Danny Greenwell to murder?

—This is the bit I'm most ashamed of. It's the bit I've been practising how to say.

Refusing to say who attacked me was one thing. Lying about it is just another level, isn't it? It was the pressure, and I was just a kid.

The pressure on me to identify my attackers as Danny and Robbie was huge after they were arrested for killing Sidney. At first I wouldn't budge. My mum tried going the nicey-nicey route, all slices of cake and cups of hot chocolate; my dad tried getting stern, but I just clammed up, I couldn't do it. I just couldn't talk to anyone. After school I wouldn't go home – I'd just wander round the streets. I couldn't go to the pond or the kilns, or anywhere that Sidney had been. It was like his ghost followed me everywhere I went. I wanted to ask him what was the right thing to do.

In the end it was the Parsons that swayed me.

Audrey Parsons bumped into me one afternoon. She was frank about it – told me the lawyers were saying it was looking uncertain, if there was a trial, that those two would be found guilty. They both denied it, and the evidence wasn't strong enough, might not put them away. If they just had more to go on, if I would just tell the truth, she said, tell the police that Danny and Robbie had attacked me just a week before Sidney, then it would tip the scales. Those two would be put away. Just tell the truth, she said.

So I did. I told the truth that everyone else wanted.

For Terry, his lie has woven itself into the very fabric of his existence. After the murder, he and his family moved away, like a number of long-term Ussalthwaite families.

—I went off the rails when I hit my twenties. I was going out to raves, off my face on pills, hanging round with dealers and idiots, basically. I know now that all of that was numbing myself against the pain of what had happened. People often look at drug addicts as if they're to blame for what's happened to them. There's not a great deal of sympathy out there. No one's first thought when they see an addict is to ask what's behind it. What's happened to you that's so bad, that's so awful, you'd rather spend your entire life blocking it out, numbing yourself with drugs or drink, than facing it?

—For you, that was Sidney's murder.

—That's right. It took me until I was well into my thirties to actually start talking about it properly in therapy. It sounds mad, doesn't it?

—Talking to me then, Terry, when you've not told your story publicly before, is it about finally laying this guilt you carry to rest?

—Honestly, none of this is about me. It's always been about him, about Sidney. All those old feelings coming back. I can literally feel my mouth drying out, my jaw clenching up. It's so weird, all of this, so hard. It's the first time I've spoken *out* to anyone, to any media, about Sidney for a long time. Maybe I'm doing it so I can finally accept that Sidney's dead?

Terry slumps in his chair. He looks deflated, spent, but there's a definite lightness to him, as if a heavy burden has shifted. He begins crying silent tears and he smiles through them this time.

—I've never just sat down and remembered him, you know? Just thought about him, thought about the nice times we had, when we were kids and that, you know? It's always been about that day, that place, that terrible place.

—*You mean the kilns?*

—Yeah, it's just … such a sad place, such a horrible place. But maybe that's where I need to go? Maybe finally I need to face the horror of the past? That sounds so dramatic, doesn't it? Like something from some eighties horror film. Fight the monsters and find redemption.

—*Maybe that's what you have to do? Finally lay the past to rest?*

—Maybe you're right?

On this point, we decide to end the interview. It seems Terry has given me everything he can. Yes, there's more I could have asked him, about demon possession, about the strange incidents at the Hartleys' house, but really, would there be any value in that? Terry Atkinson has never spoken about what happened to him in 1995 before, so I feel we've come as far as we can with this.

What is most interesting about my interview with Terry is the insight he provides into Sidney himself, and his sudden fixation with Robbie and Danny and whatever they were doing at the kilns. There's been a lot of talk about ritual magic in these episodes, and it certainly seems to me that this esoteric angle cannot be denied or explained away. But is the story of the 'charms' just another layer of mythology that had built up around the kilns? Sidney Parsons seems to have desperately wanted to believe in it.

However, we are still left with unanswered questions, and things that we will perhaps never be able to fully understand.

If Terry had told the truth about Sidney attacking him straight away – told Penny or his parents – would that have changed the course of events that led to Sidney's death? Or were Danny, Robbie and Sidney already so far down that path, Terry couldn't have made any difference to what happened?

And if he had told the truth later, *once Robbie and Danny were arrested, could that have changed the course of the case? Could it have gone to trial? Would they have continued to plead innocent, and might the evidence not have been enough to convict them? And in light of Terry's confession in this episode, could the judge's verdict now be considered unsafe?*

These questions are probably unanswerable.

What we do know for sure is the degree of grief suffered by Terry in the wake of Sidney Parson's murder. Terry is like any of us, facing the fact that he may go to his grave with his questions unanswered. At least he has been able to speak his truth and tell his story after all these years.

So where does that leave us, with two episodes to go? Where does our path take us next? I guess there's an avenue we're yet to explore, and it might well be closed off to us. That is the exact circumstances and motivation for the killing. So I want to look again at Robbie and Danny – not the children they were, the killers they were; the 'demonic duo' – but the men they've perhaps become.

Would it help the family and friends of Sidney Parsons if there was some insight available into the pair's rehabilitation? Maybe those questions that have burned for what must seem like a lifetime would be dampened by some knowledge of the two killers' process. By some insight into their paths from childhood to adulthood, and into whether they were able to face what they have done. I also wonder if the folklore that clings to this case might then abate, or will it coexist with this very modern tale of horror.

We'll see in the next episode.

Until then I have been Scott King

And this has been our fourth.

Until next time…

Dear Mum,

I'm sorry. I'm sorry I ruined it. Even though it wasn't really me who ruined it. But you were angry, Mum, and I knew it. We both knew it.

Let me explain, and you might understand. And please, please can you forgive me?

I hate it here. I hate this place. I hate the people, the buildings, the streets, the roads, the fields. I hate everything about it. Except Robbie and the special place.

Everyone here is horrible. No one cares about anyone else. No one does anything about anything ever. Darren Robson and his mates all make car crash noises at Robbie, and the teachers don't do anything about it. It sends him mad, and he starts screaming and trying to attack them, and then *he* gets in trouble, Mum. They're cowards and all run away from us, but they're always winding us up, trying to get us in trouble.

So me and Robbie have started acting crazy in school now, just to show everyone, just to make them leave us alone. The more we do, the more trouble we get in, and the more they leave us alone. Robbie says it's mad how he does something daft, like when David Watson dared him to eat a dead spider, and Robbie gets an after-school detention; but when Shannon McClearly stamped on Fatima Patel's foot on purpose and broke her toe, nothing happened because Shannon's mum does the choir at church or something.

It's good that everyone leaves us alone now, because we hate them all. Our Society of Outlaws is just me and Robbie, and no one else, and we don't care. We don't care because our charm worked, and that was the message from you, to tell us that it'll work for Robbie too.

But I know it's not just that you're angry about, Mum. I'm sorry for acting like that in school, but I don't know what else to do.

I'm more sorry about what happened at the special place.

We went up there on Sunday. It was just us two, and I

thought this was the right time. I remembered you sometimes told me to trust my instincts, and I did. I trusted them.

I honestly thought Robbie was going to laugh when I told him about how in the special place, I can hear you, and I can even smell you. I went all red and was about to run but, Mum, he didn't laugh. He didn't. Instead he looked really sad. We took our books, our *Just Williams*, and I honestly felt like a bit of a wazzock stood there with those old books from Mr Womble's shop all falling apart in our hands, but I remembered when you left us those two little stones, one for me and one for Robbie, and we saw all the burned patches of ground where you used to have fires, Mum, and I knew it was the right thing to do.

But of course, someone ruined it, like they always do. It's just like everything round here – there's always someone who spoils it.

That's why it all went wrong.

Sidney Parsons came along, and I know I'm supposed to be kind to him, Mum, but I didn't feel like I wanted to be kind, because he ruined it. He ruined all of it, and I know you were angry, Mum, and I'm sorry. He came up and started asking all these stupid questions, and Robbie told him to get lost because there were witches here. He only said it to make Sidney Parsons go away, trying to scare him, because he's special like that and would believe it. But he wouldn't go. So Robbie said he was going to summon the devil, and if Sidney Parsons didn't fuck off right now, the devil would get him.

That's when you got angry, Mum, that's when you screamed and threw the stones, Mum. That's why we ran away because we thought that maybe it was the devil. But then Robbie says when we ran away, he looked back and he said he saw something come out of the special place, and he saw it walk right up to Sidney Parsons.

I'm so sorry, Mum. We ruined it. We ruined everything.

Bad things are happening now, Mum. People in the

village keep saying we hung ropes on people's houses. They say we made Mr Graham leave the village when he told us he'd 'had enough of this accursed place full of little backward inbreds' when no one would stop talking in his lesson. That wasn't just us though, Mum. Mr Graham wasn't a very good teacher, he wasn't a nice person and no one else liked him either.

Jip won't come anymore when I call her. She spends all her time with Dad and the sheep.

I don't know what to do. I'm so scared.

Please can me and Robbie come to the special place and will you not be angry with us anymore? It's frightening.

Because if we're both sorry, will it be OK?

I just want to hear your voice again, Mum.

One last time.

xxx

When True Crime Becomes True Crime

Fraser Partridge-Rees

Where do we draw the line when our obsession with true crime begins to have consequences in the real world?

Maybe I'm some sort of modern-day Mary Whitehouse, screeching about 'video nasties' and asking why anybody won't 'think of the children', but right now it's not the children we need to be worried about.

In a case of what seems to be art imitating life, or the other way round, the obsession with life, or snuffing it out, has now had real-world consequences. When I'm listening to a podcast that discusses the grisly murder of a real person while I'm chopping onions for tonight's dinner, there's a degree of separation from the actual human being the actual murder actually happened to. So when the news broke that Terry Atkinson, friend of Sidney Parsons and guest on the *Six Stories* podcast, was in hospital after a suicide attempt, the stark reality of our obsession really hit home.

We've already had a suicide in Usalthwaite, on the very site of the Sidney Parsons murder – the tabloid press screaming for answers and publishing speculation about whether Robbie Hooper or Danny Greenwell may be the unnamed victim. To me this intense speculation is a direct result of certain media outlets' need to create compelling narratives. I'm not accusing anyone in particular, but rather the general culture.

True crime felt like a passing fad at first; like maybe the ice-bucket challenge or dubstep. But over the years it has become one of the most popular podcast genres, probably because crimes are still occurring and we're still obsessed with them. You know what they say? Podcasters gonna podcast.

Terry Atkinson is the latest person to spill out their heart to the enigma that is Scott King, adding fuel to the already controversial fire that has reignited twenty-six years after twelve-year-old Sidney Parsons was murdered by two boys his own age. The former friend of the murdered child, Atkinson finally broke his dignified silence after the eyes of the world fell once again on the village where he grew up.

In 1995 a pretty little place like Ussalthwaite was able to batten down its hatches and wait out its storms. But in the age of rolling news and social media, this terrible crime has been revisited in a brand new context, and it feels like now, Ussalthwaite has come under a new kind of focus. Already photographs are swelling a dark little pocket of the internet – the colours of the flowers muddied by filters, and the tilt-shift putting the focus on the pentagrams spray painted on ruined barns and the frayed edges of hangman's ropes that have been hung from the church. I'm sure there's already a hashtag – these days a good enough reason to record reignited trauma for likes. This is the *Tiger King* generation who want the blood and the guts and the shame spilled in front of the cameras or indeed drilled into our eardrums at the gym; no stone unturned, no grave unraked.

Atkinson's revelations in episode four of the *Six Stories* podcast add precious little to a case that is being picked through – or a 'grave' that's being 'raked over', in what has become the show's grim catchphrase.

Even his admission that he'd lied about the two killers attacking him a week before Sidney Parsons does not change the basic facts around the murder itself. There may be questions to answer about the role his evidence played in the case, but I believe his confession now makes little difference to the Parsons family. However, what can't be ignored is the sudden spotlight that was thrust upon a man who was tortured by his past – a spotlight that may well have been a catalyst for his tragic subsequent actions.

Doubts have already been cast on the very idea of the podcast itself – so eager to exploit the twenty-sixth anniversary of a terrible event. I for one was dubious as to why Terry Atkinson was so easy to share his tears with King. It is also not entirely obvious how King managed to 'track down' a man who goes by a different name and has not spoken until now.

Regardless, the consequences were there the day the episode was released – thirty-eight-year-old Atkinson was rushed to hospital from the remote site of the twenty-six-year-old murder, near the village of Ussalthwaite; a village that has recently experienced an unwelcome influx of journalists and murder tourists.

It's time, I think, to start watching the watchmen when it comes to true crime. There are many who claim Terry Atkinson's suicide attempt was a direct result of his appearance on *Six Stories*. There are many who accuse Scott King himself of manipulation, and beg that some kind of ethical standards are applied to what he is doing.

Yes, for some – for many if we're looking at listening figures and podcast chart positions – the case of Sidney Parsons is still fascinating. But now there are real-life consequences to our obsession with past crimes. It's impossible to ignore the claims that the assumed identities of Robbie Hooper or Danny Greenwell are about to be exposed, and it makes one wonder whether in the eternal quest for ratings and revenue, *Six Stories* might be preparing to do just that.

Scott King has been approached for comment.

To: scott@sixstories.com
From: <sixstories website contact form>
Name: [unknown]
Subject: U're SICK

Theres something very fucking wrong with you. Very fucking wrong indeed.

Leave this alone. Leave them alone.

This isn't about you. This is about empathy – which you clearly have none of.

2 down, how many more to go???? How much more blood do you want to spill?

MURDERER.

Episode 5: You Can't Fix Evil

—They weren't those little boys anymore – their faces blurred out like strange dolls in those court sketches. The pair of them were eighteen at this point, both technically adults. They'd changed as well, grown taller, their faces thinning, becoming more theirs. Just shadows of those two boys they used to be. They'd gone from blurred-out dolls to men. What did we, the public, expect to see when they came into the court all those years ago? Monsters? Demons? They looked like little boys. Scared little boys.

I wonder if they felt that fear in the same way?

As far as I know, both parole hearings were the same, they were faced with three people: a judge, a psychiatrist and a lay member – someone impartial. I don't know who that was. I don't actually know who any of them were on that board. It was all totally hush-hush. Both boys, now men of eighteen years, had written a statement and there were reports; from probation, the psychiatrist and from the secure units – one of which was ours.

Those reports had to explain Danny and Robbie's progress. Who they'd been when they came in. *What* they'd been. It's a funny one, that, because *what* both of them were, what they are, will never change. They're both killers. Child killers, as well as being children who are killers.

He has changed though, Danny. He's changed significantly. You can't hear much Ussalthwaite in his voice anymore. And that's just the start.

In their hearing, the parole board had to decide to what extent Danny believed, and the staff that had been supervising him for the last six years believed, that he had changed *who* he was, and whether he was suitable for release. That's not for people like us to say; we can't say conclusively whether someone like Robbie Hooper or Danny Greenwell should be released. What we can say is that he made progress when he was with us. We can say that he eventually faced up to what he did when he was twelve, and he took responsibility for it. He'd always been quiet, had Danny, and in that sense, he hadn't changed much. He was meticulous, deliberate, his every movement precise and gentle. That's actually a good word to describe the Danny that I knew – gentle. I imagine your listeners would lose their rag at that: Danny Greenwell, gentle? But he was. There were rabbits at the unit, pet ones. We had a snake as well and a couple of tortoises. Danny cared for those animals; those animals played a big part in his rehabilitation.

That's the word, isn't it? The million-dollar term. Was Danny Greenwell rehabilitated? Was Robbie?

Were they safe to go back into the world?

The parole hearing began with pretty simple questions, general stuff, you know? Obviously I can't repeat what was said, but they eased him in, got him used to them, their questions. For a kid that's spent all his teenage years in an institution, it's very interesting to see how he responded – always looking to please, to do the right thing, not to be seen as making a fuss.

Then things got intense, the mood changed. The voices got louder, the questions developed sharp edges. The name Sidney Parsons was mentioned a few times, the details of what they did to him was also brought up. The beating, the broken ribs, that rock buried in the back of his head. That was deliberate; it was all mentioned to see how they would react when faced with it, the stark truth of what they'd done.

Robbie and Danny had to answer those questions and to be fair to them, they did. I know that Danny stayed calm, he showed remorse. He talked about his rehabilitation, he talked about how he had changed and how he had responded to the therapy he'd had.

I knew he had passed. It was obvious. Danny had been calm and he'd reacted well. I say 'well'. He'd talked in an articulate way about himself, where he'd come from and how he'd changed.

They announced it the following week. Everything went rumbling on in the background, and that's why it took so long. He'd be supervised by the local parole board. They had to make it very public that Danny wasn't being let loose, just allowed to run free. He'd be on licence for the rest of his life. He'd have a new identity, documents, everything. His life, which, to be fair, had been predictable and I guess, *safe*, was about to change.

Interesting, the parallel, his life and my own, right now.

Welcome to Six Stories

I'm Scott King.

Over the last four episodes we've returned to 1995 and the terrible event that blighted the small North Yorkshire community of Ussalthwaite.

Here, on this podcast, we look back at horrific crimes like these. There's no ulterior motive, no message being pushed. This time, we're talking about the killing of twelve-year-old Sidney Parsons by two boys of the same age. Sadly, like so many similar cases, there appears to be no clear motive behind the killing. We have no discernible theory yet and it seems that however deep we try to dig, we just find more roots.

I want to say first off that my heart goes out to Terry Atkinson and his loved ones. I want to make clear that he contacted me about appearing on Six Stories, *rather than the other way around, and I sought his permission to publish the interview before the last episode was aired. Should the police want to speak to me about our interview, I'm happy to do so, but I'm not prepared to have my motives questioned by the press. This is all I'd like to say on the matter, other than to wish Terry Atkinson a speedy recovery.*

We're raking up old graves here, but we try to do so with the utmost sensitivity. We want to have a quiet, informed discussion about the case of Sidney Parsons.

Perhaps the most surprising aspect of this case so far has been its other-worldly elements, which haven't really been analysed until now. When discussing the mythology and folklore surrounding the kilns at Ussal Bank and the other esoteric occurrences in the case, it seems I've levered a cork from a long-sealed bottle. It's hard to ignore the feeling of relief that's come from the interviewees who've spoken to me. Maybe that's why those particular people have agreed to speak to me. Maybe the fact that we allow peculiar and other-worldly elements to creep into this podcast meant these people felt they could share things that perhaps may not be accepted elsewhere.

Already in this series, we've had something of a revelation about the details of what happened in September 1995: we now know that it was Sidney, not Robbie or Danny, who attacked Terry Atkinson. But does this change our view about what happened to Sidney Parsons himself. And more importantly does it tell us why he was killed?

The voice you've heard at the start of this episode is a calm one, a reasoned one. After the strange revelations in our previous episodes, I want to ground us in reality. Katie Rosen was a staff member for a time at the Willow Lodge secure unit where Danny Greenwell spent the majority of his sentence after he was convicted of Sidney Parsons' murder.

—It's not jail. It's not the dark, dank cell that people wanted for him at the time. If you believe the tabloids and read the comments sections, the country would have had two twelve-year-olds thrown into a dungeon and left to rot. But I understand that. I understand that anger. I understood it all too well. What I did isn't comparable, of course, but the same ire was shot in my direction.

Katie Rosen made the news herself in 2015. Her story was rather overshadowed by the general election result in May, and Katie's name was not at the forefront of the article either. I let Katie explain to me in her own words what happened.

—Simple really. I was offered silly money – honestly, ridiculous money – for occasional five-minute chats on the phone with a journalist about Danny and the unit. He paid me almost £25,000 and then posted loads of headlines about us allowing Danny to go to the cinema, trips to shopping centres, football matches. 'I'll not name him,' he said. It was a stupid thing to do, of course, because he told me he was going to do just one thing. I honestly thought he was listening, listening properly, taking it in. I thought his piece was going to be measured. I've still got it. I kept it for posterity, for a moment like this.

One day I knew it would come and bite me on the arse. I'd got away with it for all these years.

Maybe what's happening to me now … maybe *that's* my punishment?

The stories that surfaced in the tabloids a year after Robbie Hooper and Danny Greenwell's incarcerations in October 1995 were about the 'luxurious' conditions of the secure units they had been placed in. It had the desired effect.

—The thinking out there at the time was that the sentence for the 'demon boys', or whatever they got called, was 'soft'. Do you remember the *Daily Mail*'s 'Bring Back the Birch!' headline? That appeal to the government to bring back corporal punishment in schools? Horrible, horrible days. The anger out there was just … off the scale.

We'll come to why on earth Katie would speak out again, and especially to me, later; but for now, let's go back to 1995, when Katie was already working at Willow Lodge and Danny Greenwell was placed there.

—I'm usually reluctant to talk much about my old job, and not just because there might be legal implications if I say too much. Working with Danny Greenwell – being seen to offer him support – was a poisoned chalice. To some, it made no sense. They questioned why their taxes were paying my wages, why someone like Danny or Robbie should be rehabilitated. They wanted to see cold, hard punishment instead. But that didn't happen. And it was never intended to – whether you agree with it or not.

—*What's the difference between a secure unit like Willow Lodge and jail? Why weren't those two thrown into a young offenders' institute, like many people would expect?*

—The secure units gave them some hope of being reintroduced into society. They were twelve when they were sentenced. They were children. I make no bones about the fact that it costs a hell of a lot more money to rehabilitate, but by not punishing them, brutalising them, making their lives a succession of constant punishment and horror, surely that's a better investment? It meant they could reflect on what they had done. That's what everyone wanted, wasn't it? Really? For those two to face what they'd done and change? Secure units can offer that where Young Offenders maybe sometimes can't. In Willow Lodge, there were no bars on the windows and austere cells with bunk beds. There wasn't the overcrowding, the relentless monotony of nothing to do. The drugs.

I'll tell you now just what I told that journalist: if they'd have got jail, the pair of them would have come out worse. If they'd made it out at all. I promise you that. Young offenders institutes are child jails – they follow the same kind of structure as adult prison, the same restrictions, and they share the same problems. It's not always the right place for a child.

I'll keep saying it, despite the repercussions. I'll say it because I believe it. If Robbie and Danny's identities are exposed it will undo all the hard work and money that's been spent to rehabilitate them. I don't mind saying that in public. Nothing can scare me. Not now.

—Katie. Why on earth would you talk to me? After everything you've been through? Why on earth would you do it again?

—To be honest with you, jail time doesn't scare me as much as what's going on.

—You're being harassed I take it, now the world is refocussing on this case.

—You could call it that, I suppose.

Katie got in touch with me out of the blue. She's been listening to the series.

In 2015, there was a police investigation into allegations of inappropriate payments to prison staff and public officials. This is where Katie's email and phone transactions were eventually discovered.

Detective Chief Superintendent Benjamin Little said that Katie was 'egocentric and cold-hearted in her attempt to make personal gain from an unspeakable tragedy'.

The journalist in question was not named and was given a suspended sentence, yet Katie was jailed for two years, convicted of conspiracy to commit misconduct in public office. Her crime was making money by selling these stories. Many of you may be questioning Katie's ethics, and even mine for talking to her. Many of you may be flabbergasted that Katie's now speaking to me. But I want to hear her out.

—When the story came out, it was the exact, opposite angle. It was all the details I'd given the journalist, sure, but none of them at the same time. The sentiment was wrong. Completely wrong. It gave the public a certain view of how things were done, the complete opposite of what we were doing in Willow Lodge.

—I remember the anger at the time, the opinion pieces, people on the street being asked their views. It was like the entire country had an opinion on Robbie and Danny.

—I'm sure they did, and I'm not suggesting no one is allowed their opinion. I just wonder if, when that opinion is not informed, when it's reactionary and ignorant, when they're not aware of all the facts – what is the purpose of hearing it?

—It's a good question. But maybe there's something to be said about gauging the feeling among the public, perhaps.

—Maybe. But why? Why do we need to know what the public think? Look at any local newspaper online – scroll down and read the comments sections on any article about, literally anything, and there's always the most vile racism, sexism, misogyny.

—But that only reflects the thoughts of people who have enough time to comment on a local newspaper's online articles, doesn't it?

—Well yes, I suppose, but what concerns me more is that those attitudes are there, they're still there. And they're not going anywhere soon. I honestly thought that taking the money, talking to that journalist about this stuff, explaining exactly why Robbie and Danny were in the units, what was being done about them, would help maybe sway that opinion. Clearly, I was wrong.

I thought I was doing right by me, my own values … but what's happening now … well, maybe I was wrong?

—Katie, what is it that's going on for you right now? If it's not harassment, what's—?

—I can already see the headlines, the accusations against me. I'm seeking attention, making this all about me, trying to make money. I'll say it now. On the record. I want no money. I want no fame. I just want someone to … believe me, I suppose.

That's why I'm going to talk to you. Podcasts are different, they're not spun by journalists with agendas … I mean, I suppose some are, but not all of them. Not yet anyway.

—Six Stories, I assure you, is a place to reflect, to look at various different angles.

Katie worked as part of Danny's mentoring support team, which was separate from offender management. She will not give me specific details about her role, but it was pastoral, helping Danny adjust and become self-supportive after growing up in an institutional environment.

—*Who decided where the two would be sent?*

—Danny and Robbie were assessed by psychiatric professionals before their sentences were passed down, to make absolutely sure that they were going to the correct place, the place that could one day allow the pair to function in society again.

None of this made it into the tabloid press when Katie's words were reported, save for the amount of money it was costing the taxpayer for the rehabilitation of the boys.

—In Willow Lodge, there were intensive interventions – psychiatric and social. The institution is a system that seeks to build people back up. That's what we want, isn't it? We want our criminals, our children who've done bad things, to think about what they've done, to make amends?

—*It's a powerful argument, Katie, and the counter-argument, the one that was reported, was that Sidney Parsons and his family didn't have this luxury; what had happened to them was a life sentence. They're the ones who have to live with the consequences of what happened to Sidney. Why should Robbie and Danny get a second chance? That's what you've got on the other side of this.*

—I understand that view. Unfortunately there's no black-and-white answer; there's no way this can be addressed in general terms. Maybe that's why the 'luxurious holiday camp' angle made it to press back in ninety-six.

Yes, that pain will stay with the Parsons family forever, but that doesn't mean that Robbie and Danny shouldn't be rehabilitated. It's not either or.

A lot of us remember the school photograph of Sidney Parsons that was Sellotaped to the window of a million homes in the UK with the simple black letters above his grinning face saying: WE WANT JUSTICE!

—It's about what we want as an outcome when something terrible like this happens. My personal belief is that punishment doesn't work. You see it all the way from schools to prisons – the same faces, punished again and again for doing the same thing. Does it stop them? The same kids sat in isolation and detention, the same young men sat in cells. Returning to the system over and over again. No. My *informed* opinion is that punishment doesn't work.

How do I know? If it worked, the vast majority of reoffending wouldn't occur. So what do we want? Do we want people who have done bad things to become better people? To come back into society having learned a lesson, to be able to contribute to it? People talk about how much it costs the taxpayer for a place in a secure unit, but they're also paying for the same people to come back through the prison system time and again, committing the same crimes and getting worse. Where's the outrage about that? It doesn't make sense to me. Pay more for a system that works or pay less forever for one that doesn't.

Actually, the Parsons family were very much of the opinion that these two children should be rehabilitated. It's a pity that so many people haven't bothered to listen to them.

—*You're hinting that your own view may have changed.*

—I'm not sure I am. I've seen how both systems work – I'm informed. I'm talking from experience, that's all. Not that many people have that sort of information on which to base their opinions. Maybe it's time that they do.

Scott, I'm not going to sit here and tell you what was right and wrong. I'm going to explain what I saw, and what my opinions are, that's all. I'm not some kind of moral guide. I just want to say that.

I'm not working in public office this time so I wonder if I'll get in trouble again, for talking to you this time? There's many who'll see me as some kind of bleeding-heart and that's fine, I can't change that. There's others who may see me as something else, something completely insane.

—*Why would people see you as insane? I don't quite follow.*

—There were certain things that happened … at the unit. Things that he did. Things we couldn't tell anyone, things we couldn't explain in an adequate way.

—*What things?*

—I know what you're expecting. Shadowy figures; unexplained noises, perhaps? That didn't happen … at least not there, not then. It was other things. Let me … let's go back to then. He's, what, thirteen, maybe just fourteen? He's been in the unit a couple of years. We had someone else there too, we'll call him 'C'. Now C was about Danny's age, he had his own … situation; his own reasons for being there. C's sister, his little sister, she had … It's awful, she had been killed by their father. The circumstances were horrific. In the middle of the night, there's a call to C's room and he's a mess, hysterical, his hands, his fingers are all torn up. It took two grown men to restrain him.

—*What had happened?*

—C had been trying to open his window. There was no way of doing so from the inside though. His hands were torn to shreds, trying to get any sort of leverage.

—*Why? What was going on?*

—He said he could hear her, he said he could hear her singing, from the garden, outside. There was something in his eyes, a … He was convinced, utterly convinced it was true. We had to get medical to sedate him in the end.

Well this went on for another couple of nights, alarm calls at 3am, C's fingers bleeding through his bandages; he was crying, screaming, the boy was in agony. Then one night, I was sitting with him, trying to calm him down, when we heard it.

—*No.*

—He went rigid, every muscle tense and he began to fling himself at the door. This time, it wasn't coming from the garden, it was coming from inside – inside the unit, down the corridor.

—*Singing?*

—'When I needed a neighbour, were you there, were you there?' Do you remember that old hymn? I swear to God that all of us froze when we heard that little voice drifting from somewhere in the corridor.

'And the creed and the colour and the name won't matter … were you there…?'

We were all holding our breath.

'Were you there…?'

It was a little girl's voice. No mistaking it for anything else.

We just waited and when it got to that verse 'I was cold, I was naked, were you there?' C just lost it. He launched himself off the bed and at his door, screaming and crying, and it was like an animal, an animal in agony. Horrendous.

—*What did the staff do?*

—A few were restraining C, while me and a couple of others went off down the corridor to see where on earth it was coming from. This unit was all boys. We eventually stopped outside Danny Greenwell's room, where the singing was coming from.

—What on earth?

—It was … unsettling. We opened the door and there he is, asleep in bed, this sweet sort of smile on his face.

—Had he been doing the singing?

—He denied it. It wasn't coming from anywhere else, but Danny refused to ever admit it.

—Surely there was a lot of this though, a lot of the boys winding each other up?

—Yes. There was. As much as we discouraged it, it happened, there's no denying that. This wasn't the same, this was vindictive.

—How?

—C eventually disclosed in therapy that the hymn had special meaning to him: he used to sing it to his sister when they were little. They sang it when there was chaos all around them at home … to block out the screaming.

—How did Danny know this?

—How indeed. How was it apparently coming from the garden as well? And did Danny know that C's sister died after she was found naked, in freezing bath water in the middle of winter?

—C must have told him, surely?

—Maybe. And if he had – to do that to C, to sing that, in that voice, there was something deeply, deeply troubling about that, something sadistic, something dark. Apparently there were similar stories with the other one, Robbie, at Forton Grange.

Sadly, Katie has no first-hand insight into the care that Robbie received in Forton Grange Secure Unit, but she knows that their approach is similar. No bars, no cells, and the number of inmates is small. Both secure units provide the structure some of the young people who enter their doors have never had.

—He wasn't all roses either. There was a lot of confidential communication about the pair of them, between the units. Of course there was. Forton Grange reported other unpleasant behaviours; explainable but also strange … just like Danny.

—*What sort of things?*

—Honestly, I wasn't privy to much, but I heard things. I heard talk that there'd been an assault, an accident, they said, but … everyone knew who'd done it. There was a boy in there who'd lost the sight in one eye after Robbie Hooper 'cursed' him after some kind of altercation.

—*What do you mean, 'cursed'?*

—I wish I knew. No one saw him do it. They'd been working outside apparently and 'something black' had 'come down from the sky' and plucked out the boy's eye. Four witnesses said they saw the same thing. It could have been nothing, you know how it is. The type of people who come to the units, they're disturbed, troubled. There's some who come and they've never had restrictions and boundaries before. They've never had discipline. It's just not been part of their life. Ever. Some can't read or write, some can't even eat with cutlery; some have never cleaned their teeth before. They're from a different world. Seemingly Robbie and Danny were from another world entirely. We had to get them back.

—*Where did you even start?*

—The system at Willow Lodge was all incentive-based. Good behaviour and self-control were rewarded by 'points' – they got to spend their points on nice things: time on a pool table, television time, games console time, that sort of thing.

All of this, I explained and none of it was listened to. You saw what they wrote about Willow Lodge, that it's just a free-for-all holiday camp?

—*That's what many, many people believe.*

—Yes, they do. But I believe so strongly in what we did there, not just for Danny but for every young offender who needed us. I sold my story because I wanted to show it to the world, I wanted people to know the truth. I'm aware that wasn't the best way to do it. Hindsight's wonderful. That journalist though, he turned it into a sideshow. Everything we did, everything we've done. The paper made us look like these airy-fairy liberal bed-wetters who bestow expensive gifts on the worst offenders and take killers on day trips to Disneyland.

The damage was catastrophic. To us, to the whole system and, more importantly, to the young people we rehabilitate. Whatever your opinions on it, on what we did there, that can't be denied.

—That's not what people want to hear though, is it?

—They want what they deem 'punishment'. Actually it's the deprivation of these children's liberty that is the punishment, according to word of the law, isn't it? These perceived luxuries aren't perks. Rather than punishing bad behaviour, we reward good behaviour. It's a different way of doing it. We give young people order. They know what to expect from the minute they enter to the minute they leave. It's not long before they adapt. For those that have never had structure, it's, nine times out of ten, welcome. It rails against the chaos that they've been through.

That's something that people who want punishment don't get – some of these children have been punished from the moment they were born.

—Katie, you're talking about punishment and from what you've told me before the interview, it seems like you're also being punished.

—Yeah. That's exactly how it feels. I'm not talking about what happened to me back in 2015, it's something else … it's like it's starting again…

—What is?

—I thought I must have left something out, some food that went bad, an apple fell down the back of the cupboard, began to rot. I was actually listening to episode one, your interview with Penny Myers when they started coming.

—Who did?

—Flies. Fruit flies. Horrible things. First it was just one or two, then more. More and more. I cleaned everywhere, hung up fly paper, closed the windows, but they just kept coming. They started in the kitchen, then soon they were waking me up, hovering above my bed in a cloud.

I tried spraying them, hoovered up their nasty little corpses from my bedroom carpet, threw away the sheets. But the next day, they were back. Thousands of them, an infestation. I called someone out, Rentokil. They came and all the flies were already gone. It was like they were never there. I showed the man the inside of my hoover bag, all those little bodies on the fly paper. He nodded and I saw the look in his eyes, he couldn't get away quick enough.

I'm not insane though. They were there. And they came back a few hours after he left.

—*You must have heard about the midges in Ussalthwaite in 1995?*

—It's what prompted me to call you. I just thought, maybe it would help to tell you about what's happening to me? What I heard back then about those two. I just thought it might … help somehow.

Maybe I have lost it.

—*Can you talk to me about Danny? What was he like when he first arrived at Willow Lodge?*

—Might as well be hung for a sheep as a lamb, I suppose. I'll tell you what I can. I'll tell you what needs to be known. In what must seem a totally weird and backward sentiment, I still respect his confidentiality. So I'll just tell you what will matter most.

Lots of the kids we get through the doors are hardened; they come in with an attitude, a swagger, a reputation. Danny Greenwell wasn't like that. He shuffled in. He was scared. Scared of what might happen to him, what the others might think of him. He came to Willow Lodge with a false name, a false charge. It was the only way he could start again. I remember wondering if that would last. It did. My initial impressions of Danny were that he was socially very awkward – he wasn't interested in the other children or the staff. He was a scared little boy who'd done something terrible. He spent a lot of time in his room, he was compliant. He attended education, therapy, the meetings with psychiatrists. I do know that those meetings didn't always go … smoothly.

—*What do you mean?*

—I wasn't privy to what was said in there, but I saw the aftermath. I saw Danny when he came out of those sessions. He was often tearful, pale. Sometimes he'd go back to his room and sleep for hours. But every night after those sessions, he woke up screaming. Every single time. That wasn't uncommon, and it wasn't surprising.

—*What was going on?*

—Maybe he was finally starting to face up to what he'd done?

Documentation from Danny and Robbie's parole hearings show that both boys had, in the opinions of their psychiatrists, taken full responsibility for their actions. I ask Katie if she was aware of any breakthrough moment that Danny did this.

—No. There wasn't a watershed moment, and suddenly he was OK again. All of that was between Danny and his therapists, anyway. I was there to help him day to day, to keep an eye on his progress. What I saw was him changing, little by little, a day at a time. There were ups and downs, of course, but that was to be expected. The nights were often the worst.

—*Night terrors?*

—It's to be expected – someone like Danny working through what he's done. What troubled me weren't the terrors themselves, though, but some of the strange things he used to talk about.

—*I've spoken to someone who worked on Greenwell Farm. The year before Sidney's death, Danny's mother had committed suicide. The barn where she'd done it was locked and chained the whole time.*

—Yes, I heard as much. In fact a lot of work was done about … Danny's mother…

When she mentions Saffron Greenwell, I notice a hesitance in Katie, the first hesitance of its kind in our interview so far. I wait and hope she'll continue, and eventually, she does.

—That was a … strange situation. There was a question around how Danny saw the idea of life and death.

—*How do you mean?*

—From what I heard, Danny seemed to believe, at least for a while, that his mother wasn't dead.

—*Really?*

—He had this skewed sort of version of life and death. He would sometimes refer to her like she was still around, like she was here still, somewhere. He never referred to Saffron in the past tense. I often wonder if maybe that's why he was doing the singing – because he had another belief about death, one that we weren't privy to.

—*Did anyone ever ask him? Did you?*

—Like I say, there was a darkness in Danny, a place he'd retreat to, inside, when he didn't want to talk about something. Maybe that's where she was?

For a time, it was even thought that if he didn't understand what death meant, perhaps he wasn't responsible for his actions. But, like I say, it was talk, and I think there just wasn't enough evidence for this really.

—*Did the question arise about Willow Lodge even being the right place for Danny, should he have perhaps been in a psychiatric unit?*

—Perhaps. The reasons for these sorts of terrible crimes are much deeper than people think. There are no generalities. I've talked to so many psychiatrists, and they all say the same thing. You can blame parents, you can blame upbringing, but there's no one-size-fits-all. I'm not surprised that Danny's home life was disturbed – it's often the case that an event like this stems from a long way back.

All we know about the Greenwells are that they were a farming family, maybe slightly isolated up on the hill looking over the village of Ussalthwaite. After the death of the very much non-traditional figure of Saffron, the farm fell into disrepair, as did Richard Greenwell. The only insight we've had is from Leo in episode two, who was also mostly a stranger. I ask Katie what she and her colleagues at the unit knew about Danny.

—I'm obviously not at liberty to give you a breakdown of everything Danny said. One, because I wasn't privy to all of it; two, because it's his business; and three, most importantly, I don't want there to be some kind of direct connection between his upbringing and what he did. It's not simple cause and effect.

—*Some would say that there's a direct correlation.*

—Yes, and in some cases there is. But like I keep saying, we cannot generalise. A case like this has to be looked at for what it is.

The Greenwells went a long way back – Yorkshire sheep hill farmers. A legacy of stoic, quiet men on his father's side. I think it's fair to say that Danny wasn't encouraged to speak much about his feelings. I don't think things were especially toxic. In court, the psychiatrist talked about Danny's father being 'distant'. That's not to blame the man, that's just to describe the sort of person he was. The mother, from what Danny told me and others about her, was more nurturing. She provided the hugs, the kisses goodbye, the stories at bedtime. The impact her death had on Danny and his father mustn't be underestimated. It seemed, to me anyway, that the roles in that family were so clearly defined, the whole structure collapsed when she died. Danny and his father were never able to talk about it with each other, neither of them had the words. Mr Greenwell processed his grief and his sorrow by turning to his work – the farm, the fields. That was the only way he knew how to cope with it.

—*And Danny?*

—He was almost left to fend for himself. His father wasn't overtly abusive or neglectful, he'd just never learned how to show the degree of compassion required. It hadn't been modelled to him. Danny's father was a man who didn't show his feelings. I often wonder how Danny understood his mother's death. Children can develop strange views. That doesn't absolve them from their crimes, but it goes some way to help us understand it.

—*Did Danny ever talk to you about his mother when she was alive? Perhaps how she was seen in the village? Her suicide?*

—A little. Again, I'm not going to go into detail, but it's interesting how we see our parents, isn't it? His mother was a bit of an outsider in the village. She didn't abide by the norms of the place. Many children find that sort of thing embarrassing. But not Danny. To him, she was his hero.

—*To this day there's a great deal of rumour about Saffron Greenwell's religious practices and beliefs.*

—It's the same tabloid nonsense that has plagued the whole case, isn't it? What do they say about her – she was some kind of sorceress or something? A witch? Whatever it was, the point is, she wasn't accepted in a small, conservative place like Ussalthwaite, and by proxy, neither was Danny.

—*Some might say Robbie too.*

—I wouldn't disagree. Danny was used to being emotional with his mother, so when she was gone, it left an emptiness, a void that he was too young to know how to fill. *And* I think that's where Robbie came in. Maybe Danny saw something in Robbie: the same loss in him, the same emptiness – who can say? I believe the pair of them were kindred spirits in a way. While Robbie came from a much more disrupted background, and Danny came from almost the opposite end, from a place of silence, they both were experiencing grief. Robbie's behaviour was extreme and Danny's wasn't, but it was for the same reason. All behaviour is communication, so we have to look at what both boys were communicating with their behaviour leading up to what they did. I believe that without Robbie, Danny would have defaulted to his normal, quiet self. But together things escalated. It started as pranks, didn't it? Poor behaviour in school. Together, I imagine the pair of them felt powerful, when everywhere else they were powerless, if that makes sense?

Before I can ask more, Katie holds up her hand to stop me.

—I'm really sorry. I'm not going to be able to give you an answer about why those boys killed the other boy, I'm afraid. Of course there isn't a single, clear-cut reason. It's a complex, horrible, sad case that needs to be reflected on in so many ways. I can't sit here with you and say they did it for one reason.

You see, it's like there's two parts of me that have been fighting for so long about this. I want to say they killed that boy because of pent-up fury, a feeling of invisibility, of being shunned. I believe that had built up in both boys, and when they came across Sidney, it was released. That's the logical side of me. Then there's the flies that have infested my home; there's the fact that when we went to Danny Greenwell's room that night with the singing … he was … he was asleep. Or he was faking it, but that just doesn't seem likely.

—*What are you saying?*

—I'm saying that there's so much to this. I just want to come clean, almost; I just want to lay it all out, tell you what I saw. I want to be done with it. I want it gone.

—*Please, you have the floor.*

—There was an incident with another boy before Sidney, wasn't there? It's strange, you know, because Danny adamantly refused to concede this. He said he and Robbie hadn't assaulted that boy. Terry, that was his name, wasn't it?

—*I've actually spoken to Terry Atkinson, and he claims that it wasn't Danny and Robbie. In fact, he says it was Sidney who attacked him.*

—Really? Why? Did he know?

—It's quite a sad story. Sidney believed in something powerful up at those kilns, something magical, it seems. He got angry when his friend told him it was all just made-up.

I explain in more detail what Terry told us in the last episode, about his encounter with the pair at the kilns. Katie nods and is quiet for a time.

—That's really interesting. I wish that Terry had come out earlier to explain it. It sounds like such a small thing, but it really isn't. That kind of information, while it might not have changed their sentence, might very well have changed what kind of treatment they got from us. It sheds a different light on the escalation everyone talked about around their crimes.

But there's something else too.

There was something about that place that Danny and Robbie believed in.

—What do you think about that, considering what you've just told me, about there being another side to all this?

—I don't know. I can't say. All my career, I've been logical, pragmatic about what I do and this … I just don't know what to think. I've never been up to that village, I don't know what to believe about it. All I can say is what's happened to me. And I'm not delusional, I'm not on drugs. I'm not lying either.

—Going back to Danny, do you think there was a moment when you saw him change? When he was finally able to let go of what happened?

—There was an incident … I think it's pertinent right now to explain it.

—Please, feel free. As much or as little as you feel is right.

—It was during what we call 'mobility'. This is where people are going to get angry I'm afraid. Mobility is when the children spend time outside of the unit. Supervised, I may add, every single time. This was another aspect of life at Willow Lodge that I tried to explain to the journalist.

—Was it true?

—Yes, of course it was. But it was represented as us giving him some kind of treat. Look, if we're going to let these children reintegrate into society, they have to be ready to come out. Again, it's not like one day, Danny's suddenly let out on a jolly. These trips are built up for years, starting very small – and they're earned. They have to be able to cope outside or else they'll be back inside. All the work we've done would be useless otherwise.

Now, this event – I wasn't going to mention it, but I think it might be important.

Katie was asked to supervise Danny on a walk in the countryside. By this time, Danny was seventeen years old, and the walk was of his choosing – an end-of-term reward for 'exceptional progress' in both his education and his therapy. It was close to Danny's birthday, when he would become eighteen and be eligible for consideration for parole.

—I was chuffed when he chose me to go with him. It wasn't just me – we were driven there in the van, and there were two officers at a subtle distance. I'll not say where we went, but it wasn't Ussalthwaite, nowhere near. It was a similar environment, though. That's what he wanted – somewhere wild, he said, somewhere where there's no people. I … I don't think that was his motivation though, the lack of people. It was something more, something about the place itself.

—*Was it similar to where he'd grown up? The same sort of moorland?*

—Yes, I suppose it was. He was a lad of few words, was Danny, and fewer as he grew older. You could tell there was a lot going on behind his eyes, but he wore a stoic mask. I wondered if he just wanted to feel the wind in his hair again, face out against the sea of purple and green, you know? The heather and the wild grasses. I wondered what it brought back for him.

—*Did he talk about it?*

—He talked about his mother, how she used to take him out on long walks to 'powerful places' – those were his words. Stone circles, forests. He did talk about magic then. Like I said before, he often talked about his mother not really being dead. She was still here, that's what he used to say. She always had been, he said.

—*Really?*

—In so many words. At one point in our walk, Danny just stopped. He was quiet, and I asked him what he could hear. It's rare that there was ever silence at Willow Lodge, to be fair, even at night. Out there on that hill, we felt it though. It was heavy. Danny said he could hear the wind, he could hear the swish of the grass and the faint trickle of a stream somewhere far away. We stood and we listened. He closed his eyes and his lips were moving.

I think he was saying goodbye. I choked up, I have to say. Sometimes, in moments like these, you do. You can't help feeling things. I know that saying that, I'm going to get even worse death threats, rape threats, all sorts. For showing compassion to a lost boy, *I'm* a monster.

—Do you think that maybe this walk was Danny's way of finally saying goodbye to who he used to be as well?

—We walked a little further, and then we reached an old ironworks, I think it must have been – a half-collapsed stone structure, looking like it was left from the industrial era. A pump station. There was half a chimney covered in weeds, the rest of it sunk into the earth. I remember Danny stopped to stare at that for a very long time. He seemed to be in a dream. It was peaceful, stood there like that. After a little while, I took his sleeve, whispered that it was time to go, and he points into that ruin and says, 'Look.'

—What was it?

—I didn't see it really – just a blur, a shadow. Some animal, I imagine, a rabbit or a fox perhaps? I asked Danny what it was, and he just smiled. I don't think he even said anything, and that was OK. It was for him – whatever he saw was his, and I understood that. Everything at Willow Lodge; everything he owned, from the posters on his walls, to the inside of his head, were poked, prodded and analysed by us. That wasn't. Whatever black blur it was he saw vanishing into that old pump station, that was his to keep.

Maybe that was him able to let go, to say goodbye to the past, to whatever it was from there, in Ussalthwaite, that still clung to him?

Maybe that was the magic? Whatever it was, it stoked a little bit of regression.

—What do you mean, regression?

—After that walk, Danny went backward a bit; the night terrors returned, the bed wetting, that sort of thing. Danny Greenwell was a very frightened little boy for a lot of his life, and that seemed to be his default. I know, it's hard to see him like that. But that's what we saw at Willow Lodge when he first came – and then again after that walk. A frightened little boy. Maybe it was then that he finally was able to close that chapter of his life?

I explain to Katie about the shadow that Terry Atkinson saw in the bushes when Sidney assaulted him, the 'figure' that walked alongside Saffron Greenwell down from Ussal Top at Beltane, the 'blurry, black shadow' that was seen accompanying Sidney Parsons on his way up to the kilns the day he was killed. The figures in the farmhouse seen by Leo and the other farm workers.

Now this.

—After I'd decided to get in touch with you, the flies just left. I thought that it was coincidence, whatever; it was over. But no. I was walking home last night. I'd got off the bus at the end of my street and it was dark. I was walking and as I got closer to home, I could see them again.

—*Who?*

—The flies. It had to be them, this pulsing, black swarm, outside my front door. I could hear it, this faint buzzing as I got closer. And they sort of … condensed, became a shadow, a black figure, a woman. I just stood there, I couldn't feel my fingers or toes, I thought I was going to pass out. There was a shadow just standing outside my door, as if it was waiting for me.

It pointed. Jesus Christ, it pointed a finger at me before bursting into a cloud of flies again, that just … disappeared. I wondered if I was losing my mind. I was seeing things, right? I was so scared to go inside, but I did, and the house was quiet, dark. I could *feel* that they were gone. I messaged you that night, that very night, to tell you who I was, to tell you I'd do this interview, that I'd tell it all. I just prayed that whatever it was would then leave me in peace. I'm saying all this because it reminded me of that shadow, up on that moor. It reminded me of Danny Greenwell saying goodbye. I just wondered if … I guess that might work for me too. Maybe I can say goodbye too.

—*Say goodbye to what though?*

—To all of this.

—Katie, do you believe that there is something else going on here? Something we simply cannot explain?

—I don't know what you want me to say. These are all spurious, eye-witness accounts. Including mine. And of what? A curse? A haunting?

—I have no idea.

—Could it be, perhaps, that it's easier to find simple solutions to complex issues? The 'supernatural' history of the kilns at Ussalthwaite is just that. A witch from the 1600s? Demon possession in the 1970s, and again in 1995? I wish that was the answer. I wish that was the explanation.

We want rhyme and reason, we want cause and effect, we want to be able to have strong opinions about simple things. But none of this is simple. On the surface, Danny and Robbie were products of their environments. Both were outcasts, both of them didn't belong. I think that both of them felt that way for a very long time. And when young children only feel negative emotions, it doesn't take them long to numb themselves, to learn that feeling nothing at all is preferable. I wonder if that came into it; numbness blunted their consciences in some way? Or did something else do that for them?

—There are people who would say one or both boys are psychopaths. Will always be like that, are incurable.

—Well, in one sense they're right. Being a psychopath is certainly an incurable personality disorder. All personality disorders are incurable. Manageable, yes. But I hate a term like that being bandied around, you know, as if it somehow makes someone … I don't know, edgier. You can't diagnose someone as a psychopath unless you're qualified, and children certainly cannot be clinically diagnosed as psychopaths. Similar symptoms in children are known as 'conduct disorder'. The human brain isn't fully formed until the early twenties, so early intervention on children like Danny and Robbie can be effective. It makes me sad when people use these terms, especially for children.

—I read a comment under an article about the release of Robbie and Danny, and it stuck with me: 'You can't fix evil.' I wonder what you'd think about that.

—Evil. These biblical terms are thrown around almost as much as these pseudo diagnoses. 'The demonic duo' they were known as in the press, weren't they? Comments like that, about children being 'evil' – what exactly does it do? What does it solve? Who does it protect? No, you can't fix 'evil' but who are these people to level such a hollow accusation against two children? Yes, Robbie and Danny did a terrible thing and they should be punished for it. They *were* punished for it, and they've been able to build their lives back again and face what they did. As far as we're aware, neither of them have offended since, right?

—And you're left with what's going on with you, twenty-six years later.

—Honestly, it feels like something needs to be done to deliver us, to deliver all of us from whatever's there, at those kilns, in those boys. Because it's not going away, is it? Just recently we've one suicide and one attempt there. This hasn't gone away.

—What do you think can be done to stop it?

—I wonder if maybe we need Robbie and Danny to help us here. As much as I believe in their reform, in their rehabilitation; what's happening there, what's happening to me – maybe we need them for that?

Nothing has been heard about either Robbie or Danny since their release. From the slivers of insight that have trickled out from the press, both are living independently, both have steady jobs, apparently, and are going about their lives quietly. I want to talk to Katie about the implications of what would happen if either Danny or Robbie's real names – even their pictures and homes – were revealed in the press.

—Look, it costs around £200,000 a year to keep one child in a secure unit rather than prison. The reoffending rates are low from this kind of intervention, especially when it's done early.

If one or both of those two get identified, it'll be a disaster. It'll be everything we've done, everything *they've* done and achieved, in tatters. More importantly, at least to some, it'll be all that tax money down the drain.

—Vigilante justice is a real threat, right?

—Of course. That will be the biggest risk to them – mob justice. And I don't doubt that, with the internet the way it is, social media and everything, that mob justice will be dealt swiftly and irrevocably.

—There are people out there, a great deal of them, who believe that it's what those two deserve.

—My personal opinion was that those two passed the tests set by the parole boards – they were both questioned extensively. They were grilled, they were asked about their rehabilitation and their remorse. Psychiatrists and other professionals' reports were considered. These two weren't just kicked out onto the streets as soon as they were eighteen. They'll both be in their late thirties by now; they'll both have lives, relationships, friendships.

—But if, as you say, we need them again to stop whatever's happening in Ussalthwaite, wouldn't we destroy all of that?

—Yes, but what if destroying all of that would make it stop – would break the cycle?

—Why are you so sure that there's something to do with Robbie and Danny that would stop all of this?

—I'm not sure, but for the last twenty years, this has haunted me. Figuratively and … well, literally.

—What do you mean?

—The night I got home and saw the cloud of flies, I found something, something I thought I'd got rid of, something I thought I'd never see again.

After I got inside the door, turned the lights on, that image of that figure, stood outside my front door still inside my head, I found something lying on my living-room table. Like it had been *placed* there for me to find.

—What was it?

—A small, black stone. It creeped me out at the time, and I remember having this feeling, like I wanted to get rid of it. I didn't want it in the house. I picked it up and it felt oddly heavy, like it was made of some kind of dense substance. I don't know. I remember putting it in the dustbin outside. It was cold, frost starting to coat everything, and the dustbin lid make a creaking, cracking sound when I opened it. I remember the fusty, rot smell of the bin bags in there. I remember the rattle and clunk that stone made. I remember my hands shaking while I boiled the kettle after.

Then I remember the following morning. There it was again. The same stone. This time on my bedside table. As if it had been placed there. As if something was telling me it wasn't that easy. Then I heard your podcast and I had to get in touch.

I want to draw us back briefly to episode three and our chat with Will. He had a similar experience with a stone in the Hartleys' house:

'It looked wrong somehow, like it shouldn't be there. I walked over and took a closer look; Ken was behind me and I could almost feel that nervous energy of his, humming and crackling. I looked down at that stone – the size of a tiny fist; it would fit in your palm – and, I don't know, something inside me, some instinct told me not to touch it.'

Then we had Terry Atkinson telling us about a similar stone that Sidney had received as a 'charm' from the kilns.

'He said it was his "demon stone". I know how that sounds now, after everything, but at the time, I just thought it was part of the drama, you know, part of the game. He said he didn't want to show his mum and dad, and I wasn't to tell them because it had "powers".'

This surely cannot be the same stone.

—Maybe it's some kind of metaphysical metaphor? What I do know is that staff found both boys at both units in possession of stones with no explanation of how they had got hold of them. What can I say? How can I explain it? I have no idea. What I do know was that after that day I took Danny to that moor, after we saw that shadow, after he said goodbye, we never found a stone in his possession again.

But now it's with me. Every day I find it; every day it's there, and every day things about this case are getting worse. People are dying.

How can I explain it? I know how I sound. I know that any legitimate arguments I have about rehabilitation are negated by these … these strange things that I'm claiming have happened to me … *are* happening to me.

I need one of them or both of them to help me. I need to know what to do – how to stop this.

—*You need Robbie or Danny to help?*

—I don't know what else to do. I know how this sounds, I know what people are going to think of me. I need this over with, we all do. Stones or no stones. Whatever is happening in Ussalthwaite, it needs to be closed. It needs to stop. For good. Maybe those two, or one of them, coming out of the shadows will enable that?

It's a theory that has made me question everything I've heard yet. I'm shocked at Katie's stance, after everything she's told me she stands for, everything she's worked for her entire career. I wonder how strong her conviction is about what she believes is happening to her.

Was a myth woven over Ussalthwaite a long time ago? Is there a witch, a demon or some kind of magical power in those kilns. Are the accounts of Awd Ma Spindle, Julia Hill, Sidney Parsons and the recent suicide all evidence that something, whatever it is, is present there? Or are Katie's experiences the delusions of someone who has lost their grip on reality?

The phrase 'you can't fix evil' is often used when discussing Danny and Robbie.

Where does evil truly come into this case and how much does it encompass?

What we know is that Danny and Robbie have faced the questions of the parole board and have, as far as we know, successfully reintegrated themselves into society. But they leave a great deal of questions in their wake – questions that through the last five episodes of this podcast we have not been able to answer.

Katie herself has explained the damage it would do if one or both of the men's identities is revealed, but at the same time she wishes this could happen, to perhaps break a cycle, to stop whatever is going on in Ussalthwaite.

It seems that Katie wants to try and fix evil.

Next episode, we're going to have to ask some difficult questions and we need to expect difficult answers. We need to pull apart the last threads of this story. Perhaps we won't find an answer, but maybe we'll find some kind of resolution instead.

I've been Scott King

This has been our fifth.
Until next time.

Dear Mum,

You're still angry with us, aren't you? I can tell because everything is going wrong. We're getting the blame whenever anything bad happens. Everyone says we've been hanging ropes on people's houses, but it wasn't us, Mum. I promise you. We try and hide, Mum. We spend all our time at the old barn because people keep coming and looking for us at the kilns, and I don't want anyone to find the special place.

Dad says I'm not allowed to go up there anymore, but he doesn't care. Not really. He never comes into school when they ask him for a meeting. He says he's busy, there's too much to do with the sheep.

Then Sidney Parsons told everyone at school that we were witches and casting spells up there, and it's worse than ever for us in the village.

We went back there the next day, me and Robbie, when everyone had gone in for their tea. We went to the special place. Robbie was desperate, Mum. He was desperate to speak to his mum, and this time no one else was there to ruin it. They were all too scared.

I showed him how to climb in through the gap in the rock. Just like you used to do with me. I showed him how to lie there, on the special rock, the one we used to lie down on when I was little. I showed him how you have to hold up the book and start reading it to yourself, then sort of half close your eyes and just listen.

I could tell it wasn't going to work, Mum. I don't know why. I just could tell. You said that when you were gone, I would hear you in the wind, I would hear you in the songs of the birds and the rush of the river. But when we were there, there was no birds, no wind, just this nasty silence. and neither of us wanted to close our eyes cos it felt like there was someone there.

I've been trying to hear you, Mum, at night when it's quiet. I've been to the bridge to listen to the river and out into the hills to hear the birds, and I can't hear you. I just hear the river or the stupid birds squawking. Sometimes Robbie comes with me too, and I tell him what you said – that if he listens, he might hear his mum too. Maybe it's her turn?

That's why I thought it might finally work when he lay down on our rock in the special place, instead of me. He held up his book and closed his eyes, and I begged for something to happen. When we heard a noise, we both jumped, because the others know about the kilns but not the special place, and we nearly screamed out loud when there was a noise like something scraping on the rocks.

But it was Jip. She'd followed us, and she's never done that before. That's when we thought it must be a sign, because Robbie's mum loved dogs. Robbie lay down and held up his Just William, but instead of the usual feeling, I got a bad feeling, like the other day when you threw the stones at us. I didn't want to say anything, Mum, because Robbie really thought he would hear his mum.

But then Robbie started saying it wasn't working, and I could see he was getting angry and embarrassed, his face went all red like when people shout 'Hey you guys!' at him at school, and I was scared because I thought he was going to get up and thump me. Like I'd been playing a trick on him all along.

When he got up, something moved behind him, a shadow, like someone was at the back of the kilns and had found us. And that's when Jip started growling, you know like she does when there was a rat in the barn – dead low like a motor. Robbie stood up and started asking if I was 'fucking him about'. I wasn't, but I couldn't speak, and then Jip went for him. It was awful, Mum. I shouted at her, and she wouldn't stop, she pushed him over and tried to bite him, and the only thing I could do to stop her, Mum, was to pick up a stone and…

I can't write it, Mum. I can't write what we did, but we didn't mean to, Mum. I don't know why she went crazy like that, but if we hadn't stopped her, then she would have hurt Robbie, and he might have gone away and I would have been on my own again.

We couldn't leave her there, not in the special place. It was Robbie's idea to carry her all the way to the farm and lie her in the barn like that, open her up a bit to make it look as if a fox had got her. We only put her in that barn because Dad never goes in there, and he wouldn't see what we'd done, and the rats and things might have eaten her before he saw. We laid her on the floor, and I kept my eyes closed the whole time because I could feel something was in there, watching us. It felt like it had come with us from the special place. Was it you, Mum? Were you angry and looking down at us? I don't mind if you were.

It wasn't us, Mum, who put the rope round her like that. I swear down on my heart that it wasn't.

Then we got the blame for something happening to Terry Atkinson at Barrett's Pond, and that wasn't even us, Mum. It wasn't, but everyone thinks it was.

Robbie says there's something bad at the special place. He says it's not special at all. He says it's cursed and we shouldn't go there anymore. He said that whatever's there, it got into Jip, and that's what made her go angry and vicious like that. Robbie says that there's a bad thing at the kilns and it's pretending to be you, Mum.

I just need you to show him he's wrong, that you were angry for a bit and now you're not.

Please can you show Robbie that it's a powerful place, a magic place, and you're still there, Mum, that you're still with me?

Please?

I miss you, Mum. I miss your smell and the way you did the voices for Ginger and Violet Elizabeth Bott in Just William.

I promise that we'll do something good. Me and Robbie, we'll do something good to get rid of the bad things at the kilns, and show you that we're good and everything can go back to the way it was before.

I miss you, Mum.

Xxxx

DISPATCH*Online*

Home • News • Sport • TV & Showbiz • Money • Property

Disgraced Gold Digger 'Haunted' by Ussalthwaite 'Curse'

Parsons Killer's care staff also claims to be 'sympathetic' to child murderers in new podcast grasp for fame.

Are there no depths to which Katie Rosen won't delve? Has she made herself look like more of a psycho than Robbie Hooper or Danny Greenwell with her ridiculous claims?

Yes, you're reading right, fame-hungry ex-secure home staff member Katie Rosen is back. Despite destroying her credibility and reputation in one fell swoop when she sold illicit stories of the luxurious conditions that the Parsons killers were being kept in after their conviction in 1996, Katie Rosen (50) has now not only showcased a worrying agenda when it comes to punishing child murderers, she may have lost it completely and now wants the killers named to lift a 'curse'.

The latest episode of Scott King's true-crime podcast, *Six Stories*, which has already caused ire among friends of the Parsons family and the residents of Ussalthwaite in North Yorkshire by investigating the Sidney Parsons case on its twenty-sixth anniversary, gave an exclusive platform to Rosen's newly warped view on punishment and the monstrous murder of Sidney Parsons by twelve-year-olds Robbie Hooper and Danny Greenwell.

Rosen repeatedly claimed that punishment for murdering a child doesn't work or is futile, showcasing instead a therapeutic and holistic approach that costs the taxpayer significantly more money and basically advocates that killers such as Danny Greenwell and Robbie Hooper should have plenty of treats and positive experiences while incarcerated, as this might somehow make them reflect on their crimes.

She went on to say that, despite this, one or both should be named in order to deliver her from some kind of 'curse' that has involved an infestation of flies and appearances of 'black stones' in her house.

After the suicide of a still un-named man at the kilns of Ussal Bank, where Sidney Parsons was brutally slain in 1995, and the recent suicide attempt by former Parsons friend, Terry Atkinson, the *Six Stories* podcast has claimed another victim.

Rosen, has previously spoke out in condemnation of the pair and exposed their luxurious living conditions, and now, in what must only be a desperate bid for money, has U-turned completely, suggesting that child killers should be allowed days out for good behaviour alongside daily therapy sessions.

Rosen has also plummeted to new depths as ludicrous horror-film clichés spilled from what is clearly a damaged mind. Maybe, for someone like Rosen, who has spent her life mollycoddling murderers and taking young offenders out on jollies, her conscience might just be getting to her?

> ***Dispatch Says*** *– it's a worry when staff who we trust to keep vile killers like Greenwell and Hooper locked away seem to favour the criminal rather than justice for the victim! Dispatch wonders what sort of checks are undertaken these days to prevent someone as clearly deluded as Rosen from looking after some of the worst young offenders in our society.*

Danny Greenwell and Robbie Hooper were both twelve years old when they savagely killed vulnerable youngster Sidney Parsons in a horrific act of uncontained wickedness. Both boys had been responsible for a spate of mindless violence and vandalism across the village in the weeks before the murder, including driving a teacher and his pregnant partner screaming from their home in a vicious campaign of harassment.

It appears that Scott King's podcast is no longer happy with simply recording events, and the series is having real-life consequences – driving Terry Atkinson, Sidney Parsons' former best friend to attempt suicide. Atkinson is said to be recovering well in hospital.

Now, in the podcast's latest episode, King is colluding with convicted criminal Katie Rosen, begging the question of whether this kind of amateur sleuthing is doing more harm than good. Perhaps leave it to the professionals, eh?

Scott King has been approached for comment.

To: scott@sixstories.com
From: <sixstories website contact form>
Name: [unknown]
Subject: Where next?

Please stop. Please don't do what everyone says you're going to do and reveal the name or the location. That's what this series has been building to, isn't it?

You don't know what's going to happen to you, do you? If you do that?

There's already been one death on your hands. Do you really want another one on your conscience?

For the sake of everyone, please stop this now.

Before it's too late.

Episode 6: Ripples

—I saw it on Facebook. Our Cal says Facebook's just for old people. I was glad cos I didn't see it nowhere else. It's not like Cal watches the local news.

It was just a short article what said emergency services had been called to a report of a car on fire, up out in one of the fields. Well, round here it's miles from anywhere so by the time they got there and put it out, the body they found was almost completely gone, I reckon. There was a sort-of half-hearted appeal cos no one knew who it was or how it started. The car had been nicked. That's what people round here seemed more bothered about. I recognised it cos that's where I used to take the dog for a walk.

One of the comments was 'serves 'em right for nicking'.

Wow, I thought. Amazing what some people will say, isn't it?

A few others were saying they seen the fire, but I thought it was bollocks cos who's driving round right out there at three in the morning to see something like that?

I didn't tell him, our Cal, I never said nothing about it. I wondered if he even knew.

Five minutes later, on Facebook, they're all harping on about some story about a bloke who reckons he don't have to comply with the Road Traffic Act cos of 'the Magna Carta' or something. Turns out he was some lad we all went to school with got caught driving after being banned and having no insurance and I swear, there was more comments about him than the one what died in the car fire.

People are weird, aren't they?

Welcome to Six Stories.

I'm Scott King

Here we are, at our final episode. I'm fully aware that there's no way that this can be the final say on the case of Sidney Parsons and the 'demonic duo' – there's no way we can find an answer, an adequate conclusion, a reason, in a case like this. Child-on-child murder is held in such abhorrence by our society, is so taboo, that when it occurs, it makes us question everything. And now we also have the suicide of the mystery person up on Ussal Bank, the attempted suicide of Terry Atkinson and the revelations about not only the boys, but perhaps something deeper, something darker, from Katie Rosen.

At the heart of this case is a seemingly motiveless killing of a child.

When these crimes are committed, whether it's a child killed in a cosy, middle-class village in rural Yorkshire, or stabbed in an inner city area over a drug deal or a postcode, we leap onto our moral high horses and soapboxes, and throw out our questions about what or who is to blame. There's been plenty of culprits: video games, music, the devil – the list goes on, and will go on as long as young people commit crime.

It seems that none of these questions about blame are reflected back at ourselves. Even in medieval times, children who killed were simply deemed 'possessed' by devils or 'spellbound' by witches and sorcerers. Today's blame culture seems not much of a leap from that. The witches of old have become the music and social media of today. I wonder when we'll look at ourselves and wonder what sort of society we've created, what sort of environment has bred these killers. Where has the rage, the inequality, the inadequacy come from?

What do we expect when we actively vote in political parties who cut children's services, libraries and schools, force our NHS workers into using food banks, to whom the most vulnerable in society are regarded as workshy and disposable?

What we've learned from looking at the case of Sidney Parsons is that there's no single reason why a child kills. I certainly don't have the answer. What I do think is that, as a society, we should do better. A little bit more compassion, a little more empathy, a little less selfishness. It's not a lot to ask really. I'm not saying that's the answer, but from what I've learned on this journey, it can't be far from a solution. Or at least the beginnings of one. As many of you know, my own background was far from stable, my childhood contained a great deal of fear, but it also contained love and compassion, things that were given to me young enough, I believe, to counteract the darkness.

Because really, that's what we're doing, isn't it? Pushing back against a bitter, black tide that is forever trying to encroach on us.

I want to say these things now before I introduce my final guest of the series. My reasons for this will become clear.

You see, I've always wanted simply to be a vessel for other voices. My own character should have never come forth on this show. I feel like it's almost laughable now – the amount of times I've said this, the amount of times I've been pulled in to our stories.

However, there's something I must share, this time. Perhaps I'm taking the plunge. All will become clear after our final interview.

I'm aware of the weight of this case and it's with respect and care that I've been moving through it. We've heard from five people so far, five very different views on what happened that September afternoon in 1995.

I want to stop now and let this, our final episode, play out. The voice you heard at the start of the episode is that of thirty-six-year-old Kelly Valentine. She's been in touch with me since I began this series.

—Yeah, maybe some of the things I said, to you, those messages, I said in anger. I'm not proud. But I don't take none of that anger back, OK? I meant what I said. Maybe I could have said it better or whatever, but I meant it. You should have stayed away from this one. You really should.

The fury in Kelly is palpable. When we meet, we walk together around the streets of her home town – a small place I shall not disclose. I have to add that all the names I'll be using in this episode, including Kelly's, are pseudonyms.

It is a cold and frosty day, the tendrils of autumn starting to curl around our fingers and the tips of our noses, the chill of summer's quiet death in the air. We walk Kelly's dog – a gigantic beast. We'll call him Fred. We come to a large duck pond and perambulate around its edge. To anyone watching us, in our scarves and hats, we could be a couple, just taking our dog for a walk in the fresh air.

—We're a small place here. Don't really like outsiders. We're not racists, far from it. It's just this is a place that's kept its proper, traditional British values, OK? It's small, and everyone knows each other, and that's the way we like it. That doesn't make us backward, it doesn't make me ignorant.

—I don't think anything of you. All I have is the messages you've sent. You're angry. That's all I know.

—Yeah, and it's not just me. Anyone would be angry, in my position. You're not a mum, you don't understand. You'd never understand what it's like. Every step. Every single step of my Callum's growing up has been saying goodbye. I've still got his baby bath toys in the garage. His duck, his shark, all manky and faded and soft where he used to chew on them. He'll never play with those toys again, do you understand? I'll never get the old measuring jug from the cupboard and pour water over his head. He'll never make a beard out of bubbles. Every year that passes, every year he grows up, it's saying goodbye to something.

But it never leaves you – that fear of what might happen when you're not there with him. When he walks off by himself. Into the world. Don't get me wrong, that's what he's got to do. He's got to become independent. He's not a boy anymore, far from it. I know it. But it's hard sometimes, OK? Especially with what he's been through and what people think of him.

So when your podcast started, and it was all that gossip from that old woman, all about how them two boys was evil and that, that's what got my back up. Do you understand? Do you get it?

—I'd like to think so, yes.

Kelly has been messaging me since this series began. Now don't get me wrong, I get a lot of messages, positive and negative, about the show, but Kelly's were different. How? They actually began by railing against me for covering the case in the first place, and accusing me of adding fuel to the fire that began in the tabloid press from the moment the sentences were passed down to the two boys. I ask Kelly what prompted this.

—Subconscious or something? I dunno. I thought what you was doing was sick, to be honest. Not like my Callum says 'sick', like it's a good thing. Sick as in you're sick in the head. Why would you cover this? Why would you want to talk about that poor little boy being killed? You knew what was going to happen once you started.

—Can we start at the start?

—OK, let's go back to the start. Where though? Where do you want to begin? When I first messaged you?

—Can we go back before then, can you tell me when you first met who you call 'Jenks'?

Kelly takes a deep breath. We've planned a route out of town and up to a dual carriageway where there's a generic coffee outlet. Kelly says that if she's seen with me in the shop in town, there'll be questions. We begin moving away from the duck pond and up onto a country track that leads past tall fields of rape – a thousand green fingers, dancing in the air.

—It's for the cows, all that. Mad, isn't it? Fields of the stuff only to be fed to the animals. Anyway. I met 'Jenks' up near here, I'll show you exactly.

We continue up the path, the ground crunching beneath our boots. There's a slight incline, and a row of trees approaches. Kelly lets Fred off the leash, and he stands for a second and regards me, head on one side. Kelly's already said Fred will 'fuck me up' if I try anything funny and I'm not sure if she was joking. I certainly wouldn't come out very well if Fred decided he didn't approve. After a moment, apparently satisfied, Fred bounds up the path.

—In here. In the woods. It's not a woods really. It's a nature reserve – a load of trees and a stinky old pond what will be all frozen, probably, thank God. Bloody dog goes in there and stinks the house out. It's good for chucking a stick about, plenty of room and places for them to sniff about. You can't get no phone signal or nothing like that, so it's a little bit of peace as well up here. People leave their dogs doings in the little bags though, don't they? Hung on the branches of the trees like little presents. It's disgusting. I've been lobbying the council for a public litter bin, but do they listen? Do they heck.

—*This little bit of woodland was where you met Jenks?*

—Yeah. First time we met, it was a couple of years back. I was walking my dog, and he was walking his. You don't seem like a dog person to me, you're more of a cat bloke. Anyway. So our dogs stop and have a stiff of each other's bumholes. I get a look at him. Kind of scruffy, big, shaggy beard and hair, streaked with grey. Salt and pepper.

This sounds like a normal interaction – two strangers passing good mornings, rolling their eyes at their dogs.

—Thing was, right, I'd never seen him before round here, and, like I say, everyone knows everyone, so I got a right to ask a couple of questions. I wasn't rude or nothing, I just said, hello, mate, not seen you round here before, that sort of thing. I'm not worried, you've seen the size of … Fred, we're calling him, right?

—*Right.*

—Now, looking back, I want to say this bloke gives me the shivers or whatever, but he doesn't. No geese walking on my grave or nothing like that. I thought at first he looked like a bit of a scruff, but it was the beard. He was clean, well kept. Just a bloke. In fact he's so normal I'm a little bit disappointed. He's tallish, wearing a fleece and a bobble hat. Scarf up round him like you've got there. Nothing to him really. Wouldn't have even looked at him if I passed him on the street.

—*You got talking?*

—I wasn't being nosey. Well, I was, but it's time of day, isn't it? Says he's from up north, moved down here for work. Living up in one of them newbuilds. Oh right, I says. I'm not going to give him the Spanish inquisition treatment, and off I go, on my way. Honestly, forgot him the moment I got home.

Not long after this, Kelly began to see the man around town. She recognised him, not by his face but from his dog, who Jenks took everywhere.

—I seen it tied up outside the butcher's, and I knew I recognised it from somewhere. Fred goes over and starts smelling its bum again, and I'm trying to drag him away, when out he comes. Pound of sausages and a great big marrowbone in his bag. I says to him, I says, that bone's bigger than your dinner, and we have a laugh, and off we go again.

These chance encounters were infrequent. Kelly had no idea of the man's name or where he worked. She figured it was either some kind of call centre, of which there are a few on the industrial estates scattered outside of town, or else in one of the factories.

—It's where everyone who lives here goes to work if they've messed up in school. Half the boys I went to school with are in one of those places – and still living here, marrying the girls they was shagging in school. More kids on the way. That's why I says to my Callum, I says, you can do better than this place. If you do well in school, then you can go anywhere you want. If you don't, you'll be stuck here. Like me. Does he listen? I might as well talk to the wall. He says there's no hope for him.

Anyway, I ask a few of the other mums about this new guy, and a few have seen him about. And we don't say much more than that. We're not all nosey little Englanders. After a few weeks, this bloke and his dog becomes part of the scenery.

Weeks turned to months and every so often, Kelly meets the man in the woods. Jenks. Their dog walking schedules appear to have synchronised.

—Now, hang about, cos it wasn't nothing dodgy going on. I didn't fancy him, no way. He wasn't much to look at, and he didn't speak much. We just passed the time of day, that's all. Well, as much as we could; it was like getting blood out of a stone with that one. As you probably know by now, I never shut up, and I couldn't be doing with the silent type. But all I can get from him is that he's called Jenks and he lives on his own up on the estate. Just moved in. Works away. Week on, week off. Oil rigs or something. To be honest, I probably talked his ear off, and he couldn't wait to get away.

—*What did you talk about? Do you remember?*

—Oh nothing much really. I wasn't working at the time, and Callum, well, he was having some issues with school. I was looking round for work, trying to make ends meet, that sort of thing. Things weren't great, let's just say.

Callum, Kelly's son, was approaching fourteen years old and was having significant problems at school, specifically with his attendance and his behaviour.

—I've done my best with him, but I'm a single mum, OK? It's hard. Cal's dad left when he was just a kid; no rhyme or reason to it either. One day he's here, one day he's not. Men, *some* men, will do that to you. Bastards. But our Cal's never had a father figure in his life. I can't be both, much as I try, and what with work and the fact that everyone round here's someone's auntie or uncle or bloody cousin, the pickings are thin. I'm better off on my own. Anyways, that doesn't matter, does it?

Callum was careering off the rails, and by the middle of year nine, he had begun skipping school regularly, and many of his teachers were concerned about his grades.

—He's never liked it. Never. Not since he was a little boy. School just wasn't for him. All those rules and being told to stand up and sit down, and everything. I tell you, the amount of times I've had to go up there for a bloody meeting. I remember being sat there with that Mr Wallace, the attendance officer, and that head teacher who looked down her nose at me like I was the scum of the bloody earth. I felt like I was getting told off too. I said, what can I do? I'm not bloody superwoman. I'll do my best to get him on that bus, but I can't force him, can I?

You know, they never showed one bit of sympathy, not one bit of understanding. No one ever asked why he was the way he was – he was condemned at that school. Sounds like strong words, but it wasn't. They had it in for him. Swear on my life. Every day he was in that isolation and detention. Every day they were up in his face, shouting at him, telling him he was stupid, that he was bad, that he would never amount to nothing.

Kelly was fined for Callum's non-attendance at school. When a second fine was fast becoming inevitable, she decided to act.

—I tried taking away his phone, his Xbox, everything. None of it worked. So I said to him, right, that's it. From now on, until you go to bloody school, I'm going to take you there and pick you up myself.

—*I can imagine this didn't go down too well.*

—Well, that was the weird thing. He never kicked up much of a stink to be honest. If anything, he seemed pleased. I thought that was pretty bloody weird.

Kelly was still occasionally meeting Jenks in town but mostly on her morning dog walks after she'd taken the bus to school with Callum.

—You know, I never even realised that he'd changed his walk time too.

—*What do you mean?*

—Well, before, I would wait till Cal had set off for school, then take the dog out. Now, I had a bus ride there and back, best part of an hour, and there's Jenks, still in the woods at the same time. Never thought of that till now.

The friendship between the two was a slow burn. Kelly found Jenks to be a good listener. He was quiet, only ever speaking when absolutely necessary. Callum too, was quiet, withdrawn at home. He would attend school under the beady eye of his mother, but his behaviour and grades were still poor, and at home he would disappear into his bedroom for hours. He never seemed to want to go out with friends. Kelly was at her wits' end. Jenks quickly became her confidante on the matter.

—Strong and silent. Never told me what to do. That's the problem with other mums, isn't it? They've all got an opinion, all got a solution. I was telling Jenks cos I was embarrassed to talk to the other mums about it – their boys was all perfect, wasn't they? None of them were in isolation every day, detention every night.

I remember Jenks said one thing to me, he said, 'Talk to him. Understand what's going on for him. Don't give up on him. He'll come back to you. He will.' And I just remember properly choking up, like I was gonna start bawling right there in the woods. But he was right. Instead of shouting and screaming and telling him to move his lazy arse, I started talking to Cal about what was going on. I started asking him about him.

Callum told his mother how much he was struggling at school. He'd been finding the work almost impossible and had only been getting by, by copying others. His only friends were fellow troublemakers. The thought of going into school was overwhelming for him.

—That's why he was kicking off. He wasn't bad, he was scared. He would walk into a classroom and be expected to understand things he couldn't. He found the work too hard. So he'd kick off, chuck a chair, give someone a dig and be sent out the room. Better than be laughed at because he didn't understand the words on the bloody whiteboard. Poor boy broke down and held on to me like he was five years old when he told me that. Bless him. Suddenly I realised that he needed me after all.

So I looked at ways I could help him.

To cut a long story short, Callum was eventually diagnosed with a mild learning disability. He was entitled to extra help from a teaching assistant in school, and Kelly hoped this would be a change of direction for her son. At this moment, it felt like a start, at least.

Of course, I can see the parallels with the case of Sidney Parsons and I understand Kelly's anger at some of the voices on this series. But why is she appearing on the show? It's probably apparent but I'll let Kelly explain in her own time.

—Callum came back. A bit. It wasn't all roses, believe you me, there was plenty of other stuff at that school, but we'd made a start and we'd made it together. Rather than fighting, I'd listened, and it had helped. I'd tried to understand it from Cal's point of view. Just like Jenks had said. I wanted to say thank you. It was the best bit of advice I'd ever been given, and I wanted him to know that.

One morning, Kelly stopped by a newsagent on her way home from taking Callum to school to buy some chocolates for Jenks. She wrapped them in a bag to take up to the woods with the dog. After walking up the track we've walked today, Kelly let Fred off the lead and off he went, bounding into the trees.

—So, after a while, Fred comes back down the path and starts making a great big fuss. I'm thinking, what the hell's going on? Something's not right here. He's acting like bloody Lassie. What's happened? Is little Timmy trapped down the well?

Kelly followed Fred into the wood, and there she could hear a strange sound.

—It was this horrible voice, all croaky shouting, 'Help! Help!' and Fred starts barking again, so I follow him down a path, and there's a bloke lying there in the mud. I almost didn't recognise him. He was lying there, curled into a ball. Mud in his beard and in his hair. That dog of his stood there beside him, whimpering.

It was Jenks. He told Kelly he'd caught his foot on a root, trying to find a stick for his dog and landed on his ankle.

—His ankle was swollen up like a bloody balloon, and he was all pale and sweating. Of course, you can't get no signal out there, so I says I'll help him up and get him out of there, get an ambulance. But he wouldn't have the ambulance. No way, he says, I'll be OK. It's not broken, it's just twisted. Well, what was I supposed to do? I help him up with our dogs making a great big fuss all around us, and I help him, don't I? Anyone would have done the same thing.

It wasn't far to the newbuild estate where Jenks lived. Kelly supported him and by the time they got there, she was exhausted.

—I wanted to get him settled down, make him a cup of tea and all that. I kept asking him, should I call an ambulance, and he kept saying, no, no, he'd be fine. Dodgy ankle, it had happened before. I get him home and … well, I dunno what I was expecting really. My house is clean as a whistle, I'm telling you now, but it's full of *stuff*: old drawings of Callum's on the fridge, knick-knacks from holidays, photos in frames. I've got some of them silly signs hanging up in the kitchen. *This Kitchen Is Powered On Coffee.* You know, *stuff*.

Well there was no *stuff* in Jenks' house. In the living room anyway. It was like one of them show homes. Empty. No pictures, no nothing. Just … it was like no one lived there, and it gave me the creeps. He's got a sofa, a telly. And the mantelpiece, it's empty save for one thing. One single, solitary thing. A photo in a frame. His mum, I reckon. It looked old though. Creased and faded behind the glass.

I get him sat down and go into the kitchen to get the kettle on. All the while he's telling me that it's no problem, no bother, that he'll be fine. I could tell he didn't like me in there, he wanted me gone. But he's drowsy with the pain, knackered from hopping back all that way. I lie him down on the sofa, and I tell you, the bloke's half asleep.

Now I'm a bit worried at this point. I get the message, right. His business is his business, but I find some paracetamol in the cupboard and make sure he has it. I give him my number, just in case, and he's saying, thank you, thank you, and I know when I'm not wanted. To be honest, I was a bit pissed off cos it's clear he wants me to go. I mean, if I hadn't been there, who would have found him? Plus he's only half conscious, and I'm worried he's done himself a mischief. So I says I'm gonna stay, just for a cuppa. Just to make sure he's OK. I says if you start passing out, I'm calling that ambulance.

Anyway, I'm calling Fred, cos he's gone off upstairs. Bloody dog. I'm shouting and shouting, but the bloody thing's not coming, and I'm worried there's gonna be an accident or he's jumped on Jenks' bed with muddy paws, so up the stairs I go. I can hear Jenks moaning on the sofa, but I pretend I can't hear him. I mean half of me's nosey, I'll admit it. I'm calling the dog, and I see the bedroom door wide open, the edge of the bed. Now I know it's none of my business, but I'm gonna have a poke about, aren't I? I'll admit it, I'm a nosey bitch, OK?

Well the bedroom's just like the living room. Empty. There's a bed, a bedside table and a wardrobe.

That's it.

I was surprised because the bloke's a bloke, but he's made his bed. It was tight as well, tucked in, and it made me think of the military. I got a funny feeling then; what if he was a spy or something, working for MI5? What if this was his safe house?

I get this funny feeling in there too – almost like … I dunno, like I wasn't alone. I got the creeps worse up there. Just the bare walls and the carpet that looked brand new. No half-read books, no porno mags. I guess it's all online these days, but there was no tablet, no phone charger left lying about. Nothing. Like I say, it was like a show home.

I remember I stood in there for a bit, just … looking. There was a funny feeling in there, like a school with no kids in it or something.

When I got downstairs, I wanted out of that house as soon as possible. There was something not right in there. Not right at all.

Kelly returned home that day, determined to leave the man she knew as Jenks well alone. After a couple of hours though, she couldn't help worrying about him.

—I just thought, what if he's passed out or something? What if he *has* broken a bone and got an infection? So I gave him a ring, didn't I? Just to make sure.

Jenks turned out to be fine. His ankle was severely twisted but not broken. At least he never got it seen to by any medical professional. Jenks apologised profusely for imposing on Kelly, and explained he worked away a lot. Shift work on an offshore oil rig. It was, as Kelly tells me, almost as if he knew she was creeped out by the emptiness of his house.

—He actually asked me to come back, you know. At first I thought, the cheek of it. He said he was having trouble getting about on his ankle, and would I mind taking the dog out. Well, I thought there was no harm in that, was there? The poor bloke didn't seem to have anyone, did he? I says alright. Why not?

I went back and all, not just once, but a few times. He was nice, was Jenks, good to chat to. I brought our Callum as well – for two reasons: just in case this bloke was planning to murder me, and because I could teach him about responsibility and that.

Callum and Jenks got on well. In fact, Kelly says they seemed to 'click' almost immediately.

—Maybe it's a man thing? Maybe Cal just needed a bloke in his life. Jenks was about my age, more or less. Cal's never really had anyone like that before. Jenks taught him how to play chess – *chess!* I said it was a wonder you got him to sit down for that long.

Despite Callum's challenges, he and Jenks hit it off. Jenks was patient with the boy, listened to him, spoke to him with respect.

—He liked that. He said he liked Jenks cos Jenks talked to him proper. He said everyone else just shouts at him and calls him thick. Jenks made him feel good about himself. I could tell. When he learned how to play chess, he was chuffed to bits. He never let on, but I knew. Never shut up about it: Jenks this, Jenks that. I says to him, I says, I'll play chess with you if you want, you know, and he says no way!

Long after Jenks' ankle had healed, the three of them would walk the dogs after Callum got home from school in the copse of woodland, before returning to Jenks' strange, empty house to drink cups of tea and play chess. It was at this point that Kelly began listening to this series of Six Stories.

—Of course, I remembered the case. So sad, wasn't it? Sidney Parsons, bless his little soul. It meant a lot to me when Cal was diagnosed, cos I remembered that name, that boy what got killed and … well, I worried. Of course I did. What if Cal got picked on like that? That's when I messaged you, see? Told you to stop. It's sick what you were doing, bringing it all up again. I thought you was making profits off his death. That's what I thought.

—I can understand your anger with me. You kept listening, though, as you and Callum got to know Jenks better.

—I did. It's compelling, and I wanted to know where you was going with it. Also, I listened while Cal was playing chess for hours on end with Jenks. I'd take the dogs out while they played. He would never come to our place, always refused, never wanted to impose, he said. By this time I was starting to get a few interviews for work. I went to them when Cal was at school, but there was this open day over in [location removed], one of those careers fairs, and I had to get three buses. I said to Jenks, I said, would you mind, would you mind terribly if he came back to your place? Just for a couple of hours. I'll even give you money for the chippy. Of course, he says, and Callum, well, he can't wait. There was a little bit of me that really liked this, I have to say. I never had no romantic feelings for Jenks, and he was so quiet and cold, I doubted he had any for me. But it wasn't like that. We were mates. We were friends. But him and Callum, they had … I dunno what to call it – a connection?

—*Was there a part of you that was concerned? You didn't really know anything about this man at this point. Where he'd come from, nothing.*

—I know. I know. I was lax. It was a poor parenting decision, as they say, but it's not like the pair hadn't been alone together when I was listening to you and walking the dogs.

I just … I could just see that Callum, dare I say it, *needed* him. He needed a man in his life. I saw what Callum was getting from it with my own eyes, and Jenks too, he was always just a little bit more chatty with Callum there. They needed each other. I was sure of it.

By this time, Kelly says, she had listened to episode three, the interview with Will.

—I just thought I'd better send a more reasoned response to you to be honest. I wanted you to listen. All that demon possession stuff, I thought it was getting stupid, if I'm honest. Sorry but it was. I thought you wasn't showing no compassion to anyone, least of all those two.

—*Robbie and Danny?*

—Right. I didn't know nothing about their families before. I never knew about Danny's mum, and how she done herself in like that. Robbie as well. I found myself feeling for them, for both of them. Just a little bit. Then something got me thinking again.

It was Cal once told me that Jenks had talked to him about his mum. You remember that photo in the frame? He said she died when he was young. That photo, that's all he had left of her. 'Jenks says I've got to hold you tight, Mum. Never let you go. But I don't want to. Not *all* the time.' Cal says this to me with pure horror on his face. and I started laughing, had to explain to him that it was a figure of speech.

I think it was then, that moment, when I realised the struggle my little boy was going through. Funny how it's the daft little things like that, isn't it? Not the ed psych giving us the diagnosis, but this. I gave him a big hug, and I says to him, I says that we'll always hold each other tight, even when we're miles away from each other. I says to him, whenever you feel sad, just remember that I'm holding you. Cos I'm your mum and that's what mums do.

Callum's visit alone to Jenks' house was a success, as was the job fair. Kelly managed to get a job as a receptionist at a dental surgery a bus-ride from her home.

—It was a few trial shifts. I'd not had no experience, to be honest, and I might have told a few porkies at the job fair, but I've got common sense, and I thought that might see me through. I done my work experience at school in an estate agent. Honestly, I thought I could blag it. So long as I got there on time and learned quick. I'm good at that.

With the regular visits to Jenks' house, a couple of days a week after school, Callum's behaviour was slowly starting to improve. As was his attendance. Kelly continued listening to Six Stories *on her bus journey. The next episode she heard was Terry Atkinson.*

—Now, don't get me wrong, my boy was no angel. But he was trying, I could tell. Jenks had given him a bit of self-worth, a bit of self-esteem. Mad, isn't it? I'm his mum, and I've spent his life telling him he's wonderful, but this beardy, quiet bloke pops up out of nowhere and suddenly, in Cal's eyes, he's the dog's bollocks. I did think it was a bit weird what he said to Cal about his mum, but then something else happened which was even weirder.

On Cal's fourteenth birthday, we go round to Jenks' place after school for a cuppa. I've brought a cake, and Jenks gives him a present. It's not much, he says, and I could see from Cal's face that he didn't know what to do when he seen it. I don't think he'd ever tried one before.

—*What was it?*

—A book. An old one. No picture on the front. It was bound in this red, leathery stuff like something from the past. I could tell that Cal was disappointed, and I could tell he didn't want Jenks to know. But Jenks knew and he grinned. He had a funny smile, never showed his teeth, always hid behind his beard. You could only see his smile in the way his eyes crinkled, if you know what I mean.

'I know it don't look like much,' Jenks says, 'but don't worry about that. I thought I wouldn't like it either.'

Bless Cal, he did his best, and he said thank you, and I just wanted to say sorry to Jenks. But in the back of my head, I'm thinking about Terry Atkinson – what he said about those two with books.

This is the audio from episode four. Terry Atkinson was hiding in the kilns when he saw Robbie and Danny approaching…

'It was weird; they both had books in their hands.

—Books?

—Yeah, like, old ones, with those leather covers, and of course, we thought they must have belonged to Danny's mum. They must be doing spells or something.'

Kelly snatched the book from Cal's hand to read the title.

—*William the Fourth* by Richmal Crompton. I remember breathing a sigh of relief. I was spooked. I laughed at myself. As if Jenks would give Cal a spell book.

Anyway, that night, we get home and Cal goes up to bed. I said he could have an extra hour on the Xbox up in his room, it being his birthday. Gives me a bit of time to catch up on some TV. To be honest, I was gonna suggest we watch an old Disney, me and Cal, like we used to when he was little, snuggled up on the sofa, but I resisted.

Anyway, after half an hour or so, I can't hear no gunshots and screams and that. So I go up, just to make sure he's OK, and … well, I couldn't believe my eyes when I got in that bedroom.

—*What had happened?*

—Nothing. Nothing had happened. The screen was blank. Cal was lying on his bed, his head in that book. I couldn't believe it.

Callum, even as a small child. had never shown much interest in reading. As he grew older it was something he struggled desperately with. Especially in school.

—I don't think he was just looking at the pictures, either. I could see his lips moving, trying to sound out the words. I almost screamed. I said to him, since when did you read books for fun? Well, Cal puts the book down and he says to me, look, Jenks is in the book. Then my heart goes again. So I go over and have a look.

That's when I got one of those funny feelings like in Jenks' house, in the bottom of my belly. Farmer Jenks. He was a character in the book. This book was about this young lad and his mates in the 1920s or something. It said that they all hung out in an old barn in Farmer Jenks' field.

Well, I said, what a coincidence. Maybe that's not his real name, then? Maybe it's a nickname? I just … something didn't feel quite right.

Kelly couldn't put a finger on what was so strange about this literary coincidence, why it bothered her. There was also the photograph of Jenks' mother. These coincidences were a little too close to the bone, but none of them proved anything. Kelly decided from then on that maybe she would back off a little bit from the man she knew as Jenks. Callum as well. Kelly listened to episode five of this series and begged me to stop.

Now I understand why.

—I just thought it might be best to cool things off a bit. I mean, he was so quiet, I didn't really know anything about him, and I could never get used to that house of his. Every time we'd go there, I would go to the bathroom and sneak a peek in his bedroom. To be fair, more things appeared. One of them Kindles on the bedside table, a pair of pyjamas. Dirty socks on the floor. That made me feel a bit better, I suppose.

But then I got that job, the receptionist one. They wanted me in at nine sharp, and I couldn't walk Cal to his bus stop with enough time to catch mine. Not unless I trusted Cal to walk up the old train line on his own without doing a runner, and I could peg it to the other bus stop and pray the traffic was bad. It just wasn't going to work.

Jenks had started walking his dog down the old train tracks in the morning as well, which I didn't like because he never said anything, he just sort of *appeared*. As if he knew our schedules had changed.

Kelly was slightly disturbed by this too, it was as if Jenks knew what they were doing. But when he offered to accompany Callum to the bus stop, just to make sure he didn't do a runner, Kelly felt unable to object.

—That whole day at work, I felt sick. I kept wanting to text Cal or ring the school, and just make sure he was OK. But I didn't. I couldn't. He would have asked why, and I wouldn't have known what to say. I did though, in the end. I called that Mr Wallace, that slimy, attendance officer, and I said I just wanted to check that Cal had got in OK, that I was starting a new job. I remember there was a bit of a silence at the other end of the line. My heart was in my throat. Not gonna lie, I was expecting him to tell me that Cal had never arrived or something horrible like that.

'He's here,' Mr Wallace says, 'but his behaviour's been … odd.'

According to the school, that morning, Callum wasn't himself. He was muttering to himself, curling himself up in one of the corners of the dining room at lunch time. Kelly hoped it was simply a blip, a comedown from his birthday, perhaps.

Then she got a phone call an hour later to tell her that Callum had done a runner, hopped over the school gates and disappeared.

—I was fuming, *fuming*. So angry. Luckily my boss says I could go, and I swear down, every single traffic light on that bus ride was red, every car in front decided to drive at twenty, and every bugger wanted to get on or off at every stop and pass the time of day with the driver. I was ringing Cal's phone and Jenks' phone over and over, and they weren't picking up. I nearly called the police, but I just had to check one place first. Just for my piece of mind.

Kelly, for better or for worse, went straight to Jenks' house. She was hoping, praying that Callum had simply gone over there rather than go to school.

—If he had, and Jenks hadn't told me, well, that would have been it. No more chess, no more visits. Nothing. I thought he was better than that. But then there was that other voice in my head, the one that told me something had happened, that maybe Jenks wasn't all he seemed. That voice was telling me it was all my fault.

Eventually, Kelly arrived at the door in the estate where Jenks lived.

There was no car on the drive, the curtains were pulled closed, but there was Callum, sat on the front step.

—I nearly slapped him. I was about to launch into a tirade. He'd been doing so well with his attendance, he'd been *reading* for Chrissake. But just as I opened my mouth to shout at him, I saw that my boy, my little boy, was in bits.

Kelly sat down on Jenks' front doorstep and put her arm around her son. Callum had something in his hand. It was a folder, a cardboard folder, battered and dog-eared.

—Before I even looked inside it, I said to Cal, I said, what's going on? I want to hear it from you first, before I look in this folder. I want you to tell me what this is all about.

It took a bit of prodding and poking and cajoling. But eventually, it all came out.

'Jenks isn't his real name, Mum,' Cal says.

I'd thought as much. I thought he might be a drug dealer, scammer, a confidence trickster, or something like that.

Then my mind went to the darker places. What if he was a sex offender? What if he'd been grooming me and Cal? I started getting mad again: if he'd so much as touched my son…

I asked Cal if he'd asked for any money or asked Cal to look after anything for him. I had to ask, didn't I? Has he ever asked you to do something that made you uncomfortable?

Cal isn't a good liar. 'No, Mum,' he says, 'it's nothing like that.'

'What is it then? What's going on?'

In my heart of hearts. I knew. By now I knew who Jenks was. I'd been in denial.

Through his tears he tells me. He tells me on that walk to school, Jenks had told him he had to go away. Maybe for a long time, maybe forever.

'Why?' I said, and to be honest, I didn't want to know the answer.

'He said he done something bad.' And I swear those words buckled me. I thought of that empty house, him just appearing one day like that.

'What did he do'? I said. I could feel my anger boiling again.

'He done it when he was a bit younger than me,' Cal says, and I thought, I *hoped* it wouldn't be that bad. Maybe he was giving Cal a bit of a lesson or something. Maybe he was going to go away on the rigs and wanted to, you know, pass down some knowledge.

'Lots of young lads do bad things, Cal,' I says. 'Everyone makes mistakes, and we learn from them, remember.'

'No, Mum,' Cal says, and he looks up at me, and his eyes are all wide and bloodshot. 'Jenks done something really bad, really, *really* bad.'

I was, like *what?* And Cal shows me a Post-it note that was stuck to the folder.

It was written in block capitals:

I'M SORRY CALLUM. I'M SORRY KELLY. I HAVE TO LEAVE THIS WORLD. I HOPE THESE WILL HELP YOU UNDERSTAND WHY.

Kelly took the folder from her son's hands and opened it. The first document had been torn from a newspaper. An opinion piece about protecting the identity of a killer.

Two killers.

Danny Greenwell and Robbie Hooper.

There was something else too – a photograph; old and battered like the photo of Jenks' mother. Two boys about twelve years old standing under the arches of an ancient stone structure, arms around each other's shoulders. Stern, set faces, them against the world.

—I swear to God, I felt like my heart had turned to stone. There were more newspaper cuttings, in plastic folders – older, from the nineties, all about that poor boy, Sidney Parsons. Callum was asking me, what's that, what's that about, Mum? I couldn't speak. I couldn't. I banged on that front door, rang the doorbell, called Jenks' number. Nothing.

I was furious.

Not just for me, but for Cal. My Cal, who'd never had a father, who'd grown up with all his problems and had finally started to find some peace.

It was too late.

—*What happened next?*

—We went home. Cal was gutted. He was distraught. I sent him upstairs to his room for a while. I wanted to look through the folder, read everything about that case. I remembered it, what happened up north, that poor little boy. I felt sick, knowing that Jenks might be one of them. *Was* one of them. But who?

Kelly looked through the folder properly, with Callum out of the way. Among the newspaper articles, there was a sheaf of papers held together with a paperclip.

—They were all crumpled and stained, barely legible. Old. I had no idea what they were. Then I started reading them and I realised: letters.

From Danny Greenwell to his mum.

What was I supposed to do with these? I needed to know more about what happened that day. I needed to know if Jenks was Danny Greenwell or was he Robbie Hooper?

—*Which one did you think he was?*

—I couldn't say. They were Danny's letters but Jenks – he hid his mouth a lot, he had that beard, wore a hat all the time. He could have been Robbie? Jenks could have been either one of them.

I read those letters and my heart broke. They were … they sounded … they sounded like my Cal. I thought of my boy doing a terrible thing like that, and I wondered. I wondered what I would do. Where I would put myself.

Before, I thought I was going to blow my top. But now I felt … sad, not just for Cal but for Jenks. I'd left him alone with my son, a boy only a couple of years older than Sidney Parsons.

Would I be able to forgive Jenks for this? Would I want him punished? Put away for life?

I thought of Cal at school. All those detentions, all that isolation. All those meetings. Did it stop him? Did it make him better?

No.

The only thing that seemed to work was someone showing him understanding, kindness. It was only then that he stopped acting up so much, stopped bunking off.

It made me wonder about those two boys, Robbie and Danny, and what they were carrying, what horror show was going on inside them to do what they done.

I've never thought like that before.

I felt like I understood a bit … but it made me sick. It made me … I couldn't comprehend it. How could I feel sorry for those two little monsters? How could I feel bad for them?

I thought of Jenks. What he'd done, and also what he'd done for Cal.

I realised it was my fault he'd had to go away. I heard Cal crying in his bedroom, and I realised that was my fault.

So now, here we are, and I still dunno what to do. I want closure. But I don't know how to get it. I keep thinking of what she said, that woman in episode five, about stopping it all.

—It's up to you, Kelly. You hold the dice here. You can give Jenks' details, make them public, tell the world you know where he was. It won't guarantee he'll be discovered, but for those who want to find him, it'll make the search a great deal easier. It might bring you and others some peace.

Kelly stops. We're in the woods, beneath the trees. It's true, if Kelly discloses Jenks' location, he won't be tracked down immediately. All eyes will turn this way though. It won't take long.

—It's just … it's funny, you know, I never felt unsafe with him, with Jenks. I often wonder to myself whether, if I knew what he'd done, if he'd told us everything straight up, what I'd do. I wonder if I'd have let our Cal play chess with him. I wonder if I'd still have let him into our life?

—Huge questions.

—Yeah. But I don't have to answer them, do I? We've got no choice. He's gone. I'll give you the letters if you want them. I dunno what else to do with them. Cal's gonna keep that book, because he says he wants something to remember the guy with.

—Did you explain to him, to Callum, about it all? About Sidney Parsons, Robbie Hooper and Danny Greenwell?

—I did. I explained it all to him, and I said that he could think what he liked. If he wanted to hate Jenks afterwards, he could. If he still wanted to like Jenks afterwards, he could. It was up to him. He's never said which. I don't imagine he ever will. Maybe when he's older. It's a burden for him, I know that.

Maybe there isn't an answer, a right way to feel. Maybe it's both. Maybe he hates him, maybe he loves him too? Maybe he feels sorry for him? Maybe he feels sorry for the Parsons too?

That's why I was so angry. With you. Because there wasn't a right way to feel. There isn't a right thing to believe. There's no closure.

Maybe there never will be?

What I do know is that Jenks – Robbie, Danny; he never done neither of us no harm. Cal's been on his own with him, and all he showed us was kindness. That's what I know.

There was chat, on your last episode, about this demon-possession stuff, this haunting, this curse. At first I thought it was cobblers, but I want to ask – what do you think?

—*Me?*

—Yeah. Is it true? The curse? The stone? The haunting?

—*I'm not really here to make these decisions, to come to these conclusions myself I—*

—Here. Take this then. I found it in Cal's bedroom. If it's not true, none of it, then it doesn't matter.

Kelly presses something cold and hard into my hand.

—I just want rid of it, OK? It's yours now. If none of it is true, then it'll do you no harm, will it?

A stone, jet black, slightly smooth in the palm of my hand. I stand for a few seconds, staring at it. Then Kelly's dog begins to growl.

—What was that?

We both look around at a movement in the undergrowth behind us. Fred begins growling, a low rumble as he stands at Kelly's heel. Suddenly it feels very desolate, very quiet here, in this wild place on the outskirts of a small town somewhere in England. I wonder if there's been some tabloid journalist following us. Maybe this is a setup? It would make a great crescendo for the last episode of the series, perhaps?

Kelly suggests it's time to leave, and we do. We walk carefully back down the path, trying not to look back at the way we've come, at least not often. I wonder as we turn a corner, if the shadowy figure I see, ducking out of sight as the tips of the trees disappear beneath the horizon, is just a trick of the fading light, a shadow conjured into a figure by my heightened imagination and the stress of this entire situation.

Maybe it's time for me to take a break?

—I want to ask you something else. I don't know which one he was – Robbie or Danny. I feel like I'll go to my grave still not knowing and somehow that's worse than any witch's curse.

—*Sorry, what are you asking me?*

—Can you find out? For me? For Cal? I'm an adult, but he's just a boy, and he'll spend his life wondering too. Who was his friend?

—*OK, Kelly, I'm going to tell you something. I don't know whether I'll leave it in the podcast or keep it out, but I'll keep recording just in case.*

—Fine.

—*I knew a boy, once, a long time ago. His situation was a bit like mine. I came from trauma. It's not easy. It wasn't easy for the kind people who took me in either. I spent some weekends in respite care, to give my adoptive parents a break. That's where I met him. I didn't know him long. But I remember him. I remember we were both scared, both angry. I remember he was kind.*

—No…

—*I never forgot him. I remembered his name and I remembered his face. So when he died, of course, I wasn't able to identify his body, but I recognised who he was when no one else could, or would, or was willing to. So I came forward.*

—The police, they wouldn't never say who it was who killed himself at the kilns. And apparently that missing persons alert … it disappeared, all the details, everything.

—*Of course, they had his fingerprints and his DNA on record. After what he'd done. I suppose I wanted him to have some dignity at the end, before the vultures picked him clean. I left his grave bare for me and me alone to rake over. To find answers.*

—Jesus Christ. So you knew one of them too?

—I guess. I knew him a little bit like you knew Jenks – someone who was kind, someone who was good. You got after, I got before. Whatever happened to those boys in between, that's always going to be the question, isn't it?

—What made them do something so terrible?

—That's right. I'm not sure we'll ever know for sure, and that's the hardest part.

—So if it was the one you knew, who killed himself up at those kilns then … the other one will be Jenks.

—That's right. I'm almost sure of it.

It's on this, a sombre note, that Kelly and I part ways. Kelly takes one branch of the old railway line back to her house, and I the other. I walk along the path, the afternoon sky dark, and the skeletal thorn bushes and wizened bramble coils rising up each side of me. I am very aware of the photographs I have of those letters on my phone. I wonder, what use are they? Those intimate thoughts of a small boy who'd lost his mother? I could sell them to a tabloid, I suppose. Make my money and disappear forever. I could get experts in psychology to come on the show, and we could pull each of Danny's letters apart, line by line. But really, what would that give us? Would we get an insight into why two children killed another? Would we get the answer that we want?

I believe not.

I believe, after hearing six stories about the death of Sidney Parsons in 1995, that the more we seek, the less we'll find. Maybe with this case, more than with any other grave we've raked over, it's time to lay down flowers and move forward.

I'm not going to disclose who was who.

For the sake of a child I used to know.

You see, it's easier to condemn than to understand. It's cheaper to jail than rehabilitate someone, and in our minds, so much easier to demonise than to reflect. But to reflect and understand is the only way we can move on.

I've attempted to keep my personal views away from this podcast, but for this series, it has been impossible. Sadly though, a great majority of people often feel the need to weigh in with their view on every single matter; most often without taking the time to research, educate themselves or take some time to fully formulate their views on both sides of the argument. But then, that's easier, isn't it? It's easier to call a child a devil without knowing anything about them, it's easy to condemn someone for not thinking about things the same way you do, without ever wondering why. With the case of Sidney Parsons, I've taken six differing views of the tragedy, and I've realised that we're not going to find a definitive answer as to why he was killed.

Maybe Robbie and Danny were beyond help, an explosive mix of damage and demoniacal fury, and when the touch paper was lit, no one could put it out. Or maybe they were truly evil. Or maybe they grew up in circumstances that were evil?

Maybe they were actually victims of some kind of demonic possession, by some terrible darkness buried long ago beneath the rocks of the kilns on Ussal Bank. Or maybe they simply believed that.

We need to start understanding more and commenting a little less. All day, every day we meet with a barrage of opinions, a relentless wave of thoughts and feelings, black and white, right and wrong. Whatever anyone says is torn apart, condemned and praised without a second thought. That's not to say that opinions should not be had, it's more about whether an opinion is thought out. Have you considered everything before pressing send? You are responsible for that opinion, a potential needle under the skin or into the heart of someone who reads it. What if that was the last straw? What if your opinion has more impact than you thought it would?

That's what I've come to learn from this. Kelly's learned this too, the hard way. Maybe we need to consider every angle.

Not just six.

And that's why, in part, I feel like I need a break, a hiatus. I know what's coming for me now: questions and opinions, a relentless barrage of them. But whatever comes of this series, there will be no resolution.

One thing I do know is that Kelly was right. There is blood on my hands. The series caused a spotlight to fall again on the village of Ussalthwaite, drove one to suicide and one more to try.

So maybe it's time to pause for a time.

All I can say is that I've been here to do one thing: tell stories. To look at things six different ways, to be objective about bad things and bad people. Maybe in some kind of subconscious way I've been trying to say something, trying to get all the facts before making a judgement.

I have something else in my possession now; a memory in the shape of a black stone. I have not tried to get rid of it, at least not yet. It's going to serve as an apt reminder that stones cast ripples, that what I do here has real effects on real people.

Maybe it's time to leave the graves to rest?

I've been Scott King,

If there's a next time….

Dear Mum,

It's been a long time. I'm sorry about that. I wonder if, where you are, you're aware of the time it's taken for me to write. I still think about you, Mum, just not every day. I hope that's OK.

I feel like you'd understand. You told me, when I was little, that there was a lot I would understand when I was older, and now I'm older – much older – I think I do.

I no longer need you to come back anymore, Mum. I know you're gone, and that's OK. I'm at peace with that now.

I still hear you though. I hear you every day. I hear you when the wind kicks up over the water or the fields, or it rattles through the trees. I hear you when a bird sings, be it the burr of a roosting city pigeon or the knock of a woodpecker in a silent wood. I hear you, and I know you'll always be here, with me. I think I understand that now.

I know this might be a lot to ask, Mum, but I was wondering if he was there too, in the wind and the water, and the things that grow? If he was there too, I was wondering if I could talk to him? I'd want to say that I haven't forgotten. I'll never forget that day. It's been so long that when I remember it now, it's like it's someone else. Or a dream.

He turned up at the special place. He lay down on our rock. We hadn't asked him to come, Mum. I know that's what everyone thought. He followed us. He wouldn't leave us alone. We let him lie there, Mum, because ... we wanted to see what would happen. That was all. We gave him the demon stone to hold. We told him it would make him better.

He wanted to believe it as much as I wanted to believe in you.

When he started shaking, when he started jerking like that, we were scared. We were only kids. We didn't know about seizures or epilepsy, or anything like that. It was Robbie who said it first; Robbie said the demon had got in him – the demon had got in Sidney like it had got in Jip.

I've had all these years to wonder why he said that, Mum, what he meant. I know I heard your voice in the special place, and Robbie heard one too. That's what he told me. Maybe it wasn't his mum.

We tried to hold Sidney, and he was shaking and growling, and foaming at the mouth, and then he bit Robbie. Yes, I would say he looked possessed. He looked demonic. It was terrifying. It wasn't him anymore. I'd have known in my heart if it was really him, because I'd known him since primary school. And it wasn't him.

That's the memory I've carried. When I was at the unit, I used to wake up screaming, seeing Sidney Parsons' face. The blood. Robbie's screams. The rest is a blank.

Then there he was. Quiet. Lying on the ground now. A stone in the back of his head.

I remember we thought we'd saved him. For a second we thought we were heroes. We thought he'd wake up, and whatever was in him might be gone. We thought that we wouldn't get the blame for everything anymore. We'd come back down to the village, all three of us, and everything would be OK again.

We sat with him for hours until we realised what we'd done.

So we put him in the stream. Make it look like an accident or something.

We didn't know. We were kids.

I don't want him to forgive me, Mum, because that's too much. I just want him to know that I'm sorry.

I've spent all my life running, Mum, and here I am, running again. Tell him I've never forgotten what we did that day. Tell him that whatever I do, whatever impact I have in this world, what I did to him and his family that day will poison it. Tell him that I will never do anything good, anything positive for anyone. It's not his fault. I'm not self-pitying here. I mean that I simply cannot trust myself. I'm scared of what might happen. I'm scared that I'll come to, and there'll be another body, another broken child, another broken family. I'm scared that what happened in 1995 could happen again.

Tell him that's my burden, my punishment, and I deserve it.

Tell him that's more powerful than a demon, a witch or a curse.

In the wind and the rush of the river and the cry of the gulls, I'll listen out for him, Mum, like I listen out for you.

I miss you, Mum.

Every day.

I'm sorry.

xxx

To: scott@sixstories.com
From: <sixstories website contact form>
Name: Kelly Valentine

I dunno if you'll get this but just wanted to let you know that Callum's doing better. Much better.

It's been hard for him, but I think he finally understood. We went through the letters, and I think he now gets that it wasn't his fault that Jenks done what he done. Jenks had his own demons. Callum understands now that it was the only way for him to get them to leave him alone. I'm not spiritual or anything like that, but I hope that somehow it brought them some peace.

Those letters helped.

We took a little trip, just the two of us. Made a day of it. A train up to Ussalthwaite and a long walk when we got there. We visited their special place. People had laid flowers. There were teddies and plastic candles, poems.

We was going to burn those letters so they won't be in no newspaper or all over Facebook for old people like me to comment on. But neither of us could do it. We thought we could find the Parsons, maybe give it to them, but I was scared in case that just might make their pain worse.

That's why I've sent them to you, so you can find out the answer – so you can know why Sidney Parsons died. If you believe what the letters say, that is.

I want to say I'm sorry for saying you had blood on your hands, that any of this was your fault. If anything, you brought some peace to one person, my son.

Maybe them other two didn't deserve peace? Maybe they did?

In the press, they're saying *you* don't deserve no peace, that you're as bad as them two what killed Sidney Parsons.

I wonder if you've still got that stone, Scott. I wonder if you've tried to get rid of it yet. I wonder if it's come back. I wonder if it's let you forget?

I wonder if you'll ever find your peace?

I hope so.

Love K & C xx

ACKNOWLEDGEMENTS

I owe a huge and ever-increasing debt of gratitude to the following people:

Firstly, a gigantic thankee-sai to my wonderful agent Sandra Sawicka, who has had my back from the day she took me on, and remarkably, at the time of writing, still does.

Luke Speed at Curtis Brown for representing my more visual monstrosities.

Karen, West, Cole and Max at Orenda Books for seemingly not regretting taking a punt on me a few years ago and publishing my strange stories, or at least hiding their disappointment very well.

Mark Swan, a man whose cover designs are as exquisite as his taste in music.

James, Helen, and all the staff at Forum Books and The Bound, for simply being the best booksellers and the finest people.

All the book bloggers, bookstagrammers, booktubers and booktok folk – just know there's always a very special place in my heart for all of you.

Mish Liddle for helping me with facts about Wicca and the Witches' Rede. Any mistakes are mine and mine alone.

My family and friends – especially the conjuring of incredible ideas with the mighty Ben Bee, and the Sunday afternoon Cosmic Encounters with Richard Dawson and Sally Pilkington.

Sarah Farmer, who still somehow endures me, provides the logic to my esoteric, the pragmatism to my sentimental and the rationality to my ghostly, while still providing the greatest company anyone could wish for.

My son Harry, who is turning into a fine young man these days – my love for you keeps me pushing harder every day to improve in every way. You're an amazing person, and another year on, another book done, and it's nothing to how proud I am of you.

Lastly, you, the reader, for stumbling along these bizarre paths with me; who knows where we'll go next, but I couldn't ask for better company.